GHOST POSSE

G. WAYNE TILMAN

WOLFPACK
PUBLISHING
— EST 2013 —

WOLFPACK PUBLISHING
— EST 2013 —

GHOST POSSE

ACKNOWLEDGEMENTS

Thank you to Beta readers
Denise Kearns, Becca Payne, and Susan Stecker

ACKNOWLEDGMENTS

CHAPTER 1

TWO PRESIDENTS
1865

Washington, DC and Richmond, VA

It was a cold, bleak day. The gaunt, six foot six man in the permanent black suit felt awful. Part was his condition. The doctors knew he had something serious, but, for the life of them, they could not accurately diagnose it. The other parts were people. The White House was open to the owners; that is the American public. People came and went, hoping to foist their issues upon the tall man. The occasional issue was valid. The rest were a waste of his time and theirs.

And, then there was his beloved little wife, Mary Todd Lincoln.

The First Lady, he realized, was a bit crazy. Sometimes more than a bit. And, her obsession for state parties was driving the damn country into bankruptcy as fast as the blamed war.

He called for his secretary.

"Mr. Hay, find Marshal Lamon and have him prepare a buggy for a short trip," Abraham Lincoln ordered in his country Mid-West accent. He correctly pronounced his old friend's name "Lemon," as the U.S. Marshal did himself. John Hay scurried off. The President and his friend, confidant and self-appointed bodyguard often rode together to the cottage getaway. Whether hot coffee or hot toddy, it was a relaxing time. These were two men who, out of many in DC, trusted only each other.

Today was too gray and cold. He was not up to a horseback ride.

Lamon appeared, nonplussed, half an hour later.

"I have a buggy by the side door, Mr. President," he advised.

Lincoln drew the coat on over his usual black suit and donned his top hat. He referred to it as a plug hat and often kept letters and noted inside it. They left the White House by a side entrance.

"The cottage, Abe?" Lamon asked.

"Yes, Hill. I need to get the hell away from the hub-bub here and get some fresh air and visit with the only soul I fully trust. Which of course is my old fellow solon from Illinois days—you."

"If you don't mind, I will press on at a fair clip. That idiot Pinkerton is full of conspiracy theories, but at this juncture of the war, I believe there may be some danger for you. The Confederacy has a pretty good secret service. We, however, have the Pinkerton National Detective Agency. As you know, I believe his theory about the assassination attempt planned for the train in Baltimore was hokum. The train went through with your wife and party and not you. Nothing blew up."

"I know the two of you have been at odds from your first meeting. He is an expediency. We need a secret service and we don't have one. You can be assured as soon as this secession mess is settled, formation of a government secret service will be high on my agenda. And, all Pinkerton will do is provide us the various records he has accumulated."

Hill Lamon smiled. He was not interested in forming or running such an organization, but he had someone in mind who could do it quite admirably.

He steered the one-horse buggy towards the Soldier's Home, where the Anderson Cottage was held available for the President's use as a retreat. He went from Pennsylvania Avenue to North Capitol Street Northeast. After about three miles, he planned to jog onto Rock Creek Church Road and then on to the cottage.

The two old friends did not always agree, but their admiration and trust accommodated the occasional argument. They chatted as the horse trotted at about twelve miles per hour. The trip was four and a half miles. Just far enough from the White House to provide Lincoln with some breathing room and peace and quiet.

For one whose first and only badge was the one Lincoln had provided as U.S. Marshal for the District of Columbia, Hill Lamon was a natural at executive protection.

He was fearless, a deadly shot and a large imposing man who was as good a brawler as the man he served. He was six feet four inches and carried two Colt .44 Army revolvers. Though he did not discuss it even with Lincoln, the President suspected a Bowie knife and small gun, such as a Derringer might also be secreted upon his person.

Lamon scanned left and right, looking for threats behind trees, at intersections and looked over his shoulder frequently.

He spotted a horsemen closing fast. The horse was at a gallop, moving approximately twice the speed of the buggy. Galloping on a DC street was odd, it was also illegal.

"Abe, we have someone coming up 'way too fast behind us. Here, take the reins, while I warn him off," the marshal said.

Lincoln was a country boy and no stranger to walking miles, handling horses or wagons. He took the reins and slapped them. The horse sped up.

Lamon pulled one of his .44 Army's and turned

in the seat. He rested his wrist with the powerful revolver on the folded canopy top.

He aimed at the rider, the gun as yet uncocked.

Then, the rider brandished a revolver of his own.

"Abe, duck down. He's drawn a gun."

As the tall President crouched in his seat, still driving fast, Lamon cocked his Colt.

He took aim and fired once. The crack of the big revolver sounded like a rifle in the cold air of the capital area.

The rider had drawn within fifty feet. He jerked as the revolver fired. Through the cloud of gray-white smoke, Lamon saw the man fall off the horse. He hit the cobblestone surface and bounced like a rag doll. As he rolled, Lamon sent another conical bullet his way.

Lamon was unable to see whether the second round had effect.

"Didja get him, Hill?" Lincoln asked.

"I knocked him off his horse and he hit the road hard, Abe. I'm not sure about my second shot. It was just for insurance. You know, he looked familiar. I just don't know from where."

"Should we turn around and see who he is?"

"I don't think so. The first rule of protecting a President is to get him out of the danger area."

"I didn't know such rules existed," Lincoln commented as he pressed the horse onward at the same fast clip.

"They don't. I'm making them up as I go," Lamon grinned. Lincoln just shook his head.

"Thank God for Lamon", he thought.

Upon arrival at the Anderson Cottage, Lamon sent a runner to notify the DC police about the shooting and location.

Later, a plain clothes detective and a uniformed officer called on the President and U.S. Marshal at Anderson Cottage.

"We found a little bit of blood and a couple of threads on the stones of the street. It's hard to say whether you shot him or he was just injured when he fell of the horse. As you know, a lot of revolver wounds don't bleed much.

He was gone when we got there. I had a few officers do house to house searches. Nobody saw anything," the detective said.

"Did anybody seem nervous? Like they might have been under duress by the injured gunman?" Lamon asked.

"No, sir, Marshal. Everybody seemed normal. I think he just picked himself up and got back on his horse and rode off," the detective said.

"Thank you, detective. And, your men. I appreciate your efforts," Lincoln said and the men left.

"Hill, do ya think it was a nut case? Or, a Confederate assassin?"

"I'd hope if it was the later, they would have

sent a better man," Lamon replied. But, it was clear to the President, his bodyguard and friend was concerned. Lamon was pensive and quiet. They finished their coffee.

"Abe, I know you don't feel too chipper. And, it's cold as blue blazes and getting colder. Neither of us brought overcoats, just light coats. We'd better drive back pretty shortly. Or, we'll both catch our death of pleurisy."

He called for the waiter and obtained a wool blanket for the President to wrap around himself for the trip back to 1600 Pennsylvania Avenue.

On the way back to the White House, Lincoln leaned over to speak to Lamon above the loudly blowing wind and driving rain.

"Hill, I am going to eat steak and build up my strength. I think I will be ready by next week."

"Ready for what, Abe?" Lamon asked having no idea where this conversation was going.

"Ready to kick that damn Stanton's ass. Right there in the White House. Probably in front of the rest of the cabinet. I might take on another one or two of those fools afterwards, too."

"Will you give me some notice before you do this?" Lamon asked.

"Why? I don't need any help."

"Because I want to be there and see it, of course. I have not seen you whip anybody for nigh on to fifteen years. Remember that big mouth during one of your speeches when you were stumping all over Illinois? You sure gave him a fierce licking."

"Haha. I sure did. I wonder if he can breathe out of his nose yet? I remember I moved it a ways across his face."

"And, squashed it like a rotten plum, too, Abe."

The two enjoyed a good laugh. Lamon knew, even sick, the rail-splitter from the Mid-West could hold his own in a brawl. Especially against a bunch of pot-bellied politicians. It would be a sight to see.

******

Though a lifelong military man and robust in health, the fifty-eight year old general looked older than his actual age.

He was walking in the general direction of the former Virginia state capital, now the capital of the Confederacy. The walk was only six blocks. But, it was freezing in Dixie. It had snowed the night before. While Richmond hardly ever retained snowfall more than a day, the sidewalks were slippery for a man wearing leather-soled shoes.

The general pulled a black wool fedora down hard on his head and turned up the collar of his civilian overcoat. He was just another older Richmonder to passers-by. His head ducked down, gray-bearded chin on chest, virtually nobody would recognize the famous "Marse Bob"… General Robert E. Lee.

The War of Succession, the Southern portion of which he was mostly in charge, was going badly for the South. Lee took full blame. His decision to charge at Gettysburg was the straw which broke the camel's back. Pickett's Charge, as it came to be known was a Southern bloodbath. The fence had been invisible and his men had been unable to breach it. So, trapped, many died there. So very many.

Lee was on his way to meet with the President. He had known Jeff Davis since the Mexican War. Lee knew him to be an honorable man, but one somewhat given to grant trust to followers well before it was earned. The General considered it a highly dangerous trait for a leader.

The cold wind tried to lift his fedora and take it away. The years had not slowed the career military officer's reflexes and he grabbed the hat and clamped it more firmly upon this head.

Lee knew what Davis wanted to talk about. A long-running scheme to kidnap Abraham Lincoln and bring him through the federal blockade to Richmond. There, he would be held hostage. The ransom would be cessation of hostilities.

Lee did not know Lincoln personally. But he knew most of his generals. Some had attended West Point with him. Some had been students during Lee's tenure as Superintendent of the military academy. These men were trained to think the same way he did. They would buy into the hare-brained ransom for a minute. They would just dig in deeper and give less quarter each time the blue and gray met. It was a stupid idea. He vociferously argued against it repeatedly with no success.

Lee crossed Broad Street and turned onto Clay. He was meeting Davis at his home instead of the capital. Lee fervently hoped the President was at home directing packing of essentials to carry when he abandoned the capital and took his family to safety.

Arriving, he mounted the steps and rapped on the door. An officer answered it, wearing his sidearm. Lee was glad to note the presence of the gun. He would rather have seen fifteen men with guns and an equal number packing.

"Good day, General. The President is in the parlor awaiting you," and led Lee into a room to which he needed no directions.

Jefferson Davis arose and greeted his old acquaintance warmly. They shook and Davis motioned Lee to a small table with two chairs.

No sooner had he sat than the First Lady, Varina Davis came in, bringing coffee.

"Ah, that is welcome on such a blustery day, Mrs. Davis," the General commented as he took a cup. She smiled and departed. The two men sat and sipped for a few moments.

"Bobby, I wanted to give you the status of the kidnap plot," Davis began.

"I have had John Mosby move his band of irregulars from Loudoun County down to the Rappahannock River near Port Royal. He has a small, select band of twelve. They are, as is their habit, staying singly at homes instead of bivouacking together as a military unit.

Once our spies take Lincoln, they will cross the Potomac and bring him to our territory. Mosby will escort them into Richmond."

Lee, of course was well aware of this. At the President's order, he had been the one who directed Mosby to relocate.

"What of the spies, Jeff? Dr. Mudd is no intelligence professional. He is a facilitator, instead of an action man. I do have some faith in Surratt, however. His prowess as an intelligence operative is well-proven.

As you know, I have none whatsoever in Booth. He's a womanizing stage actor. He handled himself alright in one duel I know of, but his mettle has not been tested against professional soldiers. I feel if he is pressed, he will panic and do something rash. He has no chance against trained professionals. He's just a pretty boy. He is no proven warrior."

"I know we differ on Wilkes Booth, Bobby. But, I do have faith in his judgement and abilities," Davis retorted defensively.

"What does Judah say about him. He has one of the keenest minds in government," Lee asked, referring to the Secretary of State.

"Judah Benjamin, will surely come to see the brilliance of the plan and its agents," Davis said, admitting what Lee knew. Benjamin thought it was a fool's errand and had told Lee so privately several times.

"Jeff, I fear the tide of the war has turned irreparably against us. I need to head south as soon as possible and return to my men. We have neither the manpower, materiel, nor tactical advantage to overcome Grant. I had to sneak into Richmond alone, like a thief in the night, just to see you. I will do the same leaving.

Even if we were to somehow capture Lincoln, it is far too late in the game. He is a fair man and a smart one. I am convinced if I have to surrender soon—and, I fear I will—he will treat us more equably than the hounds of hell that are his cabinet. They will run over Vice President Johnson like a runaway train. And, the South will rue the day Lincoln left Washington."

"General, a defeatist attitude cannot win a war," Jefferson Davis scolded his most senior general.

Slipping into the formality his old friend introduced in his anger, Lee responded, "Mr. President, you should see our troops. It would break your heart. They are ragged, tired, underfed and under-armed. They have spirit, but almost no fight left in them. Gettysburg, the loss of Jackson and

Stuart, so many things have worked against us. We have already lost this war."

"If it comes to it, we will shift from a war of battles to a guerilla war of skirmishes like Mosby has fought in Northern Virginia," Davis said with finality.

Lee knew it would be futile to debate the idiocy of such a plan.

"Jeff, plan to take Varina and the children further south at a moment's notice. Grant is upon us and you have absolutely no time at all to tarry. The end of the Confederacy is very near."

"Do not worry, General. I always have a backup plan. It includes burning this city and its industrial capacity on the way out. But, I still have faith we can win our objectives here."

"If we burn our tobacco warehouses, our railroads and our iron works by the river, we will have no industry to provide jobs after peace has been prepared. The power to negotiate comes with manufacturing might and the ability to turn a dollar. Destroying our capabilities is unthinkable to me."

He saw the President frown and start to argue, then think better of it.

"God be with you and your family, Jeff. I am prepared to give you whatever escorts you need for you and your family to safely escape. But, now, I have to return to my men without further ado," Lee said as he rose and shook hands.

He left with great resignation and rode Traveler back to his men. Lee had changed to his uniform for the trip before leaving his hotel. He certainly would rather be imprisoned as a soldier than hanged as a spy. With complete humility, he realized right now, he would be the greatest catch the federals could have.

He crossed the Richmond city limits and rode southwest. Lee knew he and Davis, Vice President Stephens and Secretary Judah Benjamin had done their best for their troops and, indeed, for their short-lived country. But, they had neither the men nor the industrial might of the northern half of the former United States.

Lee was already planning his terms of surrender. He was sick at heart. But, he knew if he did not do it, many more men would die. Men on both sides. In this case, needlessly.

He saw a patrol coming towards him on horseback. He could not tell whether they wore blue or gray in the dusk. Lee lifted the flap on his holster off its catch. He could shoot his Colt Navy as well as any man he commanded. Before he felt the need to draw, he realized they were his men. The lieutenant saluted him and offered for the patrol to escort him back to camp. Lee nodded, glad for the company and they rode back. Food was scarce and Lee would not eat when his men were hungry. He supped on coffee and called his remaining generals in for a talk.

He explained he was going to contact General Grant and begin a negotiated surrender. He would seek the fairest terms possible for his men.

Several days later, he rode Traveler to the Mc-Lean house in Appomattox Courthouse, Virginia. The two men were both glad the war would effectively be over with the surrender of the twenty-eight thousand man Army of Northern Virginia. They agreed with the previously decided terms. Officers would keep their horses. Rifles and artillery would be surrendered. Men who signed paroles could return home with no further liability for prosecution. Grant, in a very humanitarian move, sent twenty-five thousand rations to the starving Confederates. He had been a relentless adversary, but was a fair man. One as relieved as Lee the whole thing was drawing to a close.

The two men parted. The man in full-dress gray, sword at his side, rode his battle horse back to the lines. A solitary tear rolled down his cheek. It was more from relief than sadness. Crying men lined his path to cheer him.

Grant sent a message by a patrol which rode through battle-scarred countryside until they found telegraph lines which had not been cut. The accompanying signal man climbed a pole and sent a telegram to advise Lincoln of the surrender.

Lee advised General Johnston and other generals outside of the Virginia campaign to follow suit and outlined the terms Grant accepted for future surrenders.

It was over. Or, was it?

******

Lincoln got the word very quickly and called his cabinet together. Led by the powerful Stanton, they recommended a full military occupation of the South. Lincoln knew it had nothing to do with security. It had everything to do with enriching their personal coffers providing materiel to the military and to retribution to those who had decided to start a war.

It was, to the frontier lawyer, untenable and he told them so. They did accept it any more than they accepted him. And, it showed.

Crowds had gathered outside, calling for a speech. Lincoln had the Marine Band play Dixie. He personally liked the song and thought it might set a precedent helping to reunite the country.

The next day, he gave a brief speech. He was ill and still fighting with his cabinet and some angry senators. The speech was neither eloquent nor patriotic. It was not what his audience wanted.

CHAPTER 2

THE ASSASSINATION
1865

Washington, DC, Maryland and Virginia

The rider felt like a steam train at full speed had hit him. Every part of his body hurt. He checked himself and saw his suit was bloodied and torn. Nothing appeared to be broken. Sprained maybe. The only bullet hole was in the shoulder of his suit jacket, not his own shoulder. He had jerked at the shot and fallen off his horse.

Luckily for John Wilkes Booth, the livery horse hung around without running off. Booth, known as one of the handsomest and most popular actors in America, painfully arose. He recovered his Whitney .36 caliber revolver and shoved it in his waistband.

Booth groaned as he mounted the horse. He knew he needed to vacate the area as soon as possible. He looked around and saw only one other horseman several hundred yards away. He seemed interested, but did not approach. Booth started back, never looking over his shoulder. His spy craft was sadly lacking.

Booth rode back to his room and cleaned up and changed before returning the horse to the livery stable. That done, he went back to his room and sat on the bed.

Another kidnap attempt done bad. This time, the damned marshal may have seen his face. He was about ready to change the plan from kidnap to assassination. It would be easier and more permanent.

Booth poured a glass of bourbon. It was so good, he had a couple more. He passed out fully dressed. His thoughts were disjointed even before the bourbon kicked in. He first noticed a lack of concentration six months ago when the pressure of being a spy with a country-saving mission began to cause him increasing stress and even depression. Drinking seemed to him to help.

******

The horseman who witnessed Booth's action on the way to the Anderson Cottage was an army spy.

He followed the injured Booth at a run. Luckily for the man, Booth's pain precluded riding faster than a good run.

He questioned the liveryman and learned the man

Ward Hill Lamon had shot at was none other than the famous actor, John Wilkes Booth. Booth's address was on the rental receipt. This was information he needed to get directly to Secretary Stanton.

An hour later, he was relating his findings to Stanton and Vice President Johnson. Decisive men, they urged the spy to contact Booth and bring him to Johnson's rooms in a boarding house immediately.

The spy secured several other operatives. They picked up the drunken Booth and fed him coffee and walked him around DC until he was fit to meet with the two powerful men.

Stanton, Johnson and Booth met. The result of the meeting was one of the greatest conspiracies in the Republic's history. Booth, now sober, but no less misguided, thought he had found the proverbial goose with the golden egg. The two politicians knew they had found their dupe.

*****

Booth met with his team of co-conspirators, first at his boarding house and then at Mrs. Surratt's home for one last time. Slyly, Booth did not share the fact he had changed sides to achieve his personally-decided goal. He was an actor. So, he acted.

"Men, all is lost and we have but one choice left. We must kill the President and several of his key

Cabinet Members.

Here is how I have outlined our path. I shall kill the President, Lewis Powell, the Secretary of State, George Atzerodt, the Vice President. Mr. Herold will guide Powell to the Seward Home, then cross into Maryland and meet me at a place we have previously agreed upon.

Do each of you have a good revolver and a Bowie or other large knife?" The men nodded affirmatively, but Atzerodt immediately began protesting he had not signed on to commit murder. Booth, still into his earlier imbibed spirits, insisted it was his duty. Atzerodt ceased arguing, already having formed his own plan of inaction.

******

Secretary of War Stanton hounded Lincoln for the next several days over the occupation issue. Stanton insisted someone trustworthy needed to immediately ride the hundred miles to Richmond and assess the situation in the former Confederate capital. Its industrial capacity was now in ashes.

He told Lincoln the U.S. Marshal and former prosecutor, Lamon, would be the ideal choice.

Lincoln relented to silence the Secretary of War.

Lamon told the President he needed to stay near him and to send someone else. The President knew he sorely needed his friend nearby for moral support and counsel.

Unfortunately for Lincoln, he denied his Lamon's plea.

Lincoln later lamented to Stanton his wife had obligated him to go to a play at the Ford Theater on the fourteenth of April.

Stanton promised another bodyguard for the night of the play. He obtained a four-man detail.

Officer John Frederick Parker of the DC Metropolitan Police was to watch Lincoln while the other three took other positions which proved ineffective.

Nobody wanted to accompany the President and First Lady to the play, Our American Cousin. John Hay contacted General Grant, who demurred because he knew his wife could not tolerate an evening with Mary Todd Lincoln. Finally, a young Army major named Henry Rathbone accepted. He contacted his fiancé, Miss Clara Harris to accompany him. Though her father was a US Senator, she had never been the guest of the President before.

Once Lincoln was seated, his bodyguard retired to a bar next door and ordered a drink. By mid-play, he had several under his uniform belt.

Lincoln enjoyed the play, sitting with his wife's hand hidden within his massive paw. He laughed and enjoyed his last minutes until the shot came.

Booth, with the door wedged shut behind him, shot

Lincoln point blank in the back of the head. The little gun with the big ball was a single shot. But, it was fully sufficient for the task. Booth dropped the Deringer pistol and pulled a long knife. The newspapers referred to it as both a dagger and a Bowie knife. It was more the latter, but with no recurve to the Sheffield blade. Booth slashed Major Rathbone, who heroically tried to detain him and leapt from the balcony.

His spur caught in the bunting and he landed badly, fracturing his leg.

What he yelled in pain sounded like "Sic Semper, Tyrannus," Latin for "Thus always to Tyrants." It was the motto of Virginia, an odd choice for a Marylander. Witnesses did what they always did. They were unable to agree upon what he said, or if he said anything at all. The dramatic Latin motto made for good reading, so it became a historical fact.

Soldiers carried the President across the street to a rooming house and found a bed. The room was tiny and the long President had to be placed diagonally on the bed. Attended by a crowd of surgeons, family members and the public, the Great Emancipator died the next day.

Booth had staggered out of the horror-stricken theater crowd, slashed the man holding his horse for no apparent reason, mounted painfully and rode off.

He approached the Navy Yard Bridge on the way out of the District of Columbia.

Using a code phrase given him by Stanton, he passed after an army intelligence officer in the shadows nodded to the sergeant manning the gate blocking the bridge into and out of the barricaded capital.

David Herold passed an hour later, not needing a code phrase. He was not the most wanted man in America. No one knew who he was.

The two conspirators met at their prescribed location. Booth neglected to mention the saddlebag full of gold coins he had exacted from the federals as his fee for killing Lincoln.

They rode to Dr. Mudd's house where Booth's leg was set. Surrat told them about Mudd as both a friend and a regular stop on the Confederate secret agent route to Canada.

Booth gave his notebook and some personal possessions to Herold. Herold would meet a Booth lookalike the next day to ride south. The man had no idea why Herold had chosen him as a partner to skirt Richmond and head on a southwesterly direction to ultimately end up in Texas.

Like real Confederate spies before him, Booth left the doctor's home with directions for the route to Canada. He turned north and rode at a comfortable pace. As comfortable as riding with a broken leg could be.

Stanton was good for his word initially. He had the nation's telegraph system shut down for a day, delaying the news of the Presidents death and any word about his assassin. Unknown to Booth, his reprieve was twenty-four hours. Afterwards, he was fair game.

Herold met the slender, dark-haired young man he and Booth selected. They had met him at a several days before in a DC bar. He could have been Booth's younger brother. He was down and out, looking for fame and fortune.

While the young man was in the privy at the rear of the bar relieving himself, Booth hatched a plan and departed, leaving Herold to pull the man in. Herold told him he had some money and was going to go south as soon as the blockades were discontinued. Once out of town, he was going to go to Texas and buy a small farm or ranch. He said he was going to need a partner. The man, Samuel Eakins, signed up on the spot. He agreed to meet Herold at midnight on the night Herold told him. Herold did not mention the murder of the President of the United States.

They ultimately stopped for a night at a tobacco farm in Caroline County, Virginia. The owner, Richard Garrett, allowed them to sleep in his tobacco barn.

Troops arrived and the barn was surrounded. Herold surrendered. The imposter, not knowing he was such, was shot in the barn and died as John Wilkes Booth.

Sergeant Boston Corbett disobeyed orders and shot the Booth lookalike through a crack in the barn. Struck low in the back of the head, the .44 Army bullet coursed down through his neck, causing a slow, painful death.

The dead man was wrapped and sewed into a blanket. He was delivered by boat to the DC Jail and buried under the floor until unrecognizable. Then, the body was turned over to the Booth family for burial on their property.

Few were the wiser. All of them had reasons to hold their tongues.

Corbett was arrested for disobeying orders. His charges were later dropped at the order of the Secretary of War, Edwin Stanton.

Corbett, a religious zealot, prior to the war had used scissors to remove his testicles in self-atonement after two prostitutes enticed him. A self-proclaimed hero and preacher after the war, the man lived convinced he had killed the wrong man and a secret society was after him for what he knew.

He disappeared from Kansas in 1888, perhaps right about something for the first time in his tortured life.

*****

Booth, living well in Canada, grew a beard to somewhat hide his good looks. He exchanged letters with Izola and inquired about their daughter Ogarita. For some reason he did not care about the son. He promised to meet them soon in San Francisco and wired funds to cover their transportation. He knew it would be a while

******

Herold, Mrs. Surratt, Lewis Powell, David Herold, and George Atzerodt, though civilians, were hung after a court martial. They had not been allowed to testify or answer questions. Of the group of eight identified conspirators in either the kidnap plot or assassination, or both, only John Surratt had a civil trial several years later.

Perhaps the only true secret agent in the group, he escaped to Canada and claimed sanctuary at several Catholic churches.

Unlike Booth, he left Canada quickly and went to Europe. He served as a Pontifical Zouave at the Vatican for a while. He was captured and escaped to Egypt. He was captured in Egypt in 1867 and extradited back to the US.

At the time of his trial, statutes of limitations had run out on all charges and he was never convicted of any alleged crime. The only real spy in the conspiracy got away scot-free.

CHAPTER 3

THE HATED MAN
1865

Louisville, Kentucky

William Clarke Quantrill was a school teacher much of his early adult life. He was exceedingly smart. His problem, or perhaps one of them, was he was not very pleasant. He tended to irritate people, whether students, shopkeepers or just about anyone else. Quantrill had some very fixed opinions on politics and was intemperate in how and where he shared them. Those opinions attracted extremists despite his personality.

When the war started, he quickly became a captain of his own group of partisans. Very shortly, he was hated by his own men. They could not tolerate his viciousness towards non-Confederate civilians. In Texas, many of his four hundred men broke with Quantrill. They included the James brothers, Jesse and Frank, as well as their friend, Cole Younger. Some followed Quantrill's lieutenant. Hardly any gentler, he was known as Bloody Bill Anderson. Quantrill even joined the Anderson band for a while.

Robert E. Lee surrendered his army to US Grant on April 9, 1865. General Johnson surrendered the most of the rest of the soldiers in gray to Sherman seventeen days later. The conditions of surrender developed by Lee and Grant prevailed.

After the effective end of the war, Quantrill was still raiding as a guerilla in central Kentucky in June. General Shelby took his men to Mexico and tried to join Maximillian, but Quantrill fought on in his normal skirmish geography.

In a skirmish at Wakefield Farm, Quantrill was shot in the back as his horse spun around in terror during a barrage of federal small arms fire.

The federal troops prevailed in the fight. From rank insignia and his face from posters, they knew they had a prize in the wounded captain.

Quantrill, pretending to be paralyzed in the lower half of his body, was taken to a prison hospital near 10th and Broadway in Louisville.

He feigned being near death and the doctors paid more attention to patients they thought they could save.

He was put into a small room at the end of a hall with another Confederate prisoner.

Quantrill repeatedly called for his wife. He claimed

he was dying and wanted to see her one last time.

The warden approved the visit at the behest of the doctors. Likely to shut him up.

During the visit, the other patient emitted a death rattle, and succumbed to his wounds.

Quantrill developed a ruse very quickly.

"Honey, I have an idea. Take your dress off quickly."

"You are wounded, Bill. This is not the time or place for such carryings on." she exclaimed.

"No, just do it so I can walk out of this hell hole."

She obeyed.

"Now, help me strip this poor soul and you put his clothes on while I begin dressing him in my uniform."

The two struggled to lift the dead weight of the deceased soldier onto Quantrill's bed.

Quantrill, seriously wounded, staggered against the empty bed for a moment before regaining his equilibrium.

"Bill, are you alright?""

"Yes, give me a minute. All the straining with a bullet just taken out gave me vertigo," he said.

She helped steady him for a minute, then watched in amazement as he slipped into her heavy satin dress.

"Bill?" she said. He looked at her.

"You look like the bearded lady in a carnival." and broke out laughing.

"Damn. I probably do. Do you have scissors or anything?"

"No. Nothing. This is a prison. They wouldn't let me bring anything sharp in anyway," she responded.

Quantrill took some bandages from the body and tied her hands.

"Now, get in the other bed. Tell whoever comes in I died," nodding towards the dead man in his previous bed. And, the other patient came to, stole your dress, tied you up and left. Cry a lot. Try not to make much sense, okay? Meet me back at the farm and we will find a new place to live."

She nodded and Quantrill wrapped her scarf around his neck. Pulling it up, it covered his beard.

He gave her a curtsy and coquettish look, causing her to break out in giggles.

Sense of humor notwithstanding, the most hated man in Kentucky and elsewhere walked out the door. He was a dead man walking.

******

Quantrill carefully sought a lookalike. He found him in a single man named Leonard Joseph Crowder. He made friends and found out where he roomed.

Quantrill rented a carriage and he and his wife invited Crowder for a picnic. They rode out to an out of the way spot and his wife, now using the name Olivia, shot Crowder dead. She was, after all, reputedly Cole Younger's sister.

Olivia even dug the grave, since Quantrill was still recovering from being shot in the back several months ago.

"Honey, you know you are the only one on God's green earth who would ask me to dig a grave. And, I'd do it," she said. He nodded and smiled.

He once the man was in the hole, Quantrill took the shovel from his wife. He filled the grave and stamped the earth down with his boots. Every stamp hurt from his waist all the way up to his neck.

Olivia set out the picnic and they ate beside the new grave.

"Excellent lunch, Mrs. Crowder."

She gave him the type smile he had given her as he escaped from the prison hospital in her dress. But, she played the coquette naturally and often with a man whose home personality was totally different to his guerilla leader one. He was a good husband and she adored him. And, he felt the same about her.

That night, Quantrill sneaked into Crowder's rooming house and to his room. He removed everything, making it look like the man had moved out in the middle of the night to avoid paying his bill.

Quantrill kept the papers and personal items and discarded the clothes in a fire barrel.

Olivia put their house on the market with a trusted attorney who handled everything. They combined their money and Crowder's surprising cash savings from his room and bought a wagon. They headed for Arkansas and a new life in a rural part of a then-rural state. His only connection with his former identity was his knighthood in the Knights of the Golden Circle. Secret organizations were his thing. And, the Golden Circle was as secret as they came. He loved it and the responsibility it had entrusted in him. He was a knight responsible for a cache.

CHAPTER 4

DINGUS AND BUCK—OUTLAWS
1882

Saint Joseph, Missouri

Jesse and Frank James sat under some trees and drank cold, pure Missouri stream water out of tin mugs.

"Dingus, I'm tired," Frank said, calling Jesse by a nickname nobody else in the world better use.

"Tired of riding, running and shooting people. We have amassed a helluva lot of money even if you don't include the Circle money held in custody.

We have to disappear. The latest wanted posters on me list crimes whose statute of limitations have run out. Hell, boy, we have been doing this robbery stuff since '66.

Seventeen years and nary a wound. Our luck can't hold forever. We got to make a plan."

"I been thinking the same thing, Buck," the younger James at thirty-six said, using his brother's nickname.

He varied between given and nicknames often in the same sentence. Frank only used "Dingus" in private.

"Something else has been worrying me," Jesse continued.

"We got us a gang member causing us great risk of getting too much attention. Two things worry me. A lot. One is his marriage issue. The other is trust. I know if he gets caught, he will identify us for sure."

"Hite?" Frank asked for verification of his suspicions.

"The very same. He is beating his wife something fierce. Now, the law won't do anything about it. But, the Masons might. They don't hold for such foolishness.

But, worse for us, he has suspicions about the Knights of the Golden Circle cache. One of us, probably me, let something slip and he put it together. That would be a helluva bargaining chip if he gets in the hands of the law.

We have a solemn oath to protect those millions in gold Confederate coins and ingots. Both of us take it real seriously, Buck," Jesse said.

"I know you do. It is a double edged knife, like an Arkansas toothpick. An honor and a pain in the ass. With what the Confederacy had in the treasury and the last few shipments of foreign aid from countries like England, France and Spain who wanted influence when we won, I doubt all the banks in New York City can touch just your cache."

"Especially when you consider, the Circle's money is liquid anywhere in the world. Bank money is part on paper with only a little in the vault, relative-like."

"Ha. Don't we know it to be true from the banks we have robbed since the war? The worth they say they have is one thing, the money in the vault is nary a drop in the bucket compared to their claims."

"So, how do we solve the Hite problem?" Jesse asked.

"Well, try this on for size. One or both of us go to his wife Zee. Say we know she must be tired of getting beat on and offer her ten thousand dollars from our robbery take to pretend he was you. Then, we get those wannabe killers, the Fords to shoot him?"

"That could work. Who should talk to her?"

"I'm thinking the good-looking younger one. You are supposed to be Robin Hood and all. And, you got a fuller head of hair," Frank grinned.

Jesse grinned back at his older brother and best friend.

The next day, the brothers rode over to St. Joseph. They were in friend and family country and relatively safe there.

Frank saw Hite downtown buying items for the farm with his take from some of the gang's robberies. He offered to buy the outlaw lunch. Jesse, seeing this, headed for Hite's house on the edge of town.

"Howdy, Zee. How are you?" he asked, noticing a dark bruise under her left eye and some defensive wound bruises on her wrists and forearms.

"Oh, I'm fine Jesse. How are you?"

"I'm fairly well. Listen, while your husband is being fed by my brother, I want to make a serious offer to you. Are you willing to listen? And, if you don't take it, to keep your mouth shut?" Jesse asked.

The woman looked apprehensive. She knew Jesse was loyal to his friends and was highly unlikely to hurt one, but she was not sure where she stood with the James boys.

"Ugh...go ahead, Jesse. I promise."

"First off, Frank and I cannot tolerate one of our group beating on his wife. Zee, he's gonna kill you one day in a drunken rage. And, he is none too nice stone cold sober."

"I wish I'd never met Hite. He's a bully and a coward, Jesse," she said, spitting the repressed thoughts out all at once.

"In my experience, all bullies are cowards. That's unfortunate for you. There's something unfortunate for Frank and me, too."

"What's unfortunate for y'all related to my dilemma?" she asked.

"Well, it's not directly related to you, but the solution could be. Frank and I know Hite is getting ready to sell us out. He could cause us to be killed or arrested. You know what the Pinkerton's did to our home and our mama. They blew the home down and her arm off and killed our little half-brother. It wasn't right. We did not get seriously mad about robbing and killing until then," he said.

"But, anyway. We cannot let him continue to beat on you. We also cannot let him turn us in. So, here is a plan. I want you to consider it and to do so quickly.

Hite favors me a bit. A little shorter, but close enough, especially with the dark beard we both have been wearing recently. We were thinking bring in the Ford brothers to talk about a plan for a robbery by just the three of them.

One of the Fords could kill Hite and claim it was me. Say Hite really was not Howard, the name he uses, but really Jesse James.

You'd have to play the grieved widow James for the rest of your life. You could think of a lot of ways to make some money off the notoriety. But, in the meantime, I have ten thousand dollars in gold and silver coins for you to sweeten the deal."

The eyes opened wide on the dollar amount. It was a fortune to her and to most people of the time.

"So, Jesse, the Fords would shoot Hite and run out claiming the man known as Mr. Howard was really Jesse James. I would back their play and cry my eyes out. Actually, instead of trying to make money off being your widow, I would probably take the boy and girl, the ten thousand, and move away. Maybe Texas. Maybe California."

"So, Zee, you are good with this?" Jesse confirmed.

"Oh, Jesse, I am *so* good with it." She gave him a big hug that promised more. But, he never mixed business with pleasure. He mounted his horse and said "When you see the Ford boys ride up—and you know them from meetings we've had here—it's gonna happen. Fix them some food or drink, then you and the two little ones hie on out and get away from the gunfire. I don't want the children to see their pa gunned down either."

She nodded and smiled. She was a fine figure of a woman. But, Jesse knew, this wife created by Frank's plan did not hold a candle to his real Mary Ellen.

He strode back to the center of St. Joseph and saw his brother and the man known as "Mr. Howard" coming out of a café laughing and smiling.

"That Buck is slick," Jesse thought. "I'm sure glad he's on my side."

******

Jesse and Frank met with Robert and Charles Ford and outlined their plan. They promised a smaller amount to them to split as Jesse had to Zee. As Frank said when he and Jesse were planning, "Those boys would jump off a cliff for five hundred dollars. Up it to a couple thousand and they'd become regular church goers."

The following day, the Fords rode up to the home Jesse had visited the previous day.

"Hiya, Tom." Bob Ford called out to Hite, using his alias of Thomas Howard.

"What brings you boys by today?" the gang member asked.

"We got an idea. Just the three of us. The James and rest would not be involved, so a three-way split. You interested?" Charles asked.

"I might be. Why don't y'all come on in and we'll each have a glass of Who Shot John and talk about it."

The Fords saw the pretty wife, Zee, and their two kids leave the house and head towards downtown.

The name Hite used for bourbon made Bob Ford sweat even harder. The two decided he would be the shooter. Both knew, unlike them, Howard nee Hite, had killed before and was better with a revolver than both of them put together.

Charles picked up on his brother's nervousness and spoke first.

"Tom, we was thinking of robbing the Platt City Bank. We went over and watched it a couple times. They have a big money delivery every Monday. That being tomorrow, we could ride over early. Hang around. Watch the delivery, then let the armed guards leave and hit the bank before the money gets put in the vault. What do you think?"

Hite walked towards a print hanging crooked

on the wall and stepped on a chair to reach up and straighten it.

Charles Ford nodded at his brother who drew his .45 Colt and shot Hite in the back of the head.

He dropped the gun and turned and ran out the house, yelling "I shot Jesse James. I shot Jesse James."

Within the hour, both Fords were arrested for murder. Within weeks, Governor Crittenden had pardoned both of them. Taking their money, they moved out of town.

Charles later committed suicide. Bob made the mistake of arguing with a man in Colorado. The man was holding a ten-gauge shotgun at the time. Both barrels took Robert Ford to an early grave at thirty years old.

Frank, upon Jesse's feigned death, surrendered to the governor. He was held in jail several weeks and moved to Gallatin, Missouri to await trial. After almost a year, he was tried and acquitted of all charges.

He had been correct. Most of the crimes with which he had been charged had long since had their statutes of limitations expire. As to the other more serious and capital charges, those states holding warrants each decided to not send good money after bad, and chose to not extradite him. He was fully exonerated by early 1883.

Frank moved his one-armed mother to Oklahoma and Indian Territory where he lived as the family patriarch with a reputable retail job.

One of the most sought after outlaws in history. One who outfoxed the Pinkertons. Frank James was just a man whose only hope was his face would be forgotten.

*****

In reality, the inseparable James brothers were not separated. Jesse following a long-term plan, bought a farm near Blevins, Texas. He lived there as James Courtney. It was not that Blevins was the center of the universe. Rather, it was operationally very near the Knights of the Golden Circle gold cache for which he was responsible. He had always been expected to gravitate towards there. Frank and even their mother, spent as much time in Texas as in the territory north of the line. He was charged, as a fellow Knight, with assisting Jesse with the security of the cache. Family, too, meant a lot to the James and Jesse believed in it. So did his older brother and lifetime best friend.

Frank had married the comely Annie. He looked forward to a long life without ever breaking another law.

The James brothers had put away their outlaw ways. But, not their guns. The guns stayed close and readily to hand.

CHAPTER 5

THE GUNFIGHTER
1878-1883

Lincoln County, New Mexico
and Hico, Texas

Billy had lived by a number of names. Henry McCarty, William Antrim, and William Bonney, were the ones he used the most in his twenty-odd years. His father's name was McCarty and his step-father's was Antrim. William Bonney was simply made up.

His sometimes friend, Pat Garrett, called him Little Reno because of reno, the gambling game they played. And, the "little" because at five foot seven inches, Garrett was at least nine inches taller.

He was slight and sandy-haired. He did not yet have enough whiskers to grow a mustache, much less a beard. For years, he would look like a kid.

Billy the Kid.

According to his mother, Catherine, Billy had been

born in New York City. He had been brought west early in his life. He left home at her death in his mid-teens.

He finally found the family he never had. They were members of the Tunstall, Chisum and McSween families in Lincoln County, New Mexico.

Billy learned about loyalty and to "ride for the brand," under the mentorship of rancher John Chisum. Chisum was a decent man. He became the father figure McCarty had been to the toddler and Antrim had never been.

Billy had been in and out of jail all of his life since his pre-teen years. The more serious allegations were connected with the feud in New Mexico, known as the Lincoln County War.

The Lincoln County War was between two factions. As many disputes were, it was about land and power. One side was headed by two Irish Catholics named Dolan and Murphy. The other was headed by Billy's friends, the Tunstall's, Chisum's and McSween's.

Riding for the brand was exactly what Billy, as he now called himself, did when Englishman Tunstall was murdered by Dolan and Murphy men.

The side Billy chose had its own enforcers. They were known as the Regulators. At any given time, Billy's side or the other, were bonafide lawmen. The Dolan and Murphy contingent were assisted by the Lincoln County Sheriff, William Brady. Brady was assisted by a gang known as the Jesse Evans Gang.

In a shoot-out, Billy killed Sheriff Brady and one of his deputies.

The act earned him a couple of murder warrants. Billy's friend, Pat Garrett named sheriff. Their friendship came to an abrupt end.

When Garrett's posse killed Tom O' Folliard, one of Billy's new friends, the end was cemented.

Billy and Pat were now enemies, on opposite sides of the Lincoln County War.

The war lasted over a year. It became unclear to onlookers who was good and who was bad. The Dolan faction had the most political pull. Their friend, the governor stated the constable, who had deputized Billy and the other regulators, had not been properly selected. With the loss of official status, everything Billy and the Regulators had done under the color of law became criminal. In actuality, virtually everything on both sides of the Lincoln County War was criminal.

Before the feud was over, Billy and his cohorts were actually fighting the US Army.

Billy was captured by his former friend Garrett and sentenced to hang.

Billy, fearing his proverbial goose was cooked, asked a visiting friend to hide a gun in the privy.

"Put any gun in the shitter. I don't care if it shoots. It just has to look like it might." The friend hid a gun. It proved fully operable.

When one deputy went to lunch, Billy told the other

he needed to be escorted to the privy. He obtained the hidden gun and killed deputy Jim Bell. Bell had been a decent sort. When deputy Bob Olinger heard the shot, he ran to the jail, Billy used the shotgun Olinger had constantly threatened him with. Billy introduced two loads of buckshot to his chest from an upstairs window. "You know you deserved both loads, Bob." he said out the window to the body below.

Billy's only possessions were his Colt Frontier Model, 1873 Winchester carbine and a .38 Colt Lightning backup gun.

When the young outlaw was collecting his guns, he found some office cash for a grubstake in the sheriff's office. He walked down to the clerk of the court's office and found the clerk cowering behind a counter. Billy pulled his .44.

"You come up with all the cash money in this place. My leaving is going to save you hanging me. So, I want some compensation for my pains," Billy said pleasantly.

The clerk came up with almost a thousand dollars in tax and fee money and gave it to Billy. He dared not share the fact Billy *not* being hung would cost the county much more than the little he stole. The economy stood to lose many thousands more dollars due to lost celebratory food and drink.

Billy doffed his slouch hat and walked out the door, money in his jacket pocket and guns strapped on.

He went to the livery where the sheriff's office boarded Reno and recovered the horse he named for the game and the two former friends who had played it.

Billy was not in much of a hurry. An affable killer, he actually whistled "O, Susanna" as he walked Reno out of town. He did not pick up the horse's gait until on the main road. Billy was known even back East. He had a reputation to maintain.

Once out of town, though, he rode like hellfire was nipping at his boot heels. Maybe it was.

Later, Garrett and several possemen went to the Maxwell Ranch in Sumner, New Mexico. They had a tip from owner Pete Maxwell saying Billy was hiding out there.

Garrett entered a bedroom where he had been told Billy could be found.

The shadow of a man whispered "¿Quién es?" or "Who is it?" Pat Garrett thought it was his old friend and fired twice, one a direct hit in the chest, the other killed an oil lamp nailed to the wall behind the bed.

The long-barreled Colt's reports in a small room temporarily deafened Garrett.

Yet, above the buzzing in his ears, the sheriff heard the distinctive four clicks of another Colt being cocked right behind his left ear. Just in case Pat missed the clicks, Billy pressed the cold steel in hard against the back of the sheriff's head.

"Big Reno. That's me you just killed. Maxwell is backing my play. He'll say it's me you killed. I am dead and gone. Take the reward and fame, damn you. Bye."

Garrett knew the voice was really was Billy this time and the shadow of a man and the voice both disappeared.

Pat Garrett never encountered Billy the Kid again. He knew Billy was faster, so avoidance now was a prudent strategy. He knew if they ever met, he would die.

Maxwell had been in on Billy's plan from the start. He deliberately put a dupe in the room Billy used, Maxwell testified to the coroner's jury "Yep. That was Billy, Sheriff Garrett killed at my place. Death changes a man, but I'm sure it was Billy when I seen him all laid out."

Maxwell liked Billy well enough. But, the Kid and Maxwell's daughter were sweet on each other. Maxwell had no compunctions about killing an innocent drifter to substitute as Billy. It was a small price to pay for not having his girl live a life on the lam with an outlaw.

Pat played it like Billy said and applied for the five-hundred dollar reward for Billy dead or alive. The governor reneged, so the angered people in the county raised seven thousand dollars for their own reward to the sheriff for killing Billy. In 1882, the legislature approved for Garrett finally to be paid his initial award. Garrett was now seven thousand five hundred dollars richer. Not returning it was well worth silence.

The Kid had outstanding capital warrants on him in both the Territories of New Mexico an Arizona. He had to avoid being captured and identified. He needed to stay both dead and far away.

So, Billy did what the Jesse James would do a few months later. He headed for Texas.

******

He landed in Hico, Waco was the nearest city of any size. It was about seventy miles away.

Reno had stopped at a stream nearby and drank. Billy liked the area, so he went looking for a town.

"I kinda like this area," Billy said to Reno as they rested. "Let's see if there's a town near-by, horse." There was. It was called Hico.

After a couple days in a hotel, Billy found a little twenty-acre place with a shack, a stable with some tack and a small corral. It had ten chickens, a rusty plow and a couple each of mules and horses. Not prime stock, but rideable.

It was not so much a ranch. Rather, it was more like a farm with some transportation thrown in. An old man had it and just died. A lawyer in town was representing his nephew in Denver who just wanted it liquidated as fast as possible. Seems, according to the lawyer, some gambling debts might be involved.

The animals were all fed. The lawyer paid the teen-aged girl on the next farm two bits a day to come over and check things and feed the livestock.

Billy, now calling himself William Henry Roberts, used most of his stolen Lincoln County sheriff's and clerk's grubstake to buy it. A lot of the rest went for feed for himself, the chickens, mules and horses.

Billy had a farm, some livestock, his guns, and a song to whistle. Not a damn thing more. And, Billy the Kid was good with his lot in life.

******

In 1883, Billy rode Reno into Hico to pick up some supplies. He got there at lunch time and decided to spend some of his sparse money on a sandwich, some hot soup and a cup of strong black coffee.

One side of the saloon was set up as a café, so Billy stepped in and sat down.

He looked at the daily menu chalked on a board on the wall.

"I'll take a ham sandwich with mustard, some of the bean soup, and a cup of coffee please," Billy said.

The man took his order back to the kitchen, then poured Billy a cup of coffee.

A half hour later, the skinny gunfighter was

stuffed and walked out into the cold, his jacket open, as always.

A farm wagon was pulling into town, the man driving was the only one aboard. The man was tall and dark haired. He wore a duster and had a full-length Winchester rifle visible propped against the seat beside him. Most riders carried short carbines.

The man in the wagon was hungry. He pulled the wagon up to where Billy had just eaten. Not wanting to have his rifle stolen in this strange town, he picked it up before walking towards the café.

A cowboy named Taos Gulden and his six friends walked out of the saloon side. He stopped aghast as he saw Billy.

"You. It's you. You're..." But, he was stopped in mid-sentence as Billy whipped out his Colt faster than the folks who saw it could believe. One of those people was the tall dark man with the rifle.

"Who I am or was is nobody's business. Keep talking cowboy and I will drill you right where you stand." Billy said.

He eased out the .38 Lightning revolver with his left hand.

"Now, I got ten shots for seven of you and I already have the drop on you. Think you assholes can draw fast enough to keep from dying? I don't. But, give her a try if you want."

"I got fifteen over here, boys. 'Pears to me y'all

are outgunned," the man from the wagon said as he levered a cartridge into the chamber of the long Winchester."

As Taos turned and looked, the man slowly raised the rifle and aimed it between the New Mexico cowboy's eyes.

Billy looked at him for a second, as did a crowd of about ten who had stopped to watch the action.

The cowboy balked and rushed off. His six companions surrounded his escape, half facing Billy and half the rifleman.

As quickly as it had formed, the crowd dissipated. The man lowered his rifle and eased the cocked hammer to half-cock.

"Stranger, if you'd let me, I would be honored to buy you the lunch I reckon you was heading for," Billy offered.

"Not necessary. But, since you already appear to have eaten, you can join me for a cup of coffee."

"I will take you up on that. I ain't much for public conversations, but I would sure like to thank you for covering my play just now."

They went in. The tall man put his rifle in the corner as he sat facing the door. Billy arranged a chair so he could see the door also. The man noticed the young man's action and nodded.

He ordered the same thing Billy just had from the limited menu and a cup of coffee for his guest.

"My name is Jim Courtney," Jesse James said, extending his right hand.

Billy shook and said "Billy Roberts."

"I'm figuring that was not the name the big mouth cowboy was gonna say," Jesse probed.

"I've had some other names. Like many, I came here to get away from somewhere else."

"I figured. Assuming he has not hurt any women or children, I don't hold much else against a man. You have to put yourself and your family first in this world. Life is not fair. The strong always come out on top. Unless seven men try to kill them," Jesse grinned.

"Mr. Courtney, you was pretty cool back there. You clearly pulled a gun once or twice. But, you seem too young to have been in the war. Unless it was one of the Indian wars."

"I was young when I wore a semblance of a uniform. But, apparently not too young," Jesse said.

"I was just a kid even when the war had ended, so I don't have a dog in the fight," Billy said.

"My family lost about everything. Then, Reconstruction and the Pinkertons hit and we lost everything else. But, I'm saying too much."

"Well, Mr. Courtney, a man's gotta protect his secrets. We all have them. I will say, having the Pinks as an enemy means you were somebody. Somebody whose name I'd know. Like you'd know mine maybe."

They were interrupted by the arrival of Jesse's

lunch and a coffee refill for Billy.

"So, what are you doing now, Billy?" Jesse asked.

"I had to leave the New Mexico and Arizona Territories real fast. I landed here and bought a no-account little farm about four miles that away," he said as he jerked a thumb southwest. "I've been playing at farming it for a while. Not a bad life."

"Yep. I find myself a farmer too, now. That's why I came up here. I read an ad for new device to harvest crops. Fella named McCormick outta Virginia is behind it."

"So, you know about farming?" Billy asked.

"Some. Not a lot. I got a small place down in Blevins. It's about ninety miles."

"A ways to drive a wagon to look at a piece of machinery…."

"I guess. I'm not used to sitting still very long. Being an honest man is a royal pain," Jesse laughed.

"Boy, ain't it the truth. One minute I was a cowboy, the next I was deputized, the next the governor said we weren't real deputies. Which made everything we had done criminal," Billy said.

"What did you do then?" Jesse asked.

Billy looked around. Nobody was within earshot.

"Can I tell you something you won't share?" he asked.

"You have my word."

"I killed the sheriff and a few other deserving souls in a face off in the middle of the street."

"And, this was in New Mexico? Maybe Lincoln County?"

Billy kind of squirmed in his chair.

"It was."

"Then, I'm thinking, if the news rags are right, you are early twenties. Not the teen age kid you appear," Jesse said with an accent on the word *kid* and a smile.

"Sounds like you might have figured out what name that fella who was about to wet his pants was gonna say," Billy said, hesitatingly.

"Pretty much."

"Thanks for keeping my secret, stranger. Letting it slip would likely get me killed. Though, other than a rifle from a long distance or a shotgun in the back, I'd go down real damn hard."

"I reckon you would. I saw you draw and know something of your history. What you just said, Billy, would be true of me also."

"You know me. Feel like returning the favor?" Billy asked.

"I miss my brother. We were partners. Partners in war and partners in crime. We are both trying to go straight now, just like you."

"Is you brother's first name Frank?" Billy asked.

"Actually, his first name is Alexander. But his second name is Franklin. Ma calls him Frank. Maybe some posters did too."

Billy lowered his voice and leaned forward.

"Looks like Ford didn't kill you," he said.

"No more than Sheriff Garrett killed you."

"So. The two most wanted outlaws in history are having lunch?"

"Seems so. Except we are dead."

"I'll be a sonofabitch." Billy exclaimed.

"The name has been applied to both of us, Billy. It gives me no worry at all," Jesse smiled. "What does worry me is I doubt you have seen the last of those seven cowboys. I reckon they are waiting to get you alone and outta sight of witnesses. Then, they are going to come after you. Well, I'm not backing out of this now. So, I will ride back to your place with you and help you out. I can look at my harvester after we take care of business. Let me finish my soup first."

Billy did not think about the offer long. Going into a gunfight against seven men alone or with Jesse James beside him did not take too much deliberation.

Jesse spied the seven going into another saloon down the street.

"Good," he thought and said to Billy, "Let 'em drink some more. Drunks make bad decisions and can't shoot very well. Hell, most cowboys can't hit much without a shotgun. We'll be just fine." Billy grinned back at his new friend. Jesse sure inspired confidence, not that anyone ever accused the Kid of lack of it.

The trip back was uneventful. There were several more hours of daylight left. They figured the riders would hit before dark.

Jesse and Billy scouted the property, focusing on the single path in from the road leading from Hico.

"We gotta get these riders in a pincher, but one where we won't hit each other in a crossfire," Jesse said as he looked around.

There was a berm of dirt on the left of the path about fifty yards from the shack. It was ten yards off the path.

Across the road at the same distance from both the shack and the path on the right was a small hollow. Jesse called it a "holler." It had a downed oak tree laying parallel with the path.

"These two places make good sniper's nests," Jesse said. Billy thought so, too.

Each set up with canteens, several boxes of .44-40 cartridges which fit their revolvers and Winchesters. They did not know how long a gunfight faced them.

Jesse walked another fifteen yards up the path and laid a long, thin branch across the middle of it.

"Billy, when the first horse crosses over the sapling branch, we cut loose on them. We will be shooting with them at the point of a V and us on the two ends. They will not expect anything until they get closer to the house. They won't have a chance."

Billy nodded and gave the endearing lopsided grin young women seemed to like. It was an unintentional trait he would keep the rest of his life.

The two settled behind their respective earth and

oak barriers and waited. It took an hour, but then they heard horses and men speaking low.

Neither sniper moved.

Jesse had proven he could hit fifteen head-sized targets at fifty yards in one minute with his Winchester. Billy, though more a pistoleer, was probably close to as good.

The men all had their guns drawn. As the first horse stepped over the branch, the two opened fire. Horses reared. Surprisingly, several men aimed their revolvers and returned fire. They did not have specific targets and just shot at random. One man in back, accidentally shot a cohort in the back of his head. He did not live long enough to feel bad as Jesse put a two-hundred grain lead bullet just under his ear.

Within a minute, seven men and two horses were down.

The two new friends inspected their work. One cowboy was still alive, but Jesse shot him point blank. Billy performed the coup de grace on two horses. They would be a disposal problem, laying across the path to his farm.

"We got a lot of work to do before dark," Jesse told Billy. "I bet if you harness up those mules, you can drag these two dead horses off. If you stay on grass, they'll slide better."

"I'll go get them and be thinking about where to drag them. There's an old farm close by. I was out hunting and came up on it. The codger who lived there was dead sitting in a rocker on his front porch. I buried him. He had at least ten hogs. I knocked a rail off the pen, but they hung around. I gave them all the feed he had day before yesterday. Do hogs eat dead horses?"

Jesse grinned. Their problem was solved.

"Hogs eat anything. Horses, men…." he nodded to the bodies piled in the path. "I will collect any guns, money and things of value from your deceased visitors. Then, we'll load 'em up in the back of my wagon. You drag the first horse over to near the hog pen and I'll check the five other horses and put them in your corral. When you get back and hook up the remaining dead horse, I will follow you over with the wagon. We'll unload those boys into the hog pen. We'll split their stuff and keep or sell it, as the case may be."

Billy nodded and went for the mules and began to harness them and hook on a logging chain.

The cowboys had decent saddles and guns. Nothing had initials or names. All could be sold somewhere other than Hico. The grand sum of money to split was twenty-three dollars.

Forty-five minutes later, Billy came back with the two mules dragging the log chain.

He helped Jesse load seven bodies into his wagon.

"I can see why they call it 'dead weight'" Billy groaned as the two hefted the last body aboard.

"We'll be done soon. I am thinking we ride back

to town, get two rooms at the hotel and have them draw up some baths. Then, some steaks and good Tennessee whiskey if they have any. We did fair work here today. Those boys will never ride after anybody again. Before a couple days have passed, there won't be any trace of them to be found."

They cleaned up enough so the blood from the cowboys to not show, rode into town with Jesse on one of Billy's horses and a plain, unidentifiable saddle from a dead cowboy. They rented two rooms and requested baths be drawn. Much cleaner, they ate later, split the money and returned their rooms to sleep the sleep of innocents.

One was almost thirty-six, the other almost twenty-four. One a rebel guerilla, the other a New Yorker turned Western gunfighter. But, they had several things binding them together. They had been two of the most wanted and most famous outlaws anywhere. And, the two of them took on seven men and killed all without receiving a scratch. Ambush? Yes. The ambush just evened the odds.

The two men remained friends. Perhaps Billy was a replacement for older brother Frank, Jesse's constant partner. Frank was in jail awaiting trial. As soon as he was exonerated, Frank moved his mother and wife to Oklahoma and Indian Territory. So, despite frequent visits, the older brother was still away a lot. Billy seemed to fill the void.

CHAPTER 6

THE ACTRESS
1883

Laredo, Texas, Canterbury, Connecticut, Dallas, Texas, Chicago, Illinois, and Tamaulipas, Mexico

Rita Wilkes liked her stage name better than her real name, Ogarita Elizabeth Bellows. She knew her real father was John Wilkes Booth. Depending on what part of the re-United States she was playing, the Booth connotation would be harmful to her career. Wilkes as her last name, not so much so.

But, to hell with it.

Soon, she was going to use her real father's surname. She had his darkly handsome looks. She had the genetic acting talent from her father, grandfather and uncles.

The Booths were the greatest family of thespians in America.

Her father had besmirched the family name eighteen years ago. Her mother still loved him and thought he had been killed in a robbery five years after his supposed death in Virginia. Rita was there in San Francisco when it happened. Her mother rushed them away, the child's eyes covered. Rita knew her mother never saw him after the robbery. Maybe her mother was right about her father dying there, maybe not.

Rita personally felt he was still alive and actually felt his presence at her performances at times.

She barely remembered the handsome Wilkes Booth at the farm he secretly owned near Harper's Ferry. He seemed to love her. As a toddler, she rode in his lap and he told her funny stories to make her giggle with glee. Maybe her mother was right. How could a loving father not contact his little girl ever again?

Rita was thrilled with the play, Foggarty's Fairy. It was written by W.S. Gilbert without his usual partner, Arthur Sullivan. She played the fiancé, a solid co-starring role she knew would help her career.

She was in Laredo, Texas. The Owen Theater was the least impressive so far. Laredo seemed to her to be a cow town. She preferred New York, San Francisco or Chicago. Not the Wild West. She had to admit, though uncouth in general, the men held a certain appeal for her.

Though not particularly religious, she was not going to be like her mother and her paternal grandfather who never saw the need for divorce before remarrying.

Rita sat at her makeup table, finishing the lip rouge and running a final brush through her dark hair. She was wearing her shoes and stockings and a see-through shift when the young male stage manager tapped on the door and stuck his head in.

"Miss Rita, you are on in one minute." She stood and faced him, giving him an eyeful.

"I shall be there in forty-five seconds, Robert. Mark my word."

He closed the door and she slipped the satin dress on and hooked the back securely as she exited her dressing room and prepared to wow the crowd. And, wow them she certainly did.

******

Jack Wise was a rancher. Maybe he would be better described as a rustler who had a ranch. It was in the State of Tamaulipas, Mexico. He moved over to Texas when Arizona Territory got too hot for him. A man had to learn his trade somewhere. Learning, Wise made a lot of rustling errors. A lot of lawdogs in Arizona wanted to talk with him.

He used his ranch to hold and rebrand cattle. Wise profited by his earlier mistakes and became a pretty good rustler. He sold under-market cattle to both

Mexican and American buyers. The buyers were aware of discrepancies in the brands. The slaughter houses were, too. But, such things could surely be overlooked for the price.

The price of graft had risen recently in Mexico. Wise needed an infusion of capital. He had seen Foggarty's Fairy in Brownsville three days ago when they sold a small herd.

An idea for the capital infusion had begun to form, so he followed the play to Laredo with some of his boys. They were tough boys, too. Unlike most cowboys who could not shoot a revolver worth a damn, these four were fast on the draw and accurate. One was his trusted foreman and number two, Otha Smith. Otha had served with him throughout his "cattle acquisition career" as he referred to rustling enough of other people's cattle to form a large ranch.

"Boss, you done drag me to this damn play for three nights in two cities. And, it ain't all that good. What's on your mind? Are you romantic for the girl actor or something?" Otha asked.

"'Or, something' is the answer. Now, mind you, I don't hate the way she looks. Nope. Not one little bit. But, I did some research on her. She's played all over the country. I believe her family and the play people both might pay to get her back, if she was to be taken and held somewhere," Wise said.

"Somewhere like a ranch down in Mexico?"

"Somewhere just like a ranch down there," Wise agreed.

"How do we get her?"

"Wal, she is at the Drover's Hotel just down the street. I figure she'll be tired out after her acting and will sleep pretty deep, don't you?"

"Probably, Boss. We gonna bust in and get her then?"

"Maybe quieter than bustin' in, but yeah," Wise said.

"What time?" Otha asked.

"This play ends within a minute or two of eleven o'clock every time we've seen it. I figure maybe two-thirty or so."

"What if somebody is with her?"

"I considered the possibility. We cannot leave a witness or a body. We will have to take them and dispose of them over in Mexico. We want Miss Rita to just disappear. We don't want no lawmen poking around. At least not until we are safely back at the ranch. They can't come down there. And, I am 'helping out' the local Rurale captain on the side, as you know."

"Yeah, the money has been well spent so far."

"Tell the boys we have a little mission tonight. Have their horses saddled and left at hitching posts near the hotel. But, not right in front, okay? Just nearby. And get the buckboard ready and out front, too."

"We'll sneak in, guns out, but nobody fire a damn shot." We don't want to wake up the town. If anybody gets in the way, tell the boys to bust 'em over the head with their shooter," Wise ordered. "And, we'll all wear bandannas around out faces," Wise added. His foreman nodded assent.

******

Rita finished the final act and she and her leading man had three curtain calls with the cheering audience. This was the final night in Laredo. They were off to Denver next and she could not wait.

The troupe gathered and each toasted with glasses of champagne. Rita knew the bottles were too warm and did not like the taste anyway. She begged off and walked over to her hotel and climbed the stairs to her room. This was the first time her place on the program allowed for a private room and she liked it.

She stripped and gave herself a sponge bath in the bowl. The pitcher water was tepid, which unlike the glass of champagne, was a better temperature to enjoy. She looked in the streaked mirror and admired her curvaceous shape.

Rita slipped on an almost transparent thin cotton shift and brushed her dark hair her usual sixty strokes before dousing the oil lamp and getting under the sheet.

It was a hot night. The little bit of breeze coming in the open window was not much help. Nor was the constant sound of yelling and occasional shots.

She finally fell into a sweaty, fitful sleep around midnight.

Just before three in the morning, she was awakened by a small noise. It was like a click. The click was the tip of a Bowie knife pushing the bolt on her door's lock aside. The door opened with the tiniest of squeaks.

Four masked men silently entered. One still had the large, ominous knife in hand. Her first image was her father jumping off the balcony at Ford's Theater, Bowie in hand. But, the image faded and stark terror took its place.

Two of the men guarded the door. Two approached her silently. One cupped her mouth before she could let out the scream she planned. He tied a gag around her mouth so tightly it hurt. It was followed by a pillow case over her head. She was effectively blinded and muted.

"You resist us, you make a sound, you die. Get it? I am not kidding Rita Wilkes. You will die. But, the four of us will have our way with you first. And, it will not be gentle."

She nodded, terrified. One sat on the bed with her. He, she assumed correctly, was the leader. The other man who had approached the bed now packed her clothes and personal items in her valise. She knew this by sound. The room was still dark and her head was still covered by the pillow case.

Within a minute, she heard the valise close and the strap cinched. The man on the bed with her stood and roughly dragged her to her feet.

Taking her by the arm, he guided her through the door and down the hall to the stairs. He whispered the stair location and helped her down the first step, leaving her to find her own way on the rest.

Rita realized he was not being a gentleman by helping her. His guiding hand was not in the middle of her back, but varied from her bottom, covered by the sheerest of cloth only, to her breasts, similarly covered. It was not a time to worry about dignity, she realized. Rather, it was a time to stay alive.

The half-asleep night clerk awoke with a start as the four men and one almost naked woman came down the steps.

Wise brought a Colt Frontier Model down on the man's head. Two men each grabbed a shoulder and dragged him along to the rear door.

Two saddle horses and a two-mule wagon awaited in the alley beside the hotel. Wise threw the oiled canvas cover back on the wagon's bed. They bundled the unconscious man into the bed, followed by the actress.

The butt of a Colt slammed into the man's head several times. He would never awaken from the blows.

A cowboy pulled the cover over the woman and the body as Wise and Otha climbed aboard. Flanked by the two horsemen, they eased out of the alley and down the street at a leisurely speed. They were what they appeared to be, a rancher and his cowboys heading back home, but only after a brief stop.

Otha slapped the reins and the mules picked up their pace. They crossed into Mexico well before daylight and headed towards the ranch some fifty miles distant.

The stop in Laredo was at the post office. Wise had questioned the girl about the address of her next of kin. She reluctantly gave her mother's address in Connecticut. Her mother is Martha Lizola Mills, called "Izola" by friends and family. Wise posted the ransom letter before leaving Laredo. It would take at least a week, perhaps two, before it was in the mother's hands. Mexico would have taken longer yet.

Ten miles into Mexico and nary a Rurale patrol in sight, Wise called for a halt. They stopped near a small hill with rocks laying on the earth.

Wise had his men remove the hotel clerk's body and cover it with rocks. They used his coat to wipe most of the blood from his head wound out of the wagon's bed.

Wise and his men got a full look at the beautiful, dark-haired actress in the bright sunlight. The light almost made the chemise shift disappear. She was even prettier without clothes than in any array of costumes. Wise thought, had he not been strapped for money, he would have kept this one just for fun.

Hell, he still might after he got the money.

They pressed on, thirty-five miles to go.

******

A week and a half later, Wise's ransom letter arrived at Izola's home in Canterbury, Connecticut. She read it with horror.

She immediately dug through papers Booth had left with her in San Francisco after the war and his earlier faked death. Their life there had abruptly halted when she saw him struck in the head during a robbery and killed. That her one true love had never again contacted her proved his real death this time.

She found what she sought. It was what he called her panic address. A post office box in Dallas, Texas.

"You ever get in trouble, money trouble, legal trouble—hell, any kind of trouble, Izola. Wire this address and mention my name. Help will come," Booth had said. He refused to elaborate further, despite her questioning.

She wrote the following wire: "Daughter Ogarita Wilkes kidnapped Laredo Texas. Stop. Five thousand ransom. Stop. Letter follows. Stop. Lizola Booth."

She hesitated to use Booth's full name on a telegram others would see before the recipient. That could wait for the letter to Dallas. She would post it the same time as she sent the wire. She quickly drafted a letter with her contact details and bonafides, as well as the ransom demand letter itself, folded inside.

Lizola immediately left to send the telegram and mail the letter.

******

At the same time, a letter from the owner of the stage troupe arrived at the Chicago offices of the Pinkerton National Detective Agency.

It was screened and quickly found its way to founder, Allan J. Pinkerton.

Pinkerton, whose firm contractually served as Abraham Lincoln's secret service, had suffered a stroke. He was only working a few days each week.

But, his staff knew whose daughter Ogarita Wilkes, nee Booth, was. They further knew the assassination of Lincoln had been the company's and its founder's, greatest failure, accompanied by a distant second. Second was the inability to bring the James brothers to justice.

It had been eighteen years since Booth's death at the Garrett tobacco barn in Caroline County, Virginia at the hands of a crazy federal sergeant named Boston Corbett.

The Pinkertons had tracked at least fifty "Booth sightings" since 1865. His staff knew Booth and Jesse James were their founder's obsessions. The Scot would want to see this letter with his own eyes.

The contention of the owner of the traveling act was Rita had run off with the hotel clerk. Since she was under contract for another ten plays, he wanted her back. He had no clue she was a kidnap victim.

Pinkerton had Detective Nash in Corpus Christi and another, Pollard, in San Antonio. He had the Corpus Christi man on the Texas-Mexican train to Laredo and the San Antonio detective on the I&GN line within hours. The troupe had already left, but Pinkerton, America's greatest detective, wanted his men to interview people on the scene more than to speak with the owner. He was now in Denver, if necessary, Pinkerton could sent a Colorado detective to interview him. Maybe even one of his new cadre of female detectives. But, his instinct told him the scene of the crime would be where the necessary information was. It always was. So, he sent two of his most experienced detectives to Laredo. All of his detectives could shoot. In 1883, Pinkerton was careful to place the best shooters in Texas and Arizona. They needed the best gunmen there.

CHAPTER 7

THE KNIGHTS OF THE GOLDEN CIRCLE
1883

Laredo, Texas
and San Clemente, Mexico

Michael Kane had not been a Confederate officer. His father had. A very senior one in the Confederate Secret Service.

The elder Kane had reported directly to the real brains of Confederate administration, Judah P. Benjamin. Benjamin was a Jew. He was the first Jew to serve on any President's cabinet in US history. The president, however, had been the President of the Confederate States of America.

Benjamin had served as both Secretary of War and Secretary of State. He was a Louisiana attorney before the war. The overall intelligence effort reported to him, though it was not widely known.

He turned to an old group, founded outside the

Mason-Dixon line, called the Knights of the Golden Circle, to help preserve the hard assets of the Confederacy.

The secret society had been an expansionist, then pro-slavery and pro-secession. It had as many Northern officials leading its various regional "castles" as Southern. As the war proceeded, its goals became almost solely confined to the Southern effort.

Before Richmond was burned and abandoned by the Confederacy, Benjamin had elements of the society and his secret service move gold coins and some bullion to several secret locations. These locations were in the custody and the files of the Golden Circle. And, there they remained.

The society's final post-war headquarters was in Dallas.

Kane was late-teens to early twenties during the war. His father groomed him for the career he planned for his son. He sent him to the University of London for studies in accounting and economics. Young Kane, at twenty, had the best equestrian, shooting, military tactics and hand-to-hand fighting tutors in Europe.

He could ride and shoot as well as any ranger on either side of the war and could use a sword or rapier as a real weapon, not just a ceremonial part of a uniform.

Texas suffered less than any Confederate state during Reconstruction since each of its governors, whether Republican or Democrat, were native Texans.

Regardless of politics, they each had Texas's future as their primary goal. Their moderating effect on Reconstruction had contributed towards the headquarters of the Circle being placed in Dallas.

Michael Kane, brilliant and deadly, had worked for the Circle since his return from Europe. He had been its Superintendent since just before his thirty-fifth birthday.

Now, Izola Booth's letter in hand, he had to decide which Circle members to activate.

Unfortunately, the best equipped were hiding in plain sight under new identities.

He could not make them resurface to retrieve Rita Wilkes. But, he hoped their sense of loyalty and duty would. Most were the Circle's custodians of large caches of Confederate treasure and men who had amassed large fortunes themselves during or after the war.

They had done dishonorable things. All were killers.

They knew about honor, though no longer honor and duty to country. Honor to each other. Warrior's creed. Maybe a little honor among thieves.

Kane thought about all of this as he chose his team. Most were already in Texas or adjacent Arkansas. One was in Oklahoma and Indian Territory, but he was crucial.

He sent the coded wire there first. To the only one

who went by his birth name. Frank James. Perhaps not as well-known as his more charismatic brother. But, deadlier and the better tactician by a smidgen at best.

Then, another wire in code went to Blevins, Texas. To a man named James Courtney. He had only been "dead" a year. It was going to be risky for him. Real risky.

He was Frank's brother, Jesse. Jesse James.

The next one Kane really caused Kane to wrestle with himself. The man had seemed a psychopathic killer. Though one whose tactical operations were textbook. He had been "dead" for exactly eighteen years. Now, he was known as Leonard Crowder. He was a state away. Probably nobody would recognize him now. But, anyone who did would either shrink away in stark fear, or shoot him on the spot.

His name was William Clarke Quantrill. The rebel guerilla leader who had slaughtered virtually every man in Lawrence, Kansas. None were soldiers. Male civilians in their teens to nineties. Often in front of their families. Frank James diverted from the main body of rangers and warned men and boys to hide so they would not die. Quantrill's bloodthirsty furor on raids prompted Frank and Jesse James to separate from him during the war, along with their friend, future outlaw Cole Younger.

They were all members now. Kane had not picked the members. His predecessors had. He just inherited them. But, he had chosen and submitted the possemen to his board of trustees.

Jesse and Frank were co-custodian knights, though their cache was the largest one. Quantrill was a custodian knight. The final one was a knight for life, but inactive and with no ongoing responsibilities. Until now.

These men individually had killed more men than Hickok, Earp, or even Hardin. Probably put together. In war and in outlawry, without counting Lawrence, Kansas.

Kane had to include this final one. He had a vested interest. A member with his own money, he had no cache responsibility. But, he knew the codes. He would come.

He had killed only one man Kane knew about. Abraham Lincoln. The last member of the ghost posse, besides Kane himself, was John Wilkes Booth.

Jesse was the youngest at thirty-six. His brother, Frank, was four years older. Kane was Frank's age. Booth was forty-five and Quantrill was forty-six. Prime. All of them.

Kane did not know it yet, but there would be one more. A surprise posse man. Maybe the fastest, coolest gun of them all. Maybe as good as Kane himself. Probably not. Just maybe.

It took two days for the posse to get their telegrams, decode them, encode responses and send.

They would meet in Laredo in four days. Kane would leave today and snoop around Laredo. He would look for clues.

Kane packed his clothes and gear in saddlebags. He put his horse, Hadrian, in the stock car on the train to Laredo. Hadrian was an exceptional black stallion. His coat matched Kane's trail outfit and gun rig. Solid black.

Kane sat in the best car and lunched on steak and red wine served upon a starched white cotton table cloth. He had every right to this lifestyle. He was effectively the head of the bank with perhaps the largest amount of liquid assets in America, if not the world.

Kane was moral and apolitical. The initial reason for the vast treasure he oversaw was to fund the resurgence of the Confederacy—a purpose which had faded long before he assumed his responsibilities. It was no longer a Southern Cause trust. Now, it was generally either used for what the committee deemed to be a good cause, or was simply protected. It was a trust. One often used for charity. And, Kane was its living, breathing, deadly due diligence trustee.

Kane realized with the black horse, him dressed in black at his six-foot four, he was an imposing figure. It was good; he would divert attention from the wanted men trying to spend their new lives as farmers.

He arrived in Laredo in the evening and checked into the hotel where Rita Wilkes stayed. The hotel manager was long since home. Kane would chat with him in the morning. For now, he carefully folded his business suit and laid out his black shirt, vest, jacket, trousers and gun rig. He dusted the black Stetson with the cigarette roll on the edge of the brim. He checked to assure his backup pocket gun was ready. It was a British Webley Bulldog in .44 Webley. He had become familiar with the gun while training in England. For a two inch barrel, its accuracy was amazingly good. Kane slid his perfectly tuned .45 Colt Single Action Army under his pillow.

Kane was asleep within minutes.

The next morning, he had steak and eggs. "May as well stock up before trail food," he thought to himself. After breakfast and three cups of strong, black coffee, he sought and found the hotel manager.

"I am Michael Kane. I'm conducting inquiries into the disappearance of the actress Ogarita Wilkes," he said to the manager.

"Another? I had two yesterday. Pinks."

Kane did not flinch, though shocked.

"Who hired the Pinkertons?" he asked.

"I reckon the man who owned the actor company. They mentioned his name."

"If you do not mind, please repeat your answers to them. For me to ask the same questions would waste your valuable time, Mr. Baum."

"Well, I got in early and the night clerk was not

at his station. I checked the office and the privy. He was nowhere to be seen. I noticed he gave the eye to the actress every time she was in his presence and she smiled back. So, I thought I'd go up to her room and see if she'd seen him. Her door was open and she'd cleared out. Without paying, I might add," the man said.

"So, I put two and two together and figured the two of them had run off together. So, that's what I told the Pinks."

"What else did they ask?" Kane interjected.

"What kinda fellow Roberts was. He was the clerk. Was he a handsome devil who'd attract a beautiful stage actress."

"And, Mr. Baum?"

"I said he was fit and presentable. He was an orphan with no family, no fortune and no prospects. He was a go-getter though. I figure he'll have money of his own one day. Just not now."

"When do you reckon they left?" Kane asked.

"The Pinks figured she must have gotten in after a cast party around midnight. So, it had to be between midnight and when I found her empty room at about seven-thirty in the morning. The night clerk could have left anytime."

"Was the room messed up? Like a fight or some-thing?" Kane asked.

"No. A little messy. I find women guests make more

mess than a trail riding cowboy anyway."

"Interesting. Did anybody else check out early?"

"Not a soul."

"Any strangers hanging around here or around Miss Wilkes?"

"Not that I saw."

"Would your day clerk have seen anything?" Kane asked.

"The Pinks questioned him and he said 'no,'" Baum replied.

Kane verified the exact date and thanked the hotel manager.

He went to the theater. The man in the office served as the ticket taker, which was exactly who Kane wanted to question.

"My name is Kane. I've been asked to look into the disappearance of Ms. Wilkes recently. Do you have a list of names of attendees the final night of the play?" he asked the man.

"I do. We have found sometimes the guests get riled up or likker'd up and shoot into the ceiling or start a fight or try to get up on the stage. Especially if there is a female looker like the Wilkes woman," he said.

"May I see the list?" Kane asked.

He could see the man hesitating and placed a five dollar gold piece on the counter between them. The money help the man decide in Kane's favor.

It appeared fifty people attended the play. The man

had remarkably clear penmanship.

"It you make a duplicate copy this, and copy it really neat for me, I will include another gold piece when I pick it up. Deal?"

"I could copy it again," the man said.

"Anybody stand out for any reason?"

"Naw, just a mix of townspeople and riders off the trail. Like everything else we have here."

"Any people from outside Laredo in pairs or larger you remember?"

"Maybe one pair. Guy in his forties and what looked like his foreman. Got the impression they were off a ranch out of town. Thought this was not the first time they'd seen the play from something one of them said," the theater employee said.

"Do you remember what it was?" Kane asked.

"Just a feeling. I don't remember exactly what, but I am sure I got it right."

"Where did they play before coming here?"

"I think somewhere in East Texas, but I don't know where."

"These two men," Kane began, "what did they look like?"

"Both tough-looking fellas. Older one was the boss for sure. Short, stocky. He was bald with brown hair on the sides mixed with gray. Had a Van Dyke beard. Other fella was the opposite. Tall and lean like a rider. Looked to me like both had guns under their coats."

"Is that unusual for 1883 Laredo," Kane asked.

"For town folk, yes. Riders no," the man responded.

They chatted a few minutes more, but Kane had learned all he reckoned he would from this man. He would pick up the list of attendees in a while and take it with him to the two livery stables in town to see if he could identify the rancher and his associate.

He walked over to the town marshal's office and inquired whether there had been any herds outside of town about the time Rita Wilkes went missing. There had not been. The brand associated with a herd would have been good information to add to his investigation.

As he walked out of the hotel, he spied a businessman in suit. Like he was wont to do, Kane looked closely for something. There it was. A Masonic symbol hanging on his pocket watch chain.

Kane nodded to the man and stretched out his hand to shake. The particular handshake advised the man he was a fellow Mason.

"I am just visiting Laredo. Do we have a lodge here in town?"

"Not yet. We are using the Presbyterian Church," and he nodded to the nearby building, "until we raise funds to build one."

"I see," Kane said. "Is the pastor a fellow Mason?"

"He is. Pastor Duff. A fine fellow and a good Mason."

"Thank you. I may walk over and extend my regards to him."

"I know he'd like it if you did."

They parted and Kane headed directly to the church. He introduced himself the same way and soon he had arranged a meeting room for the next day.

Kane picked up the list of play attendees and took it to both liveries.

He hit pay dirt on the first one. It was where he left Hadrian. The stable owner kept names and addresses of customers.

One name from the theater list was a livery customer the night of the play. Jack Wise from an unnamed ranch in Mexico. He had left a two-mule drawn ranch wagon and two saddle horses. He claimed them the night of the play, which the liveryman thought was odd.

"Most folks claim their mounts early in the morning. These fellows claimed the mule wagon and their horses about dinner time. Helluva time to hit the trail for Old Mexico, by my reckoning," he told Kane.

The description of Wise and the one other matched the theater man's description. Kane also obtained descriptions of the other two.

He checked on Hadrian and started canvassing the several hotels in town. He found one where Jack Wise and one Otha Smith had single rooms and an additional double room was reserved in Wise's name the night before Rita Wilkes went missing.

For the hotel's address requirement, Wise and Smith listed "San Clemente, Mexico." San Clemente was the return address for the ransom demands. It was a small town in Tamaulipas State.

"Hopefully," Kane thought, "these are our suspects." He knew it was not cast in stone, but the probability was better than anything else he had. The timing fit, the retrieving the horses and mule wagon at an odd time fit, and Wise and Smith attending the play fit. Further, it looked like the end location fit. It was enough to work on.

******

The Knights of the Golden Circle had a room reserved in a different hotel from the one Rita Wilkes had used. Kane had a list of the room numbers and bought some stationary and envelopes. He put them in as many hotels as the town had so they would not recognize one another ahead of time. His exception was putting the James's in one.

He addressed each envelope by room number only. The rooms were in his name. Kane placed a coded note inside each, telling the Knight to report to the Presbyterian Church after lunch tomorrow. They were not to acknowledge one another in the hotel or an eating establishment, if they were acquainted or otherwise recognized each other.

Kane spent the rest of the day walking around town and observing. He dropped the envelopes at each of the three hotels.

He took Hadrian out for a ride to loosen him up after the train trip. The black stallion would rather run and fight than he would eat. He was still almost wild, but he and his master had a bond. If Kane called him or whistled in an emergency, he would nearly pull down any object to which he was tied. He would stand motionless almost anywhere if Kane left him reins down. At most, he was hobbled on the trail at night. Man and horse were partners.

The following day, Kane had determined he had accumulated all the evidence still available about the kidnapping several weeks before. By the time he received the mother's letter, the troupe had moved on. Kane thought the letter was histrionic, but admitted he could not put himself in the place of Martha Lizola Mills, nee Booth and several other married surnames.

The only one of Kane's original deadly crew who worried him was Quantrill, now using the name Leonard Joseph Crowder. He had a reputation as a psychotic serial killer, generally not liked by his men. Kane included him because his tactical planning was reputed to be the best available anywhere. Kane would keep his murderous tendencies in hand, or kill him if needed.

He was less worried about the James brothers except for one fact. Frank walked freely and used his real name. If he was recognized, might Jesse, whose face had appeared on many wanted posters be also? But, these two were men who had not hesitated to ride from Arkansas to Minnesota to rob two banks. The robberies went wildly awry, everybody but Jesse got shot up, but he and Frank got away. The Youngers were in prison.

The men selected all rode hard and shot straight. Kane did his risk assessment and stayed with his plan to keep America's recent two most wanted outlaws in the posse.

Booth was riding because of the vested interest his daughter being kidnapped represented. He reportedly traveled to a number of cities to see his daughter perform. He was an actor. He was not a great rider or shooter. He had prevailed in several duels, but that did not make him a gunman. It did not take a tremendous amount of skill to put a single shot pistol made by Mr. Deringer to the back to someone's head and press the trigger. Even if the someone was Abraham Lincoln.

Kane had not included him on the list of possemen he presented to the Circle's trustees. A majority added him.

Kane ended up with four men. Three as deadly as could be found. One, a loose cannon actor at best. But, if not included, Kane feared Booth might take matters in his own hands and do something stupid, jeopardizing the mission and the life of his daughter. After almost two decades of Reconstruction hardships, most Southerners were not Booth fans.

Their lot would have been better had Lincoln lived.

Kane determined if Booth jeopardized the mission, he would kill him. He should have ample time en route to Mexico to observe both Booth and the others' reactions to him. He was betting all would consider the actor expendable, his daughter notwithstanding.

Kane had not identified the members to one another in his coded letters to each. He thought the element of surprise might be instructive to him, as he watched their interpersonal reactions.

He looked at his watch. A man in a suit was approaching the door. It was Quantrill or, Crowder, as he was known now. Kane recognized him from library research. Quantrill had changed in the eighteen years since his "death," but Kane still knew it was the former guerilla.

"Mr. Crowder? I am Michael Kane. You can just call me Kane. Everybody does. Thank you for coming, sir."

Crowder stuck out his hand and shook. His handshake was firm and confident. He looked Kane in the eye. Kane, who was not afraid of a soul, living or dead, successfully hid a shudder. Crowder—or Bill Quantrill—had eyes as unfathomable as the ocean. And, cold. This was the man who annihilated Lawrence, Kansas. In cold blood. A man even his as yet unknown cohorts, the James brothers, had parted from. At forty-six, he was clearly still a force to be reckoned with.

His voice was even and did not give a hint of madness. Kane already knew he was brilliant.

In a pleasant tone, he said, "Call me Bill. I chose to use my former name as a nickname. If it gives me away, so be it."

"Bill, you will know two of the knights chosen for this mission. One may surprise you even more. It is his daughter, who very few people even know exists, who is the reason for the mission. Or, as I refer to it, the posse."

Quantrill nodded politely and sat in one of the wooden chairs placed around a scarred church table. They heard the sound of rider's boots. Two tall, dark men entered. Jesse and Frank James had arrived.

Jesse and Quantrill looked at each other without saying anything. Both moved their hands closer to the revolvers hidden beneath their jackets. Frank James stepped between them.

"Damn, Bill. We heard you were killed in Kentucky," he said.

"You heard wrong, Frank. Here I am, frisky as a colt and meaner than a copperhead."

"So, I see," Jesse responded.

"Jess, how you been?" Quantrill asked.

"Dead like you. But only since last year, not 1865. I'm still not used to it. How'd you pull it off, Bill?" he asked his former and hated commanding officer.

"Allow me to interrupt, gentlemen," Kane said, "We will have time to swap legends on the trail. But, once the fourth man arrives, I need to brief you and we have to begin to formulate a plan. The three of you will be crucial to the tactical planning due to your military and umm, extralegal experience."

"Kane, I left another man standing outside. I met him after I 'died,' and was pretty impressed with his draw speed and accuracy. You'll know why, when you see who he is. But, first, he's not a Knight of the Golden Circle. He's only twenty-four and has no allegiance except to himself. But, he's a man I'd ride the river with."

"Who is this young man who has so impressed you, Jesse?" Kane asked.

"He goes by Bill Roberts now. But, you would know him as William Bonney, Henry McCarty or maybe Antrim."

"Billy the Kid?" Kane asked, almost incredulously.

"That very same. I've been around the boy since I died and went to Texas last year. Billy was already there. He's loyal and deadly. I don't reckon I have to sell you on his skills as a gunsel."

"No, you don't. Before we let him in…. Bill, how do you fell about letting one more man know Quantrill lives?" Kane asked.

"I'll go with Jesse and Buck on it," Quantrill said, using Frank James's nickname. Kane looked at the James and got nods.

"Jesse, if you would, bring the young man in," Kane asked.

Jesse James showed Billy the Kid in and introduced him. Kane repeated this would not be the time to exchange stories about how each falsified his death.

He was a good-looking young man. Kane found out he was twenty-four. He barely looked sixteen. Billy had not begun to shave yet. He had a ready smile and seemed both bright and affable. A good judge of people on first meeting, Kane liked him.

Kane looked around the room as the men chatted about old times. The Kid just listened. The odd man in the posse was late.

At twenty minutes after the appointed meeting time, there was a knock at the door. Kane approached it, his hand loose and near the butt of the horn handle on his .44 Colt single action.

Every man in the room was a killer. Many times over. Each watched how Kane moved. Each wanted to see him draw. Draw on someone else. They suspected they would get their chance soon.

Standing at the door was a man who currently used the name John St. Helen. John had been his first birth name, though people called him Wilkes.

Once the most wanted man in America, John Wilkes Booth was now only somewhat recognizable. Few outside of DC had seen the wanted posters. Virtually everyone in the country had seen his likeness in the newspapers which were now eighteen years old. His trademark dark mustache drooped down below his lower lip. The mustache was considerably thicker than when he jumped from the balcony at the Ford Theater after assassinating Lincoln. He had added muscular bulk to a previously lean frame. But, he was, indeed, Lincoln's assassin, standing there in the flesh.

They shook, wordlessly and Kane showed Booth to a chair. The three former Confederates looked at Booth, knowing he looked familiar, but not quite able to place him.

"Gentlemen," Kane began, "this is the final member of the posse. He goes by the name of John St. Helen. I think you will recognize him as John Wilkes Booth."

The four men at the table were clearly surprised.

"I had heard rumors, but didn't believe them," Jesse said, unintentionally speaking his thoughts aloud for everyone.

"Wilkes, we will use the cover names in our travels on this mission. For now, I will use real names," Kane said.

"May I present in seating order, Jesse James, Frank James, Billy the Kid, and Captain Bill Quantrill?"

"My, my. This is quite an assemblage of mayhem

for our little project," Booth said.

Without waiting for further elaboration or questions by anyone, Kane resumed control over the meeting and began his briefing.

"Wilkes was married and had a daughter well before the events of April, 1865. He was an operative of the Confederate Secret Service tasked with kidnapping Abraham Lincoln.

John Singleton Mosby, known as the Gray Ghost, was diverted from Northern Virginia to meet Booth, a couple of henchmen and Lincoln on the border of the Virginia. Mosby would escort the party through the federal blockade to Richmond. Once in Richmond, negotiations would begin for the cessation of hostilities and the return of Lincoln. The plan was rendered unnecessary by Lee's surrender. I can only assume, Wilkes, you decided to assassinate Lincoln without orders from Richmond?" Kane asked.

"I had cooperation from the federal White House. The cooperation facilitated my escape across the Navy Yard Bridge, had the War Department turn off every telegraph in America for a day and facilitated the legend of my death. The reasons for the assassination were prompted by money and personal wealth by highly placed members of the government. Had I known the horrors of Reconstruction, I would have never done it."

Kane watched as the former Confederates sat iron-faced. The Kidd fidgeted in his chair, not interested in something before his time and which did not affect him a damn bit.

"It is Wilke's daughter Rita Wilkes—she uses her father's middle name obviously—who is the subject of our endeavor here. She was kidnapped from the hotel a block down the street about ten days ago. Her mother received a ransom note and forwarded on to the Circle's address. I received it, called a board meeting, summoned you and came here to do some detective work.

The detective work has given us a suspect and his domicile is the same area as the place the ransom letter demands money be sent. I believe rancher Jack Wise, with a spread south of the border, kidnapped Rita. I further believe he had help from his foreman, Otha Smith, and two riders. They likely put her in a wagon and transported her over the border and are holding her there right now. Mexico will be our destination. We need to decide on what weaponry and equipment we are missing, get it here in Laredo and proceed to San Clemente in the state of Tamaulipas, Mexico to recover Miss Wilkes, or Booth, as it were."

Kane paused to pass out theater programs showing her likeness to each of the members.

"I found out something disturbing in my detective work here in Laredo," Kane said.

"The owner of the theater group considered he

lost a valuable asset in his actress. He contacted the Pinkerton National Detective Agency to investigate. Two of their detectives were here several days ago. I do not know if they found out the same things I did, but have to assume so."

The James brothers clearly rankled at the mention of Pinkertons.

"Perhaps, Frank or Jesse, you would explain to the group how the appearance of the Pinkertons hampers us," Kane said, picking up on their body language.

"The government paid Pinkerton to kill us and level our family home. They got Greek Fire bombs from General Sheridan and threw them into our family home. The place blew up, killing our nine-year old half-brother and blowing our mother's arm clean off. Chasing after Frank and the boys and me is part of the game. Attacking a child and an old lady is damn unforgivable murder. If we see the Pinks on the trail, we will kill them and bury 'em so damn deep nobody will ever find the bodies," Jesse promised.

"I have no problem with your plan," Kane said.

"We have a mission. That is to recover Miss Wilkes. Anyone who gets in our way is disposable," he added.

He looked around the room. Nobody batted an eye at his words. He focused sharp blue eyes on Quantrill and the James for the next sentence.

"While I doubt we can formulate a final operational plan until we get to Mexico and conduct surveillance, we need to determine what we need in the way of materiel," Kane said.

Quantrill spoke up.

"Our old practice of riding in shooting with a revolver in each hand would only have a place in our plans if it was to create a diversion for part of our group who was actually freeing Miss Rita," the former captain observed.

"But, nonetheless, I believe we should each have two revolvers, a carbine, and a shotgun or two as backup and plenty of ammo. A little dynamite might be nice, too," he added.

"Wilkes, do you know if your daughter rides? Or, will we need a wagon?" Frank asked.

"She rode all over the farm in the Shenadoah Valley. I assume she has not forgotten how."

"Then, Kane, we need a fit horse for her and complete gear for it—canteens, blanket roll, tarp, saddlebags," the elder James concluded.

Kane was taking notes. All but Booth had two guns and a carbine. He took a quick survey of calibers and asked about camping gear to be carried on horseback.

"San Clemente is about fifty miles into Mexico. It is a fair size town and should have a church, stores and hotels. Probably several saloons. I don't know about cafes separate from saloons. If we ride in like a posse, we will attract attention. I'd say set up camp away from target ranch, send a man or two in for food and checking out military or police presence. We should not have to be there more than a day or two."

"What about those Rurales?" the Kid asked, speaking for the first time.

"Good question, Billy. We should try to avoid them and have a cover story if we encounter any. Who here speak Spanish other than me?" Kane asked.

"I do," Billy the Kid answered. Nobody else did.

"Okay. We will have a good cache of gold coins with us. I think portraying a group of land buyers would fit our demographics best. All agree?" Kane asked. Nobody dissented.

"Billy, as to the Rurales. Despite what President Porfirio Diaz would have us believe, his Rurales are no Texas Rangers, except for maybe some around Mexico City. Most are seven to ten man patrols led by a Mexican officer. They are largely peasants conscripted from villages and I understand few are either good horsemen or shots. I'd hate to kill off a whole patrol, but if we have to, we will. Like the Pinks, we will have to bury them deep."

"Mebbe we should have a buckboard to carry all these shovels and some decent camp gear and a protective box for the explosives. The girl can ride in that. One of us can drive with our horse tied to it," Quantrill suggested.

"Perhaps I should drive the buckboard," Booth began. "While I have ridden all over this land for eighteen years, the rest of you are proven military men and long riders."

"Makes sense to me," Frank said.

"Preference on guns, Wilkes?" Kane asked.

"Not really. I am not an expert. I have only killed once in my life. Colt or Smith & Wesson. Winchester for the carbine. All same caliber would be good."

"Done." Kane looked around the table. Anybody need anything while I am getting equipment? No? What do you think about scattering and going to lunch? We can leave before dinner and cross into Mexico around dusk. If there's a moon, press on until nine or so. If not, look for a decent camp off the road. It would be cooler than leaving in the morning."

All nodded and the meeting broke up, men leaving in separately or in twos.

Before dinner time, Kane had bought two .44-40 Colt revolvers with holsters, a Winchester 1873 in the matching caliber, a ten-gauge shotgun, several shovels, an axe, campfire cookware, some tarps and a horse and light buckboard. The horse was also broken for saddle. Kane purchased a saddle and accompanying gear to carry in the back of the buckboard, if needed for Rita. He added provisions and was done.

CHAPTER 8

THE PINKS
1883

Laredo, Texas

Jesse was out on the front stoop of the hotel smoking a cigarette. He saw two men walking down the broad dirt street. Dark suits and derby hats better suited to back east than to Laredo, Texas. Better suited too, to Chicago. Chicago was the headquarters of the Pinkerton National Detective Agency. The Pinks. As he had told the others, the Pinks were the ones who had burnt their family home to the ground. They killed their little step-brother. Their explosion took the right arm off their beloved mother. Allan J. Pinkerton, had been hired by the federals to get them. One way or another. He failed. But, he had not failed in gaining the lifelong enmity of Frank and Jesse James.

Jesse, coatless and unarmed, stood and followed the two men. There was no way in hell they would ever recognize him. Especially not here, far from his usual grounds.

The two men walked a block. One turned and made Jesse. Jesse began to stagger and the man made a joke about him to his partner. They went on and Jesse staggered across the street and followed from the side in the shadows. "Idiots." he thought.

He watched them go into a hotel. Giving them a few minutes, he went in and spoke to the desk clerk. A five dollar gold piece bought him two room numbers.

"I'm an undercover government man. Those two are frauds. Pretending to be Pinkertons. Did they tell you they were Pinks? They did? I figured so. They have a scheme and it's my job to stop it. You warn them before I get my partner and I'll charge you with aiding and abetting a felony," Jesse said, making it all up as he went.

He knew bull, spread convincingly, would fertilize any situation. He had used it in war and especially in robberies with great success.

Without a stagger, he went back to the hotel at a fast stride and tapped on Frank's door.

Frank opened it, S&W Scofield first. He dropped the long barrel hog leg and let his brother in, concerned by his expression.

"Buck, I found the Pinks and paid for their room number."

"How do you know the clerk isn't telling them right

now?" Frank asked.

"'Cause I told him we were federal men on their trail. They were fakes. He bought it lock, stock and barrel. Now, get your pants on. Won't be right walking down the street with your hat, guns, night shirt and those skinny-ass legs shining, big brother or not. You are Frank James. You got a reputation to uphold. So, let's go uphold it."

Five minutes later and the brothers were dressed and gunned up. Frank also had a Bowie knife and Jesse a lead sap with which to bust a Pinkerton head.

They walked part way to the hotel, took a right and walked the rest of the way on a parallel street running a block over. When they got near the hotel, they cut across a couple of lots and ended up in an alley behind the hotel. There was a back door and they went in quietly to the back door. The two climbed the rear stairs and walked as quietly as they could to the two rooms. Luckily, they were beside one another.

Taking out the sap and Bowie, which Frank held with its big blade pointed up and the sharp edge towards himself for a reason.

Both tapped lightly on their respective doors.

Jesse's door opened first, a Webley revolver stuck in his face. Jesse looked the Pink the eye and brought his sap down on the man's wrist, fracturing it. A left jab staggered the man back into his room with Jesse on top of him.

About the time they both hit the floor, Frank's man opened his door.

He greeted his caller gun first as his partner had.

Instead of a sap, he received the top, square edge of the big knife on his wrist. It did not cut, but it fractured nicely. Frank shoved his body against the Pink and they both went down. Frank pushed the door shut with his foot.

Jesse was astride his man, throttling him with both hands. His brother had his forearm across his man's larynx and all his weight pressed against it. Both detectives died quietly and quickly.

The brothers packed the two men's valises, taking money, badges and their Webley's. Both swung their victims over their shoulders and did a quick room check. No blood, no overturned furniture. Picking up their men's valises with their left hands, they peeked out their doors.

It was clear. They headed down the hall and down the rear stairs. Jesse tripped on the final step and dropped his man outside on his head.

"Damn."

"Don't worry any, Dingus. He didn't feel a thing." Frank observed.

Both men were on the ground, valises beside them.

"Now what, big brother?" Jesse asked, adding, "we can't claim the buckboard or our horses in the middle of the night."

"Can we get them to the river?" Frank asked, referring to the Rio Grande.

"Carrying dead bodies right through town?" Jesse asked rhetorically.

"Stop talking, Dingus. I'm thinking. There is a solution we passed. I just have to formulate it," Frank said. His brother shook his head, as he was wont to do.

"Wait here with our Pink friends. I'll be back, either with a solution….or, not."

Frank almost sprinted off. Jesse dragged the two bodies further into the shadows and sat on the steps with one valise in front of him like he was waiting for someone.

Frank returned ten minutes later with a push cart and two wooden coffins.

"What in hell?" Jesse asked.

"This is what we passed on the way here. I did not pay it no never mind until we were in a quandary, Jess. We walked right past a funeral parlor. These were outside waiting for the next couple of murders in Laredo. Which we just committed. How about our luck, little brother?" Frank said in a historically long tirade for him.

"There's a cemetery in town right on the river. We saw it yesterday. We are gonna be gravediggers on the way for an early job," Frank said.

"And, Frank, what are we digging with? Our fingers?"

"Not at all. We will be digging with the two shovels I put in the coffins."

They looked the part in their black suits as they wheeled the two coffins across town and to the cemetery.

Several large rocks changed their minds. Digging would be hard and take too much time. They added rocks to the coffins and closed the lids. The two tapped the nails already in place with their gun butts, sealing the lids. Jesse took his trousers off and waded almost waist deep in the water.

Frank slid a coffin down a slight bank to Jesse, who pushed it into the water.

Jesse kept pushing the sinking coffin into deeper water before it flooded and dropped the the bottom of the Rio Grande. Frank slid the other one down. Jesse repeated his launch and soon, both body-laden vessels were sunk.

"I wonder if two Pinks dead in the river vindicate Ma's arm?" Jesse asked as he pulled his trousers back on.

"Naw. We have to kill a few more. Now, old Allan himself would even out the debt."

"I was talking with Kane. He said Pinkerton had a stroke and was on his last legs now," Jesse said.

"No loss to mankind," Frank observed. Winded, the two former outlaws walked back to the Pink's Hotel. Jesse was dry before they arrived.

"We are here to arrest those fake Pinkertons," Frank announced.

"Who are y'all with again?" the clerk asked.

"Justice Department," Frank growled. "You want to get your passkey and lead us up to their rooms so we can arrest them?"

"Unlock it real quiet-like. Stand back if there's shooting," Jesse whispered to the man who looked very alarmed all of a sudden. Frank and Jesse drew their revolvers.

The clerk almost silently unlocked one door and stepped down the next. Nervously, he opened it with a loud "click."

The James's simultaneously kicked both open doors wide and went in more drama than they had almost two hours ago. They made a great deal of searching and walked out to the man with threatening looks.

"You are under arrest for conspiring to interrupt an arrest." Jesse said to the now-terrified man. "I warned you, didn't I?" he added to the made-up charge.

"Now, Fred, he may be innocent and a good American. Let's see if he really warned them to clear out before dragging him off to jail," Frank suggested.

"Naw, I know he warned them. I told him what would happen."

They went back and forth for a few minutes before Frank prevailed and questioned the man.

"I'm convinced he never came up to warn them,

Fred. They must have seen one of us on the street or something. Look, they even packed all their stuff. This is a clean getaway. We gotta get back on the trail come daybreak," Frank continued the charade.

The three walked downstairs and, without further ado, the two federal officers left.

A block down the street from the hotel, Jesse said "I'm pretty sure he would tell anybody who questioned him we were legit and the two Pinks were fakers who ducked out in the middle of the night, don't you?"

"Likely. It was as good a coverup as we had available. Just having them disappear might have been better."

"Sometimes, I get tired of the killing, Frank," Jesse observed.

"You sure are softening up, little brother."

"Mebbe. But, I'm not a shoe salesman."

Frank James, the most dangerous shoe salesmen in history, cuffed his younger brother playfully and almost knocked Jesse off his feet.

"I might be losing my hair, but I can still kick your ass." It was true.

CHAPTER 9

THE POSSE RIDES
1883

Near San Clemente

State of Tamaulipas, Mexico

Rita was used to a better lifestyle than she was experiencing. In the weeks since her kidnapping, her thin shift had been washed only once by the old Mexican woman who fed and tended to her. The shift was more threadbare than ever and provided less modesty than when she was taken.

Her meals consisted primarily of pinto beans, corn tortillas, and water. Sometimes, she received strong black coffee at night. It tasted like lye water, but the smell was wonderful to her.

Rita learned the owner of the ranch was her kidnapper. He was named Jack Wise. While she was used to men looking at her lustfully, Wise gave her chills. He did not miss a chance to grope, either. She had slipped a small, blunt butter knife under her bed. It was accidentally brought the first night with her dinner. Thereafter, she only had a spoon with which to eat.

Rita did not know if the knife was an intentional gift on the part of the middle-aged Mexican woman who was her only contact other than Wise. If the woman noticed the disappearance of the knife, she did not say anything. Each night, Rita sharpened it against the stone fireplace in the corner of the room. It was now worthy of both slashing and jabbing. She fanaticized about shoving it into Wise's gut and twisting. The rush it gave her survival instinct another day. It was not time to kill him. She would know the time all right. And, she would strike.

She did not know what her ransom amount was. She knew her mother was virtually destitute, unless in the year since she had been touring, Izola had remarried money. Rita knew Izola had more experience marrying without divorce than she had marrying anyone of substance, legally or not.

Rita had been a mere child with her mother in San Francisco the late afternoon they were going to meet her father for dinner.

He had been on the run for five years. They saw thugs attack him by the docks before he could meet them. Through her mother's fingers over her eyes, she saw the club crack his skull. And, the blood. So much blood.

Her mother hurried her away from the scene. Both thought they had just seen the true end of John Wilkes Booth. Who could they tell? No one. No one at all.

Booth was a scoundrel and killer to most. To her, the man whose dark hair and features she shared was papa too. He always would be.

Though long past it, Rita shed several tears. Papa would do something. He would rescue her. But, he could not. He was probably in a pauper's grave in San Francisco. Unmarked. Unloved. Forgotten, except to students just past McGuffey's Readers.

Rita sat on the edge of the bed, head in hands sobbing. After an hour, she heard the quiet padding of her keeper's feet. Marina. She was probably a nice woman. She always smiled at Rita. They could not speak because neither spoke the other's language.

Rita pulled up the shift, baring all which should be private. She wiped her eyes on the hem and lowered it for the barest modicum of decency just before the door opened and Marina walked in with a dinner of beans and corn tortillas. She also had coffee and an apple tonight.

Tomorrow, if past history predicted the future, Marina would bring a pail of hot water and a wash cloth and towel in with dinner. It would be for Rita's weekly bath.

The next day was like the past seventeen. Uneventful. Rita knew it was seventeen from the hash marks she had cut in the floor beside the bed with her repurposed knife.

She stripped and bathed. There was no mirror. She could not see her face. Her face and breasts were, she reckoned, her best attributes. Her legs would have been, except nobody ever saw them under the style of the day….perhaps style of the century. She looked at and lifted her breasts. They were noticeably smaller.

She shook her head and proceeded washing herself. At the end, she washed her shift. She could sleep naked, knife in hand and it would dry overnight.

Rita draped the wet shift over her single chair and went to bed. Hot and humid or not, she pulled the dingy sheet up around her neck and squeezed the knife tightly in her right hand. Sleep was a long time coming.

******

Kane, Billy and Quantrill led the posse out of Laredo late in the afternoon.

Booth drove the laden buckboard pulled by a strong horse, sixteen hands tall. As recommended, Kane chose a horse broken to both riding and towing.

The two James's brought up the rear.

It was too hot for dusters, but each man wore a long coat covering his pair of revolvers. Used to wearing one revolver and a small backup, Kane added a matching Frontier Model seven and a half inch barrel with a matching white horn grip to his primary.

They had agreed Bill Quantrill, or Len Crowder as he was now known, would be the prospective ranch buyer, Booth using the name John St. Clair, Crowder for the mission, was his brother. Frank would pose as his foreman and Jim Courtney and Billy Roberts were cowboys. Kane decided to be whatever the viewer imagined. Most likely, he would be imagined as a hired gun.

The road was hard and flat from the wagons of goods and people who transited it between Laredo and Mexico. It was a moonlit night and the posse rode until ten o'clock. Kane went ahead and found a likely camping spot a quarter of a mile off the road.

Knowing a fire might attract a Rurale patrol, they built one just large enough to see by and to lay out bedrolls. Kane assigned two-hour watch duty and the men finished coffee and climbed into their bedrolls. Booth managed to find room in the bed of the buckboard.

The night was soon full of coyote, cicada, and snoring sounds. The sky was clear and stars bright. Kane, on first watch, thought it was a good omen for the start of their mission.

He thought about Maria Elena Gonzalez de Vasquez. He had met her in Spain twenty years ago. Her family liked the money his family represented, but held his lack of both title and Catholicism against him. She married very quickly and was a *viscondesa* now, with two grown children. The oldest, a boy, was Kane's son. They had written no less than monthly each of the ensuing years. One day, he would go claim his one true love. And, his son. One day, perhaps.

He checked his pocket watch in the moonlight and carefully roused Frank to spell him.

Kane's allowable moments of contemplation about what had not been and may or may not be in the future were expended. He fell asleep immediately.

Billy made a small, smokeless fire in the dawn hours. He used one of the shovels to craft a Dakota fire pit and stoked it with enough twigs and small limbs to make a pot of coffee. Once made, he filled the air pit and fire pit with the dirt he scooped out and any vestiges of smoke were gone.

For Indians, there would have been the faint smell of smoke and the aroma of coffee. But, he reckoned a man had to take a few chances for the first cup of morning.

The aroma awoke everyone. Kane washed his face by pouring water from his cup held in his teeth into the palms of his hands.

He then got the last cup out of the pot and savored it while the rest of the posse broke fast with bison jerky and biscuits from the general store in Laredo.

By the time the sun was just over the horizon, they

rode back to the road and turned right, or southeast. San Clemente was another thirty-five miles.

Slowed by the buckboard, they only made a few miles in the first hour.

Kane spotted a dust cloud ahead and called for a halt to confer with the posse.

"There are Apaches who duck across the border into Mexico. That cloud could be Indians. Most likely, it's Rurales.

What happens will be determined by the officer in charge. The men will have no say in it. Down in this part of Mexico, I am betting they will all be untrained peasants," Kane said.

The men drew their rifles and proceeded forward. Booth had the double-barreled shotgun propped on the buckboard seat.

As the men neared, it was obvious they were Rurales.

The officer looked young and was well-uniformed. Kane thought it boded well. He feared an old, fat officer with an unkempt uniform would be more prone to either demanding graft or just attacking.

The patrol was one officer and seven men. From the looks of the men, the six possemen could make fast work of the eight Mexicans.

The patrol stopped fifty feet from Kane, who was at the head of the posse.

The young officer postured and tried to look intimidating.

Kane just stared him down.

In Spanish, the man who Kane thought must be a lieutenant, demanded to know who they were, why they had rifles out, and what their business was. All reasonable questions, Kane thought. Interestingly, Kane thought, the young officer's accent was educated Castilian, like his.

When Kane responded, the handsome young officer picked up on the similarity in their accents immediately, but said nothing.

"First, *Teniente*, our rifles are out in an abundance of caution. We feared you might be robbers or hostile Indians until you got close enough for us to see your uniforms.

As to who we are, we are the Crowder ranch employees accompanying Mr. Crowder," and he nodded to Quantrill, "on a ranch-buying trip. We are, in addition to Mr. Crowder, his brother, his foreman, several of his cowboys, and me. I am the one who speaks Spanish."

"I see," the officer began. "How do you propose to buy this property when you find it?"

"We have sufficient gold for a down payment," Kane responded, still speaking Spanish. He watched the Rurales as he spoke and noted how they perked up at mention of *oro*, or gold. He could see gears turning in some of their minds. The young lieutenant had no idea how much immediate danger he was in from his own men.

One of the men moved the muzzle of his rifle towards the officer's back. He yelled "*Teniente. Levanta los brazos. Ahora.*" ordering the officer to raise his arms now.

Kane, still on Hadrian, watched carefully. The man ordering his lieutenant cocked his Remington Rolling Block rifle and Kane drew and fired in a blur and his bullet struck the man in the side of the head. He crumpled off the horse as the James's and Billy the Kid began toppling Rurales with their rifles. Booth fired the ten gauge and one man almost lost his head as the load hit him.

Two Rurales dropped their rifles and threw their hands in the air in surrender. Kane motioned for his men to stop firing.

Shifting to excellent English, the lieutenant asked Kane where they were going and if they might help him get the bodies of his mutineers and two prisoners back to San Clemente.

"That is exactly where we are going Lieutenant. But, before we put the bodies on the horses, what is your story going to be? Because if it varies from us helping to save your life, I will drop you dead in front of your captain, then the boys will take him out and anyone else in uniform. Are we clear?"

"Perfectly clear. I have no reason to cause you trouble. You saved my life.

The Spanish army, where I was trained, also used peasant conscripts like these Rurales. But, they spent a lot more time training them and observing them before turning them loose with only one officer. It is a wonder this sort of thing has not happened before."

"Well, make sure you tell the true story. You will live to enjoy the drink I will buy you at your favorite San Clemente cantina," Kane said. The officer stared back at him, both contemplative.

The Americans watched the lieutenant direct the two survivors in throwing the dead over their horses and tying their feet together. The two prisoners were ordered to lead the horses carrying their dead former riders.

They rode into San Clemente by the end of the day. Several patrols were assigned to the town, so there was a captain who commanded the Rurales outpost. He accepted the lieutenant's story and asked questions of the posse, which backed it up.

The unexpected turn of events officially validated their cover story, so the posse members were able to secure hotel rooms for the night without arousing suspicion. The horses and buckboard were put in a livery stable and the group met for dinner and drinks with their new Rurale officer friend.

Between tequila and dinner, Billy and Jesse stepped outside to roll some cigarettes and get away from the din of the cantina.

"Did you see how fast Kane was, Jesse? I never saw somebody who I knew right away was faster than me. But, he sure as hell was." Billy almost whispered.

"Not only was he fast, he put the ball in the side of the man's head from twenty feet on horseback. I never saw the likes of it. Frank may be a bit faster than me. Or, maybe not. But, neither of us hold a candle to the man in black," Jesse responded, his voice also low.

Back inside, the lieutenant introduced the group to an *abogada,* or attorney, who specialized in land sales and closings. Somewhat stuck with their cover story, Quantrill and his "brother," Booth, agreed for a tour of available properties.

Kane, the James and Billy decided to spend the time riding around the area of the Wise ranch and reconnoitering.

Good luck struck the posse a second time, as the attorney, Jaime Diaz-Garcia, took them to the Wise Ranch as their second stop.

"I was approached by Sr. Wise some months ago. He needs to raise capital for his cattle operation and has more land than he needs. Out of a thousand acres, he is willing to sell a several hundred acre parcel," Diaz-Garcia advised them as they approached the ranch house.

"That is less than I want," Quantrill said, "But let's talk with him. The promise of gold coin might make him enlarge his offering." Booth nodded, as did the attorney, eager to earn a commission.

Otha came out and met them.

"Is Sr. Wise in? I have some prospective land buyers to speak with him."

"Yeah, he's here. Get down. Marina will get you some water while I get him."

Wise was upstairs getting ready to have his way with Rita when Otha caught him before he entered her room.

"Boss, that lawyer is here with some fellas looking to buy land."

"What do they look like, Otha? Mex or American?" Wise asked.

"Definitely American. Two brothers, mid-forties. Tough looking sorts."

"Think they are detectives, like Pinks. Or, maybe U.S. Marshals?"

"I can't tell. I'd say we have to talk or they'll come back. We just gotta be careful," Otha said.

"Alright," Wise said, buttoning his top buttons and putting off his first tryst with the girl until later.

Otha turned and led him down the steps of the *hacienda*, a smirk on the foreman's face.

"Sr. Diaz-Garcia. Good to see you. Gentlemen, welcome to Rancho del Oro."

The two nodded at him and all three men climbed out of the lawyer's carriage.

"Gents, I got three hundred acres west of here.

Good graze for cattle. Got some on it now. We can ride out after sitting and having some water. Or, whiskey if not too early."

"I'm sure it's late enough somewhere," Booth commented.

Quantrill, the tactician, was eager to get inside the house and see the layout. To look and listen for some sign of the girl. He might open the party if the girl was there and kill these two idiots now and ride out with the girl.

He decided on water instead and Wise yelled for Marina. She appeared and he ordered a pitcher of spring water and some glasses. They sat on steerhide chairs in a comfortable open area with a fireplace. Quantrill noticed several chimneys on the flat roof of the adobe two-story villa. Probably one for the living area, one for a cooking fireplace and two for bedrooms. He assumed the girl, if still alive, was upstairs. The outbuildings consisted of a bunkhouse, a small cottage for the foreman, a stable and small barn. He doubted if a valuable captive would be kept in one of those.

Jaime Diaz-Garcia told Wise and Otha the Crowder brothers were from Texas and had a large ranch north of Laredo. They wished to expand into Mexico and thought this area would be the most convenient to move back and forth between.

"You sure you want to buy a ranch? Mebbe we

could partner up and you could use some of my thousand acres instead of owning. We could figure a mutual benefit deal. Either on percentages or rent or something," Wise offered.

"We are open to changing our plan. But, before we do, we'd like to see some ranches about this size first, then think about alternatives. You sure you would not like to sell your whole ranch? You could retire young and we'd keep Otha and your riders on as part of the deal," Quantrill said, getting into his cover identity as a rancher. He had quickly figured out Wise was a rustler.

It might not be a bad thing for Wise to think he was, too.

Wise paused at the offer. Making a large amount of money and heading to California, or maybe further south than Mexico with the girl had some appeal.

"I might consider selling the whole ranch. If the deal was right. Of course, Jaime and I would have to privately meet and discuss what to ask for it. And, whether we'd be better off selling the cattle or moving them back across the border and up to a railhead to sell them back east," he said, clearly intrigued.

Booth was getting into the guise and spoke up.

"My brother and I are not familiar with Mexican style houses. This one looks pretty nice. Could you show us around a bit?" the assassin asked.

"Mebbe downstairs, this trip, the upstairs is messed

up and I'd want Marina to finish cleaning before you saw it," Wise said.

"So, the girl *is* upstairs." Quantrill and Booth thought at the same time. Booth, like Quantrill a minute ago, also thought about the immediate efficacy of pulling their guns and killing Wise, Otha, and the attorney right then. Their problem was the unknown. Not knowing how many riders were in the barn, corral or stable. How soon they could get to the house. Lastly, what would be their alibi? If they pulled it off and took the girl back towards the US in the attorney's carriage, how would they contact the rest of the posse? Could they elude the Rurales?

Quantrill concluded it would be better to wait and have the whole posse hit the *hacienda*. He winked at Booth without the others seeing and hoped the man who spontaneously had decided to kill the President of the United States would not do something stupid. Again.

"Sr. Diaz-Garcia, perhaps we should take a look at the three hundred acre parcel and leave the house for Mr. Wise's convenience. I believe we have several other ranches to see today, so we'd better get going," Quantrill prompted.

"Otha, why don't you show them the parcel up for sale. I have something to finish here," Wise said.

Everyone rose and the two strangers shook hands with the rancher and followed Otha and the attorney out the door.

The father suspected his daughter was upstairs. What he did not suspect was what awaited her the moment he was back in the attorney's carriage following Otha's horse.

******

Wise poured a shot of whiskey. It was not rotgut, but also was not a fine Tennessee aged whiskey. He hurried upstairs and encountered Marina.

He motioned for her to go downstairs. She understood what was going to happen. It had happened to her in the past in this house.

Sadly, she went downstairs and cleaned up the glasses and pitcher from the table.

Wise unlocked the door. Rita heard him on the stairs and got her knife. Surprise was going to be her friend.

She laid on the bed, the short shift awry in an inviting posture.

Wise walked in. One look at him showed what his interest was. That interest was piqued when he saw her.

He took his clothes off. Terrified, the actress hid it behind a stage smile. He sat on the bed for a moment and groped her.

Rita Wilkes arced the sharpened butter knife into

his side with all the strength she could master.

Wise screamed like a scalded animal and rolled onto the floor grasping his side. Blood ran through his fingers.

Rita looked down and laughed.

"Guess you aren't so ready to show me a good time now are you, you bastard." she screamed.

She ran downstairs barefooted and wearing only the threadbare shift.

Wise's revolver and belt were on the table. She grabbed them, wishing more for shoes than a gun.

His horse was saddled and tied at the hitching rail outside.

She untied the reins wrapped on the rail and scrambled on, wincing as the hot saddle hit her bare nether region. Rita saw a rifle in the scabbard, saddlebags stuffed with who knows what, and a canteen.

Reins in hand, she turned the horse. She had no sense of direction. So, she just rode, spurring the horse with her bare heels. The horse went as fast as she could say on.

For the first time in weeks, she was free. Her dark hair blew straight out behind her and she smelled the desert. It was a glorious smell. The sun burned down on her back. She knew it would be a problem until she found some sort of covering for her head and body. But, for now, she had to put distance between her and anyone related to the Wise ranch.

Rita rode like the wind, smiling all the time.

She knew enough to spare the horse and slowed him down from a gallop to a trot, then a walk. Rita saw a stream ahead. It was barely a trickle, but she stopped to water the horse.

The horse balked at it and refused to drink. It must be alkaline or some other poison. She rode ahead slowly, the sun burning her back though the thin shift. The feeling of freedom diminished the sting of the sun.

Rita saw a small canyon ahead and pointed her nameless horse towards it. It offered the possibility of shade and a chance to go through the saddlebags and see if there was anything useable for her in them.

She could smell juniper and some pine as she entered.

Looking down, Rita saw a ten-foot wide groove in the sand. She thought it was a dried up creek bed. There were green plants and grasses growing at one point. Maybe there was water underneath. She had the canteen, but reckoned the horse needed the water in it, if not more after his hot run.

Rita slid off the horse. With his reins hanging, he stood still and did not look like he was going to run off. She spoke soothingly to him.

Looking in the saddlebags, she found a couple of sacks, tied with twine. One was tobacco. It was of little use to her.

The next was jerky of some sort. She bit off a piece. It was flavorful, but salty. She would finish chewing it, but put off eating more until she was sure of adequate water for her and the horse. She could tell the saltiness was making her thirsty already.

The next find was a good one. A rolled pair of clean socks. She put them on immediately. She had not gone barefoot since a little girl and the bottoms of her feet already were painful from the stirrups on the saddle. She found a folded bandana, which she used to make a head covering. Rita wished for something to cushion her nakedness on the leather of the saddle seat, but found nothing workable. There was a box of .38 WCF cartridges. She slid the Winchester out of its scabbard and saw the caliber was .38 Winchester Center Fire. Her purloined revolver must be the same caliber. Moving the lever a bit, she saw the rifle had a cartridge ready to be lifted up into the chamber with a full lever rotation. The last sacks were cornmeal and coffee. The other saddlebag had a small iron grill and a coffee pot and tin mug.

Rita found a small metal box with a valuable find. It had about thirty Lucifer's, or wooden matches. So, given some juniper or pine twigs, she had the makings of a fire. She didn't have anything to cook and doubted the desert would get cold enough to need a fire for warmth, but it was still a comforting find.

Lastly, there was a sheathed hunting knife. She

removed it and squatting, bare kneed on the grass, Rita began to dig. By the time her hole was a foot deep by a foot wide, she saw muddy water beginning to gather in the bottom. She and the horse shared some canteen water. She poured it in her cupped hand for him to drink. He went through half the canteen before she stopped. The hole was almost full.

Rita took off her makeshift bandana hat and used it as a strainer. She placed it over the coffee pot and used the coffee mug to scoop water out of the hole and pour through the strainer. The water in the pot was not crystal clear, but it was not muddy brown either. She gave the horse a coffee potful and strained another to make actual coffee for dinner with a piece of jerky.

Her diet had cost her to loose weight. She took off the threadbare shift and stood naked in the sun, wearing only Wise's socks.

Rita put her head in the hole and soaked her hair. She squeezed as much water out as possible.

She then put the shift in the water and washed it as well as she could. Taking it out, she wrung it and put it back on wet. It was cooling and made her feel better.

Rita walked towards a juniper bush and a diamondback rattler slithered across the sand several feet in front of her. The sight of the poisonous snake made her skin crawl.

She hacked some branches off the juniper and saw another oily looking plant. She did not realize it was creosote and would make fast-burning tinder. She gathered some and added to her growing fuel pile.

Rita left the horse munching on grass and walked out of the canyon.

Looking up, Rita reckoned she had another hour before dusk. She circled, looking at the horizon from each perspective. No dust clouds of riders searching for her. She returned to the canyon and unsaddled the horse. The sweaty saddle blanket was her only source for ground cover, so she spread it under a low-hanging pine. She added a few chopped off pine boughs to add a pleasant odor to the less than pleasant saddle blanket. There were not boughs enough for a pine mattress.

Rita built a tee-pee of twigs and touched a lit Lucifer to a smaller pile in the center. She got it right by accident and the creosote twigs in the center flamed up and ignited the tee-pee. Soon, she had a fire with the bail of the coffee pot on the end of a long branch, the bottom of which was held down by a couple of large rocks. Getting the rocks scared off a pair of scorpions. Rita began to understand, even without Wise or his men, this was naturally dangerous country.

She munched a piece of jerky for dinner and drank strong coffee. It was not properly brewed, but it was satisfying to a woman who had been a prisoner for almost a month.

Rita's clothes and hair had already sun-dried.

She leaned against the saddle, bottom and legs on the blanket, revolver, rifle and knife pulled in close. The horse was free to roam and she said a little prayer he would be there come morning.

The howling of coyotes did not deter from sleep coming to her early. She slept deeply through the night.

*****

Diaz-Garcia dropped Quantrill and Booth at the hotel to contemplate the properties he had shown them today.

The others arrived shortly.

They gathered under a tree in the square and Quantrill shared the story of seeing Wise and his property. He took a stick and drew a diagram of the house in the sand, which each man memorized.

Quantrill proposed they return before sunup and plant dynamite in the privy behind the bunkhouse and have a large charge near the bunkhouse door for explosion by rifle shot.

Since Kane and Billy spoke Spanish and the housekeeper did not appear to speak English, he suggested they be the two to quietly enter the house.

He said, "We should assume Kane and the Kid are inside the main *hacienda* by six o'clock and I will blow up the privy to get their attention. Since there will be more men in the bunkhouse than main house, Jesse and Frank should cover it with rifles. They should shoot the first man out the door and tell the rest the bunkhouse has explosives planted and if one more man exits, it will be blown to bits, them included. I will return to the front of the *hacienda* after placing the privy charge and Booth and I will cover it and the adjacent cottage," Quantrill finished.

"Billy and I will take care of Wise and any other threat in the house, then get the housekeeper to lead us to Rita. If she panics, we will just find her ourselves. Once we have her and any luggage she has, we will yell we are coming out the front," Kane said.

"Your exit, of course, will be timed by whether we have an active gunfight going," Frank James said. Kane and Billy nodded their total agreement.

"I will advise the livery we'll need our horses and the buckboard just before he closes at six tonight. If a couple of y'all will accompany me, it will be easier to get the mounts and buckboard tied near the hotel," Kane said. As he looked around the group, three nodded.

"We should, based on how long it took to get to the ranch, start out around midnight. While midnight will get us there an hour or so early, I think we need to build in enough time to handle any Rurales patrol we might bump into," Kane said. "So, everybody get some dinner and maybe some shut-eye before gathering one at a time here.

Don't forget to pack all your items. With any luck, we won't be back to town. We will put Rita in the buckboard with her pa and cut for the border.

Tonight, we will walk one or two at a time to the horses and leave, instead of riding out as a group. I think we will attract less attention that way," Kane said.

"And, thus rides the Ghost Posse tonight," Booth said with a theatrical flair. Kane noted some faint smiles.

He knew there was no need to have the men, with the possible exception of Booth, look to their guns. All but Billy were military men. Billy had not stayed alive by carrying dirty or faulty guns.

Kane walked over to the livery and placed the order to have the buckboard hooked up and the horses saddled for pickup at closing time. He gave the man a nice tip to assure timely compliance. The probability was, however, the man would have complied with anything the gunfighter dressed in black had requested. Kane looked serious in his business suit. In his black trail clothes with the Colt worn low, serious did not begin to describe the thoughts engendered in people who saw him.

He went back to the hotel and packed his valise. He would toss it into the bed of the buckboard on the way out of town.

******

The Ghost Posse assembled at the square at midnight and went by ones and twos to the hotel hitching posts and mounted. As a set rode off, another walked across and mounted. By six minutes after midnight, the last man, dressed in black, walked over to his black stallion and mounted. It would not take Hadrian long to make it to the front of the procession, once out of hearing of anyone awake in Laredo.

They rode quietly though the night, finally telling their stories of how they had faked their deaths and moved on from a life of murder and mayhem.

The three military men, Quantrill and the James, felt comfortable, even happy, to be back in formation riding to an objective. Billy, awestruck by Jesse James, was equally fascinated by the man in black. He was especially so after seeing the speed of Kane's draw. He wondered who was the fastest. But, did not wish to learn in a draw-down.

Kane was a natural leader. He knew how the men were thinking. A possible exception was the former actor. He suspected Booth was still acting. And, he was so damn good, one never knew whether he was genuine or on the stage for his audience. He was an enigma at best.

Kane did not question Booth's willingness to kill without hesitation or passion. He read the killer instinct in the actor's eyes. Kane also was pretty sure Booth had killed a number of men along the way during his long fugitive run. Men he did not claim or boast about. Just men he felt needed to die. Kane wondered about former Secretary of War Stanton's early death at age fifty-five. It happened just before Christmas in 1869 following a long period of declining health. Booth had told Kane at a dinner with just the two of them he considered Stanton had betrayed him into killing the "greatest man who ever lived."

Kane had taken the comment with a grain of salt at the time, but the more he got to know Booth, the more he realized how deeply the man's still water ran. He now believed Booth was a stone cold killer. And maybe his skills had grown to equal his lethal compulsions.

"Perhaps, just perhaps, we'll learn if I'm correct about the actor tonight," Kane thought as he rode along, Billy the Kid at his side.

Periodically, the procession would stop and listen. Once, they heard horses. Rurales or, Indians? The lieutenant had told them at their first dinner Lipan Apache war parties were riding across the border from Texas and raiding their former territory in Tamaulipas.

All the members of the posse knew they would be a greater threat than Rurales.

The men dismounted and gave bits of feed to their

horses to assure they stayed quiet. The sound passed a half mile away and disappeared in a direction almost exactly opposite to their destination.

"If it's Rurales, we will need to head due north and cross the border 'way east of Laredo to avoid them on the way back with Rita," Kane noted quietly.

"And, if it's Apaches, we better hope they just keep on going." Jesse added to expressive nodding by all. Even one of the deadliest groups of six men ever did not want to go up against Apaches of any similar or greater number.

They arrived near the ranch around four-thirty, having made better time than they planned. Billy, the most recent cowboy, rode a circle around their position to make sure none of Wise's cowboys were tending cattle nearby.

They drank water and chewed either jerky or plugs of tobacco. Lighting a cigarette or cigar was too dangerous. The smell would carry on a still morning.

To the military men, the waiting reminded them of waiting before an attack. Buck looked over at his brother and winked. Jesse gave him a big grin. Their former captain, later nemesis, had a wild look in his eyes. It was obvious Quantrill relished the prospect of battle again.

Fifteen minutes before six, the men gave their guns and extra ammunition one last check. Quantrill loaded an indeterminant number of sticks of dynamite into his coat pockets. He tucked the sheathed Bowie knife in his belt to cut the coil of detonation cord he carried in his left hand. He had his Sharps rifle in his right as he silently zig-zagged his way to the privy.

He put two sticks in the privy. He placed a blasting cap between the two sticks and tied the three together with a short length of the detonation cord fuse. Quantrill attached the cord fuse to the cap and ran what he estimated a burn time of five minute's worth of fuse. He struck a Lucifer and lit his end of the cord. He paused to see how fast it was moving towards the explosive, nodded to himself and ran to the bunkhouse.

He place an unplanned six sticks under the raised bunkhouse and ran cord to the stoop where he placed two more. The cord connected two blasting caps.

Quantrill then ran to the foreman's cottage and placed the remaining three sticks from his pockets under the wooden steps, close to the front where he could see them from his and Booth's vantage point.

Quantrill ran back to Booth and waved to the James's, who acknowledged.

Nobody had questioned his pauses for surprise explosions, but Quantrill knew it would be a delight.

In the meantime, Kane and Billy entered the front door of the *hacienda*, the main house. Nobody locked doors, so they walked right in.

They went up the stairs without a creak in the

steps and saw Wise asleep in his room, snoring like a buffalo in rut.

They checked the next room and found a dirty bed, some plates with crumbs and some cut ropes.

What they did not find was Rita Wilkes.

"Damn." Kane mouthed silently to Billy the Kid.

They went downstairs and found the small room occupied by Marina. Kane put a hand over her mouth and shook her.

She awakened, eyes filled with terror. He spoke to her in Spanish.

"*La señorita. ¿Donde esta?*" he said asking where the girl was. He showed her the playbill with Rita's picture on it and she nodded her head.

The scared woman told him Wise had tried to rape *la captiva*, or female captive and she had stabbed him and escaped yesterday afternoon.

"Which was did she go?" Billy asked in Spanish. She told them the girl had taken Wise's saddled horse from the hitching rail and ridden due east. She described the direction by pointing.

At this moment, the privy blew with a loud explosion. The two left the room and entered the main room of the house.

Jack Wise limped to the top of the steps with a double-barrel shotgun aimed at them.

Kane and Billy both drew. It was difficult telling who fired first because it sounded almost like one loud shot. But both knew it was the tall man in black.

Both bullets pierced Wise's heart and finished what Rita Wilkes Booth had started. Wise tumbled forward and then fell, end-over-end down the steps. He landed at the two gunmen's feet. His unseeing eyes were wide open.

Billy went up to Wise's room and came back with his wallet and a bag of gold and silver coins. He gave them to Marina. She nodded at him and went to her room to dress and, they reckoned, return to her village.

Kane examined where Rita had been kept. There was fresh blood on the bed. Dried, but not faded. There was a weak trail of it from the edge of the bed, out the door and down the hall to Wise's room. Kane walked down the steps and rolled Wise over. He saw the fall had opened a fresh wound in his side. A stab wound. So, Rita had stabbed him and escaped on his horse. Good for her.

"How had she survived the night? Where?" Kane wondered. He started to share this with Billy, but all hell broke loose outside.

Outside, the exploding privy had awakened the cowboys in the bunkhouse and Otha.

Otha appeared first and stepped onto the first step in his nightshirt. He carried a Winchester.

Booth aimed and fired his rifle. The ball hit him in the forehead. Quantrill fired at his sticks of dynamite under the steps before Otha could fall.

The explosion sent him twenty feet into the air, flipping twice.

As the first cowboys rushed the bunkhouse door, they saw their foreman land from a height. He landed on the top of his head with a crunch.

Frank dropped the first cowboy at the bunkhouse door.

Quantrill aimed his Sharps buffalo gun and exploded the charge under the steps. Several seconds later, the flame on the detonation cord made it to the large charge and the bunkhouse raised ten feet straight up above its foundation and crashed down, a pile of boards burning fiercely.

He turned to Booth, then the James's and grinned evilly.

"That sonofabitch. He hasn't changed a bit since Lawrence, Kansas," Frank said. He had seen Kane and Billy leave the house without a hostage. He knew the search was not over and they would need every gun.

For that reason and no other, neither Frank nor Jesse James shot their old commanding officer. But, the urge was there. Jesse looked at Frank and said "Later."

They rallied back at the horses. Marina was coming out with a bag holding her life's possessions. She knew she had an even chance of either dying or getting help.

Kane approached her and asked if he could help. She told him she would like to get to her village. It was, she said, just off the road the captive girl had taken.

Kane told her to get into the buckboard with Booth. She did and he began to formulate another plan.

He motioned the other members over as they road east.

"If there are men in the village and Rita is not already there, maybe they know the country. I am not opposed to spread some coin among them to help us look for her. Maybe a reward. What do you think?" Kane asked.

"Forty sets of eyes see more than six," Quantrill said for all.

They took off for the village at a fast pace.

Marina pointed them towards the chapel and the priest.

He immediately told them Rita was not there, nor had they seen her.

Kane asked if he thought the men of the village could provide assistance searching.

"These men, senior, are poor farmers who seldom go farther than their fields, or into San Clemente to buy seeds and such. They are not like Indians who range around the desert," the priest said in good English. Kane recognized his faint accent from is travels in Europe. Italian was his native tongue.

"Father, are there perhaps Indians in the area we can recruit?" Kane asked.

"None have lived here for many years. There is

talk about a Lipan Apache war party somewhere in Tamaulipas for ill purposes. We have seen a couple of braves scouting us. They know we do not have any weapons with which to fight them. The Rurales say they will keep us safe, but," the priest spread his arms and motioned around the whole area with them. "where are they, these Rurales? I do not see them. Do you?" he asked Kane rhetorically.

"No, father, I do not see them either. Do you know how many Apaches are in this band? And, are they just braves? Or, do they have families traveling with them?" he asked.

"I only know what I have heard. I have heard there may be thirty or forty braves with no women, old ones or children. The Rurale officer said so.

I believe they are looking for horses and cattle to steal. And, perhaps scalps for prizes. I pray every day they do not come here. I know in my heart they will, though."

"Perhaps we will encounter them," Kane suggested.

"That would be bad for such a small group."

"It may also be bad for the Apaches, Father. These men, young and older, are very well trained in warfare. But, above all, we need to find the girl. Her father is the man in the buckboard. His daughter was kidnapped by a man named Jack Wise, who owns a ranch west of here."

"I know of this Wise, Senor Kane. It is said he

steals cattle in the states and brings them here to Mexico. He either sells them here to people who do not care what the brand says or he alters the brand and drives them back to the United States and to a railhead. There they go to big cattle buyers who pay much," the priest advised.

"My two associates who spoke with him surmised as much. He has paid for kidnapping the girl and whatever else he may have done with her. Now, we just have to find her and take her home. As soon as possible."

Kane went back to the men.

"These folks are living hand-to-mouth. They don't have any knowledge of much outside their village beyond the road back to San Clemente. We need to press on to the east. According to the padre, there is a thirty or so brave band of Apaches out here somewhere. I just hope we get Rita before they get her. Let's ride."

*****

Rita hated to leave her relatively comfortable home with its semi-clear water and scrubby trees for desert. But, somewhere out there, she believed was a town. Unfortunately, she had no idea which direction and was riding exactly the wrong way.

Riding on a sun-scorched saddle with nothing on had yielded blisters in a place she really did not want them. She stopped the horse and took the knife and cut a corner off the saddle blanket and put it on top of the saddle's seat. It did not help the blisters there already but, she thought, would prevent more from forming.

Rita saw dust in the distance. "Mexican army or police?" she wondered.

As they neared, she realized they were Indians. And, a lot of them.

She turned the horse and kicked him with her bare heels in the opposite direction.

Rita rode like the wind and heard a bullet whistle past her ear before hearing the crack of a rifle. She tried to make herself as small a target as possible and still have enough reach to control a horse running faster than she had ever ridden.

She heard more "whizzz" sounds followed by cracks as bullets went past her.

As she came around a rocky hill, she saw a group of riders coming and a buggy or wagon of some sort. They were dressed like Westerners, neither Mexicans nor Indians.

"Are they people Wise sent after me?" she asked herself, not even sure Wise survived the night with his stab wound.

She saw the horses pull up hard and the men got off and formed a formation of some sort. A very tall man in black waved her on.

Kane saw what was happening and knew it had to be

Rita in the nightclothes and being chased by Apaches.

"Men. I think it's Rita. Dismount with rifles and plenty of ammunition. Form a vee-shape pointed out, but keep it open in the middle for her to ride through. After she does, close ranks. Only men on the end of each wing should fire at the Indians. After all this, we don't want to chance hitting the girl."

Kane was glad to see Quantrill move to the outside right with the big buffalo gun. He had several times the range of the revolver caliber Winchesters and proved it as he took the lead Indian off his pony.

The Apaches, and Kane was sure they were now, were within fifty yards of Rita as she galloped through the open point of the Vee. The men closed ranks and began firing as fast as they could aim and lever their guns.

While shooting, Kane saw Quantrill set his Sharps down and pull something long from his pocket. He lit it with his cigar and threw it, flipping through the air, into the middle of the native horsemen riding towards them.

When it blew, the dynamite killed several braves and actually knocked surrounding horses over as if hit by a lightning strike.

The other braves stopped, more in wonderment than fear. Fear was not a trait Apaches shared with most other humans.

The Ghost Posse used the confusion as an opportunity to pour fire into the braves.

About ten were down, critically wounded or dead. Kane could not get an exact count in the gunsmoke and dust.

The rest retreated, a few wounded pulled up on ponies and riding double.

Kane realized an almost naked woman was blazing away at them with a nice Winchester right beside him. It went cold and she whipped a S&W Schofield out of a holster on her saddle and emptied it at the retreating Indians. Her shots fell a hundred yards short, but she seemed to be deriving some positive emotional release out of doing it.

Kane took off his black coat and draped it over her. She looked down at herself and slipped her arms in the very long sleeves and buttoned the front. She gave him a dirty-faced but glorious smile.

"Anybody hurt?" Kane asked.

"I got a little bullet crease on the right arm," Jesse said.

"Afraid I have a hole in front to match the one a Yankee gave me in the back in June of '65," Quantrill said, not knowing the severity of his wound.

As the James's reloaded and watched for a second wave attack, Kane looked to Quantrill. He was already prone. Kane unbuttoned his vest and shirt and saw a hole with a little blood around it under his left rib cage."

"I'm thinking it's a .44 Henry rimfire," Kane said.

"How in hell can you surmise the caliber from a hole, Kane?" Quantrill snapped.

"From the fact an 1866 Yellow Boy brass framed Winchester is a real popular Indian rifle. There are about five of them laying on the trail up by the bodies."

"Well, what the hell. Did it pass through?" Quantrill asked.

"I'm afraid it's still in there," Kane said, as he took the protruding bullet between two fingers and pulled it out. He pressed a clean handkerchief on the shallow hole.

"Damn, Kane. Feels almost as good as new." Quantrill said. Kane winked and walked away. Quantrill held the pad on a few minutes. Bleeding had stopped. He was fine and got up to see to his rifle.

During this time, Rita and a dark-haired man had been staring at each other. She was looking at the ghost of a man she saw killed through her mother's fingers over her eyes almost fifteen years ago.

"Daddy?" she said in a little girl voice befitting a six year old.

"Yes, Ogarita. Your daddy lives and has come to take you home."

"I knew you would, daddy. Somehow. I knew."

Tears flowed over Kane's black suit jacket she was wearing

They approached each other slowly and then she ran to him in her sock feet. They embraced. Lightly for a moment then so tight it was hard for either to breathe. To Rita, it was as if her prayers had been answered and God had sent her daddy down from heaven to save her. She never doubted he would save her. She just didn't know how it would manifest itself.

"We'd better get any rifles and cartridges from the fallen Apaches and put them in the back of the buckboard. They will be back and probably raid the unarmed village behind us. They're madder than enraged hornets and twice as dangerous," Kane yelled as he ran towards the fallen Apaches.

Kane began grabbing an armload of carbines, mainly 1866 Winchesters with brass tack decorations in the stocks. Frank, Jesse, Billy and Rita joined him.

"Take any .44 rimfire cartridges you can find. The brave nearest the rifle ought to have 'em in a leather pouch or some conveyance," Kane instructed.

He dropped the rifles from his arms and drew in a blur as a shot sounded. Billy had shot a brave.

"He was playing possum," the young gunfighter said matter of factly. "He's deader now. A helluva lot deader."

Kane picked his rifles back up and walked back to the buckboard. He returned for another load. At least the village would not be totally unarmed now. Assuming they could get back alive.

It took ten precious minutes to move the Winchesters and a few odd Spencer's and Springfield trap door single shots to the buckboard and get under way.

They pushed the horses hard, but soon saw dust behind them. The Apaches were coming back.

Three of his men were experienced shooting from horseback. Even at pursuers.

The Apaches were still out of '73 carbine range. Jesse's longer barrel was close to being able to shoot to point of aim. But, Quantrill's Sharps was easily deadly and he turned in the saddle, grimacing at the pain. The first shot of the big fifty knocked a pony down and caused several to trip over him.

Kane noted the incident only killed one pony and no braves, but may have bought a few seconds time and slowed the approach of the Apaches,

They were five minutes away from the village. Kane did not even know its name. Probably Santa Josepha after the church's name. But, right now, it did not matter. He just hoped the priest was gathering his flock into the church. It was the only building in town with any semblance of being bullet proof.

Kane was right about the village's name being the same as the church's. And about the priest ushering his parishioners inside. They brought urns of water in from the well outside. To be caught without water during any sort of siege would be a fatal mistake.

As he got the last person in and was getting ready to close the massive door, Father Geppetto hesitated.

It now clearly sounded like two groups, one pursuing the other. He told one of the men to close and lock the door if he was not back in two minutes and rushed to the edge of the village.

He saw two clouds of dust, the front one was smaller than the rear.

He was right. He could see the front group was slowed by a wagon of some sort. Anglos. Apaches did not use buckboards.

There was nothing he could do to help. He just watched, fascinated as riders turned and fired rifles from a full gallop.

Kane and he was sure it was Kane's group by now, had said his men were military trained. One had long, streaming black hair. Could it be a woman or girl? She was shooting also.

The first group roared into the village and Kane called for village men to grab rifles from the back of the buckboard and take them into the church. Ordinarily, Father Geppetto would not allow such a thing. Today was an extraordinary one. He grabbed a Winchester and some cartridges himself. God and the Holy Mother would forgive him. He was protecting ones unable to protect themselves. The priest filled the tubular magazine and levered a cartridge into the chamber.

Most of the Ghost Posse, the girl and the priest took up positions behind the well, the newly overturned buckboard and any barrier available. Kane,

Jesse and Billy led the horses into a small corral and returned to their positions.

The Apaches rode into town in full glory. The first volley brought down five braves and seven ponies.

Another dust cloud appeared. The lieutenant led his Rurales in a charge to the rear of the Apaches. Their single shot rolling blocks were no match for fast-firing Winchesters and they were decimated. The first to fall was the captain. He had chosen a bad day to ride on a patrol.

Kane watched as a brave shot the lieutenant off his horse. Jesse James returned the favor to the brave. Dead or alive, the lieutenant was vindicated. Another jumped off his pony with a scalping knife at the ready. Kane was right there instantly. He drew a Bowie from the back of his belt and they circled. The brave feinted, but Kane stood firm. Then, in a move learned from the fencing master at Spain's military academy, he lurched and the blade sunk seven inches into the brave's solar plexus. On his back step, Kane withdrew the Bowie with a twist. The brave fell dead.

The lieutenant recognized the fencing move, though not with a big American knife. He looked up at the tall man in black and nodded. The man pulled the dark bandana from around his neck. He folded it and placed it on the lieutenant's shoulder wound.

"*Presione en esto,*" Kane said, telling him to press on

this. Kane walked away, work still to be done.

With the confusion and shots from every direction, the leader of the war party chose to regroup out of range. He lost another two braves.

However, he had a whole village and some defenders corralled. He knew he had the upper hand.

The Ghost Posse members gathered more weapons and dragged three surviving Rurales into the church. They were the captain and a trooper. Kane picked up the lieutenant and carried him in.

Village women began to administer first aid. Marina ministered to the captain who was the most grievously injured.

Kane found out three of the older men had served as Rurales several years ago. Billy quickly instructed them in Spanish on the loading and operation of a lever action carbine. Three more sentries had been added to the defense.

Jesse and Frank collected the several rifles and ammunition from the newly fallen Apaches.

"Bill, how much dynamite have we got left from the original box?" Kane asked the former guerilla captain.

"Mebbe ten or twelve sticks."

"Fancy a little raid about midnight?" Kane asked.

Quantrill's answer was a chilling grin.

******

Back inside the church, Kane spoke to the priest for a moment. The cleric nodded his head and Kane began speaking to the gathered villagers in Spanish.

"We have to mount a guard of at least three sentries at all times. This is going to be a tough place to protect since the Apaches can hide in your homes, stables....virtually anywhere in the village to launch an attack. It's not like protecting a fortress. It's going to be house-to-house fighting. We have a plan tonight which might lessen the threat of attack.

In the meantime, our men will have to search your homes to make sure no Apaches have slipped in and are waiting for us. While we are there, we will try to pick up all the food and dishes and cups we can to bring back here. We don't think this situation will last long, but we want to make sure we have adequate supplies in the meantime.

Does anyone have any questions?" Kane asked.

"Do we have medicine to treat wounded?" one woman, who had been caring for the lieutenant asked. Marina, beside the captain shook her head in agreement.

"No. We don't. We have to do the best we can. I have thought about trying to send a man on horseback out the back to circle around and go to San Clemente for help. I am afraid we do not have enough men to risk one. We have to improvise with what we have. Thank all of you. I need to go out and make sure we have a sentry schedule so we will be guarded. Then, we will begin the house-to-house search."

He went over to the pallet where the lieutenant lay. Kane knelt down and looked at him. His eyes opened and met those of the tall gunman.

"Are you alright?" Kane asked.

"My shoulder hurts like hell, but I will recover."

"I am counting on it." Kane smiled at him.

Rita, still wearing his coat and Wise's socks, caught his arm as he went past and drew him close.

"I want to be part of the sentry list, Kane. You all are down here because of me. I can shoot and I want to carry my weight."

Kane stared at her long and hard before answering. She could be his daughter chronologically.

"Damn, she's beautiful with a dusty, gun powder stained face and a rifle in hand." he thought.

"Alright, Miss Rita. You are on the roster. What are your calibers and do you have enough rounds?" Kane asked.

"Something called .38 WCF. I have the rifle and Colt loaded and about a half a box of bullets."

"Keep the cartridges for the revolver. I will get you an Indian carbine and cartridges. The Apaches have well supplied us with their legacy firearms. It loads a bit differently from yours, but operates the same."

She followed him out the door.

"Billy, do you have a pair of trousers and a shirt

Miss Rita can borrow? You two are somewhat similar in height at least," Kane asked the Kid.

He went to his saddlebags, now in the alcove of the church and withdrew a shirt and pants. She put them on in a study and came out, handing Kane his jacket with a smile. She had tied the bandanna around her head like an Indian. Rita Wilkes looked ready to fight. And, the look in her eyes proved she surely was.

Kane worked out the sentry guard schedule, including the three villagers. Then, they searched the houses while Booth and Quantrill stood watch, rifles at ready.

The men brought food and kitchenware into the church and the priest and several women put it at the end of a long table which would be used as a buffet table for meals.

They only had enough cups for family's to each share one. The number of bowls was sufficient for all.

Apaches preferred attacking pre-dawn. The Westerners knew this, but were still vigil. A guard saw one brave moving furtively and quietly called Quantrill as planned.

When the brave next appeared, Quantrill was ready with the big .50 and killed him with a four hundred yard shot.

Kane sidled up to Billy.

"Billy, I want you to stay here tonight when Bill and I pay a surprise visit on the Apaches. If something was to happen to me, we will need you to be the Spanish interpreter, alright?"

"I'd like to go, but what you say makes sense."

Kane had spoken with Billy at some length in camp and on the trail. The Kid had suffered a rough home life and been at odds with the law since before he was ten.

Except for killing an abuser, most of his crimes had been property and were to eat. It was not until he got messed up in the Lincoln County War did most of his crimes become hanging offenses. Killing the county sheriff and several deputies was the crowning blow. He had to stay dead or would be dead for real if caught by the law.

Being with the posse was a big risk. One which showed the high regard in which he held Jesse James. James was obligated. Billy was not. He rode along to help his friend with his greatest talent. Handling a gun.

That night, the village women cooked dinner. They invited the posse members to partake. Five went out and spelled the sentries. They would eat later.

After all had eaten and the new sentries posted, Kane sat with Booth, Rita and Billy. He had noticed the two almost competed for attention from the young lady. Odd, since one was her father. Kane, as a leader, wanted to determine what was going on between father and daughter. They could shoot each other for all he cared after the mission. But, until she got back into the US of A, he was interested. As for Billy, he chalked it off as young man and a very pretty young woman of the same age. It was natural.

Booth was not his frequently tipsy self tonight. Kane had taken up all the liquor and given it to Marina to use as painkillers for the wounded.

As he sat, back against the church wall, hat tipped over his face as if he was sleeping, he listened.

Kane thought Booth was competing for time with his daughter because the better she got to know him, the less she liked him. Frankly, Kane told himself, he felt the same way.

Kane detected a genuine chemistry between the somewhat famous actress and the very famous gunfighter. He did not make any judgements, on this or much else. "Let the cards land as they are dealt", he thought.

Booth followed Kane's approach and leaned against the wall, his head covered with a dark slouch hat and soon was snoring. Rita and Billy continued to speak. Kane was not eavesdropping, his proximity made not hearing impossible. He was pleasantly surprised the conversation was both serious and erudite. Not what he would have expected from an actress and an uneducated young gunfighter.

Just as he dozed off, he was awakened by a shot. Then, several more.

Kane was on his feet immediately, followed quickly by Billy and Rita. They moved to the front. Kane virtually clothes-lined Rita as she started to run out into the dark.

"Easy, Lass. Make sure you know what you are stepping into before you commit." She nodded, gun in hand. Kane looked around the door frame.

He saw the flashes of rifles to the left, so he swung his Colt to the right. As his eyes adjusted to the pitch blackness of the night, he made out an Apache form gliding slowly between buildings. He made sure of his target and straightened his right arm. As soon as his elbow locked, the Colt bucked in his hand. Billy and Rita saw the Apache stumble forward and fall.

Kane was already swinging his revolver in concert with his eyes. It paused again and fire blew four feet out of the long barrel and another target fell.

Billy knew he, himself, was a great shootist. But, watching this man was simply mesmerizing to him.

Kane eased out with the two close behind.

As they rounded a small adobe house, three Apaches jumped Kane and he want down. A rifle barrel across the top of this Stetson put him down hard. Billy pulled the Apache rifleman off Kane before he rammed the butt into Kane's head. The two fell back against the wall of the house and Rita fired at the second and third Apaches point blank with her Colt. One fell over the unconscious Kane. The second staggered back and she shot him twice more. He fell permanently as her gun clicked empty.

Billy and the first brave, who was much larger than he was, were engaged in a fight to the death.

They twisted and turned so much in the dark Rita was unable to help.

She looked at the brave sprawled over Kane and saw his knife stuck in a sash around his waist.

Rita holstered Jack Wise's revolver and slid the knife out of its sheath.

The Apache muscled Billy to the ground and straddled him. He put his hands around the gunfighter's neck and squeezed as hard as he could.

Rita, knife above her head in two hands, brought it down between his shoulder blades. It sunk up to the hilt.

She would never forget the sound of a blade penetrating muscle and bone she heard then. Spinal cord severed, the Apache fell dead on top of Billy.

"I killed him for you, Billy honey." she whispered as she drew the .38-40, reloaded, and scanned for more Apaches.

Any raiders still living slipped off into the night. She heard Billy grunting as he fought to get out from under dead weight eighty pounds more than his live weight.

They both pulled the dead Apache off Kane who was slowly regaining consciousness.

Kane knocked his Boss of the Plains Stetson off and rubbed his head. His fingers came back dry, thanks to the hat. But he felt a knot the size of an egg under his hair.

Rita slipped his Colt back into the shiny black holster and the young man and woman supported Kane back into the church.

The two James brothers searched the village, picking up weapons and ammunition and assuring each attacker was dead.

"Whatever the two of you did saved my bacon out there. Thank you," Kane said, still not able to stand steadily and sliding intentionally down the wall to sit on his butt, legs outstretched.

"Kane, are you alright?" Billy asked.

"Yes, just a few minutes to clear my head and I'll be right as rain."

"I'll get you a cup of water," Rita said and rose from the floor beside him to get it.

"What did the three of us get? Five of them?" Billy asked.

"Not sure. I think so. I shot two and the lights went out."

"Well, you got two, and three jumped you," Billy said.

"And, you got them."

Billy grinned.

"Nope. Rita killed all three. Shot the one who

clubbed you and his buddy. Then, knifed the one who was beating living hell out of me." Billy said with obvious pride.

"I might have to talk her out of the theater and into being a farmer's wife. I guess dreams like that one are stupid, huh?"

"Billy she's coming back now. So, I'll say something real fast. I didn't fight for a woman named Maria Elena when we were your ages. I have always regretted it. I might not have won, but at least I would have given it my best. I have been thinking a lot about going back and trying," Kane said.

"What are you gunmen scheming about?" Rita asked.

"You," Kane said as she handed him the cup of water and he quaffed it.

Billy stood in shock as she looked at him for an answer.

Kane swallowed the water and looked hard at both of them.

"You two make one hell of a pair of gunsels. I'd have you back my play any day."

"You would?" Rita asked in surprise.

"I would. You two are good together. Team-work and all. You ought to figure out some sort of partnership."

Billy still had his mouth open, not knowing quite what to say. Finally, he blurted out. "Rita, that sounds good to me. We should work out some sort of something."

"I think so too. We are a great team, you and I." she said.

"There you go." Kane said. "Billy, will you check with Frank or Jesse and find out if everyone is okay and what the count was on our attackers?"

Billy sped off.

Rita turned to Kane.

"Frank and Jesse. There are only two brothers named Frank and Jesse I ever heard of. And, Jesse is dead. Right?"

"Damn concussion." Kane thought.

"Jesse is dead. Your father is dead. A number of people are dead to the world. But, here we are to rescue you. A dangerous crew. My advice is don't ask any questions. A lot of people risked their lives to bring you home. And, the danger is far from over. If someone wants to tell you who they are, so be it. But don't push them," Kane advised sternly. Rita figured out two. She probably wouldn't know who Quantrill was if formally introduced. Kane was an enigma whose name was real. She could not begin to figure him. Billy….Billy's identity would shock the hell out of her. Kane knew Billy would impulsively tell her. He just hoped the Kid would wait to see if they had any sort of future first.

Kane was actually relieved he told Billy about Maria Elena. Saying it aloud after twenty years of not

mentioning her name to a soul was a sort of commitment. He may really go to Spain after this mission and
implore her to run away with him. Which may require
as much shooting as rescuing Rita Booth.

Several hours later, he went out to relieve Quantrill
at his post. Before returning to the church he motioned Kane closer.

"Booth is a deadly shot, regardless of what claims
he might make to the contrary. He put a bullet between the foreman's eyes from a decent distance. It
was no lucky shot. Kane, I believe he has killed before.
And, I'm not talking about Lincoln. He was more
identifiable than Jesse or Frank or Billy. Yet, here he
is alive and kicking. I don't believe he's the madman
or drunk he sometimes portrays."

"Bill, I've been thinking something similar. He
comes from the greatest family of actors in America.
I think he not only *was* a good actor, I think he still *is*. I
believe we will all get to our respective homes without
ever knowing who he really is. The more I know him
though, the less I want to know him," Kane said.

"Do you think the same about me, Kane?" Quantrill
asked bluntly.

"No, I don't. We are both killers. We don't make
any pretensions about it. And, we understand each
other. It's scary to both of us, but we somewhat think
alike. So, again, my answer is no," Kane responded
with raw truth.

"I 'spect you are right, Mr. Gunfighter. It takes temperament such as yours to lead the Ghost Posse. Booth couldn't do it. Maybe Frank could. But, you can see in his eyes, while this is fun, he's no longer the outlaw. He's straight now. Told me he sells damn shoes for a living. Frank James. Shoe salesman. What is this world coming to, Kane?"

Kane smiled at Quantrill, one of the few people who did.

"Beats me, Bill. Now, get some sleep. Heal up the shallow hole in your chest. You know the Apaches like to hit an hour or so before dawn. So, keep one eye open and your big 50 Sharps ready." Quantrill nodded and walked to the church, a building he doubted he would be welcome in anywhere near Kansas.

******

Kane's post was near a small peasant home. He decided to leave the door open and sit just inside in the shadows. He had a wide view and was out of sight. Additionally, no Apache could sneak up behind him and lift his scalp.

As he sat cross-legged in the floor, his Winchester across his lap, he did a lot of thinking.

"What if I went to Spain and Maria Elena did not want me? What if she changed and I did not want her? Would she give up being a *viscondesa* to come home with me? Would I have to kill her husband? I don't care about killing him, but what if she secretly would hate me if I did? And, what about her son and daughter. The son is a real and present danger right now. And, he is probably across the courtyard laying in the church. "

Kane finally concluded if he did not go, he would always wonder about those questions. So, he would resign from the Circle and go. He had been paid well and had sufficient money set aside to live quite well on. If he needed more, he could always become a roving gun and help only people with righteous problems. He heard there was a man in California who made a living helping people who needed a fast gun and hard fist.

At three in the morning, he awakened his men, including the village conscripts.

"This is the favorite time of day for the Apaches to attack. They know the people back at San Clemente are scrambling to put together a strong force to come out and find the patrol they lost. The Apaches don't want to get caught between us and three Rurales patrols joined together. So, I figure this morning is their last best chance. Now, another thing." He repeated this in Spanish for the armed villagers, then continued in English.

"This morning, the wounded lieutenant asked me if we hit the Wise ranch and killed all those folks. I did not answer him. He told me he has no problem, since Miss Rita here told him she had been kidnapped and held there. But, he said Wise was paying some higher ups in his structure and they would be pretty mad about us killing their golden goose regardless of why. So, I have a plan, assuming we stop the Apache attacks in an hour. I will take some of the villagers and maybe two of you men. We will all first pile some of yesterday's dead into a wagon I saw earlier. Some of their rifles, the least desirable ones, like the old Spencer's should be left near bodies and the proper ammunition on or by the bodies. We will create a skirmish site. And, ride back here.

When the Mexicans get to the ranch, they will think the Apaches attacked it. They will ride this way with righteous indignation to find we have already solved their Apache problem."

"There might be two flaws, Kane," Frank James said. "One, is if the Apaches *don't* attack in an hour, or we don't either kill them all or set them to running back home. Two is if the lieutenant has a change of heart and tells what he and his captain saw and concluded yesterday. I figure the safest thing is, if the Apaches cooperate, we should kill the lieutenant and put him in this skirmish as a casualty."

"Frank, your points are good. I trust the lieutenant. I cannot kill him or allow any of you to kill him for reasons I cannot disclose. You will just have to trust me. The captain is another matter. If he lives through the night, I will personally kill him. As to the other angles you brought up, they are valid. Like in any military action, sometimes one has to make a battle plan and execute it. I propose we follow such a strategy here," Kane said.

"He's right, Buck. There is no guarantee in love or war. The plan is as solid as we are going to have. I'm with Kane," Quantrill said.

The rest nodded, including Frank James. Kane had not led them wrong yet.

"Let's get back to our posts, this time three at a post. Be careful where you shoot and identify your target first. As you know, we set up the posts to prevent cross-fire and shooting each other, but let's be careful anyway. God speed men," Kane said then repeated in Spanish.

True to expectations, the Apaches struck quietly at four in the morning, the time when most people were sleeping the deepest. They came in furtively, wraiths in the dark, planning to stab and slash as long as they could before the attention shooting would prompt.

They did not find sentries standing outside posts. Two raiders entered a small house. Kane, Booth and a villager opened up and the two died in the doorway.

The fight was on in earnest with those first shots. Men in darkened rooms fired at shadows and the shadows fell. Two made it in to where the James brothers were with a villager. The James's dropped their rifles and pulled Bowie knives. The fights were silent and fast. The Apaches were superb warriors. But, Frank and Jesse James grew up on Bowie knives and could wield them as well as Jim Bowie himself. They wiped bloody hands on the clothes of the vanquished and pulled their six-guns. Jesse carried Colt's and Frank S&W Scofield's. Both were .44-40s and both men were experts. Several more shadow warriors fell.

Kane could not continue to wait for the fight to come to him. He stepped out of the door, his seven and a half inch barrel Colt's in each hand sending feet of flame with each shot.

Outside, Billy and Rita stood back to back shooting rifles until they were empty, then pulling iron and shooting their revolvers.

In very few minutes, it appeared to be over. The moon was behind a cloud and the darkness was like a pall over the village.

Kane had half of his men stand together as a watch and took the other half around the village, searching each house and checking every fallen body to make sure no one was feigning death. A fast tally suggested their estimated strength of the attackers had been accounted for in the several days of fighting.

******

As planned, yesterday's bodies and a weapon and matching ammunition for each were put in a wagon and hauled to the Wise Ranch. The bodies were distributed around. They were positioned as if they had fallen in a firefight.

Using creote bushes, Kane set the remains of the bunkhouse and Otha's cottage afire. He wanted the destruction to appear from fire, not explosives. A crime scene created, the men returned to church dedicated to Santa Josepha.

Kane reported the results of the evening and morning to the priest and to the wounded young lieutenant. The captain had died of his wounds during the night. Kane was relieved he did not have to kill him to protect his men.

The next day, the Ghost Posse and its newest member packed for the trip back to the US.

Kane went back into the church and quietly gave a thousand dollar contribution in gold to Father Geppetto.

He also checked on the young lieutenant. He was a graduate of Spain's national military academy. He was striking because of his bright blue eyes.

Kane put his hand on the lieutenant's uninjured shoulder.

"Get well quickly and go home to see your mother. We will meet again."

The young officer looked into Kane's blue eyes

and nodded. He knew they would meet again, and he suspected he knew why with a dawning realization.

Kane handed him one of his prized Colts. Lt. Miguel Vasquez had never seen such a beautiful gun. He turned it over. The initials M.K were engraved on the base of one side of the white grips.

"You? M. Kane?" he asked.

"Yes, Michael Kane, of Virginia. Keep this with you. Show it to your mother. The initials may have significance to her, Lt. Miguel Vasquez. Leave this mean land and go home to Spain. You are needed there. Let this Colt protect you and remind you of the man who appeared and had your back for too short a time."

Kane turned and walked out the door, not looking back. He was pleased and saddened at the same time. He mounted Hadrian.

Lt. Miguel Vasquez watched him ride away, more conflicted than he had ever been.

******

As they approached the Wise ranch, they saw a large contingent of Rurales there. Probably fifty Rurales and three or four officers. A patrol with several officers rode out immediately and challenged them.

After the requisite identification, the officers asked if they knew when the Indian attack on the ranch had occurred.

"It must have been yesterday morning. Maybe the night before. We were returning from a land buying trip and were attacked some miles east of where Santa Josepha church is. We exchanged shots with a large group of Apaches and they chased us back to the village.

As we got to the village, returning fire to the Apaches, a patrol of Rurales came to our rescue. They were cut down.

Everybody was holed up in the church. We took the wounded into the church. A captain died last night. The lieutenant was wounded, but is recovering. We fought off a dawn attack and think we killed most of the raiders.

Our plan is to get back to Texas before more Apaches come after us. The boss," Kane nodded to Quantrill, "Mr. Crowder, has decided things are too dangerous down here to invest for a while," Kane finished in Spanish.

The officer, probably a major by his rank indicia, nodded and said something to his captain. The junior officer rode to where the men were examining the skirmish site at the ranch and rallied them. In formation, major in front, they galloped off towards Santa Josepha.

CHAPTER 10

DEAD AGAIN AND REINVENTED
1883

State of Tamaulipas

Mexico, Texas, and Virginia

Within an hour, the Americans were passing through San Clemente. They crossed the border before dark and got rooms at Laredo.

Kane reserved the whole dining room at the hotel for a late dinner meeting.

Before the dinner, Booth gave his daughter cash and accompanied her to a clothing store. Billy tagged along behind. One member of the Booth family was pleased. The other glowered through his mustache.

The dinner was scheduled for nine o'clock. There was both red and white wine on the table. Everyone showed in suits. Booth was fashionably late.

He made his entrance at ten minutes after nine, Rita on his arm. She wore an emerald green satin dress and her long, dark hair was fashionable coiffed. To say she was beautiful would have been a gross understatement. William Roberts, almost unrecognizable with trimmed hair and a dark suit, motioned them to the two chairs he had held open.

"The belle of the ball has arrived," Kane began, standing at his chair. "First, I'd like to propose a toast." He raised his glass.

"To the reason, we are all here. The lovely actress, Rita Wilkes."

The men all stood and raised their glasses to her. She blushed prettily from her chair.

"Before our dinners are brought in, I'd like to say a few words. We must be circumspect in our conversations tonight. We do not know who may be listening. So, we are still on mission status. Our mission has been a successful one. Of course, we had the most apt riders available anywhere. The person we sought is safely back in the United States and none of us are seriously wounded."

Kane smiled as he continued. "And, none of us are any more dead than when we left Laredo.

Each of you took a risk participating in this mission. I have been empowered by the board of your organization to reward each posse member with one fifth of the gold I bought in case we had to negotiate Miss Rita's return. It greatly exceeded the ransom amount. After the purchase of the buckboard, sundries and a contribution to Father Geppetto, that amounts to eight thousand dollars apiece. You will find equal bags of gold coins tied to the right rear legs of your chairs. Spend your stipends in good health gentlemen. And, Miss Rita. You were not just a hostage, but one who pitched in and defended against the Apaches at your risk, too. Here is a small token to acknowledge your contribution." Kane passed a bag down the table to a surprised Rita. It was only slightly thinner than the others.

Billy was shocked to find his bag, though not a member of the group. It would go a long way with the plans he had. Eight thousand dollars in gold made him a very rich man in a day when the average worker made less than three hundred fifty dollars a year.

Kane stood and walked towards kitchen. He intercepted the head waiter and asked for the dishes of food to be delivered. As was tradition among Westerners, there was little talk at dinner. Most was led by the two Booths, the senior, a Marylander and his daughter who grew up around the country.

Outside the door, the waiter listened for more information. He had heard the part about eight thousand dollars gold to each and had some friends who would help him steal it. He put together a list of the room numbers by having a waitress help him watch where each patron went following the meal. He reckoned the tall man who presided and had presented the bags of gold to his guest would be the first to hit. Then, the two older men, the man and daughter, the kid, and, finally the two who he gathered from eavesdropping were brothers. He had no idea about names. Their rooms were all in the name of the money man, Kane. But, this would be a pushover. Names did not matter in the middle of the night when his thug friends came calling.

The head waiter, Abraham Cloninger, gathered four friends. After they spoke, they decided for two to hit Kane and two to hit the first of the two older men, then the second. Assuming the robberies were quiet, they would successively strike the rest in room order. A plan which might have worked on a group of Eastern dudes, but was weak at best given the real identities of the proposed victims.

At one in the morning, two approached Kane's door and two Quantrill's door.

The waiter had secured passkeys from the area behind the front desk as the desk clerk slept.

Kane's eyes popped open at the first click of the lock. He rolled off the bed and aimed the Colt from behind it. Kane knew the bed was not much of a bullet stopper, but hid his form somewhat as a target. He would have liked to get away from the bed, which was where an intruder's gun would be pointed. But, time did not allow such a luxury.

He saw two men enter. The faint light from the

hall outside showed a knife blade glint and the outline of a club of some sort. That was enough to justify use of deadly force to Kane and virtually any judge in America. Though Kane could give a damn about the judge part.

The flame from the two shots almost reached the two targets as they stood, dead on their feet. The noise in the room was deafening.

Kane, ears ringing from his big .44, hardly heard the shotgun blast just once in Quantrill's room.

Kane pulled on pants and stepped over the dead bodies into the hall.

Doors flew open as the James's and Billy the Kid came out crouched and ready.

Quantrill's two bodies, riddled with buckshot, were on the hall outside his room. A set of passkeys were beside them and a revolver and a knife were clutched in cold dead hands.

Booth's door stayed closed, but Rita's swung open and she appeared in a shift and her .38-40 cocked. She looked at Billy standing there in just his shirt with his bare ass shining and began to giggle. The men wanted to join in, but were too smart to embarrass such a dangerous friend.

Kane bit his lip and said "I'll pull something on and get the marshal. Leave the crime scene as it is."

He walked to Rita and whispered. Only she and the Posse members could hear.

"Miss Rita, you are a known quantity. Swap rooms with Mr. Crowder before we get back. Hold onto the shotgun and tell the officers I gave it to you for protection. That way nobody will look too closely at the real shooter." She nodded.

They heard footsteps. It was the awakened desk clerk.

The muzzle of Kane's Colt stopped him cold.

"You damn well better not run into something you cannot handle, boy." Kane said as he uncocked the Frontier Model.

"Now, go get the marshal and be quick about it. We have had two attempted robberies with passkeys in your fine establishment. I will be talking with my lawyer about it. By the time we get through, the young lady and I will likely own this place and be your boss. Now move."

He did and Kane turned to the others and shrugged. He went into his room and dressed for the law. Rita and Quantrill obtained clothes from their real rooms then exchanged.

As Kane knew it would be, it was a long night. He got to bed at five.

He met with the owner and the manager at eight and repeated his threat. The rooms became free and breakfast for his party was, too. Kane did not care about the money or about owning a hotel. He wanted to be an indignant center of attention to divert any attention from people either dead or, in the case of Frank James, alive. He said his young female friend was devastated seeing the damage the shotgun inflicted on the two who had broken into her room. Kane said she wanted to go straight to the local newspaper and tell how dangerous and ill-run the hotel was. He told them if they left her alone, he may be able to talk her into not damaging their reputation further. The owner and his manager quickly agreed.

Kane joined the whole posse in Frank's room. They discussed the evening before and decided dissolving the posse as planned might be premature. They would ride together until Booth found a train station with lines going somewhere appealing. They would go to Belkin and Hico. Frank would visit with Jesse as he often did, then return alone to Oklahoma and Indian Territory. Quantrill would go as far as Dallas with Kane and then head to Arkansas.

Rita had not decided her fate or its destination. Billy found great hope in her indecision and the additional time he had to work his plan on her.

Once his posse was securely dead again, or in Frank James's case back home working innocuously, Kane had decided to resign as the superintendent of the Circle. Meeting the young officer in Mexico was fate. Kane knew he had somewhere to go. He had put it off far too long.

After dinner, Kane called everyone into a corner

of the private dining room where they could speak quietly without being overheard. He proffered his idea to stick together and drop off members one by one instead of just disbanding. Jesse spoke up.

"This thing about us being targets....Frank and I have been holding back on something. Going into it was not mission-specific earlier in the game. It is now.

Before we left for Mexico, I spotted two suits in town with every earmark of Pinkerton. I followed them and sure, enough, they were Pinks all right. I brought Frank in on it. We agreed they were here because of the kidnapping. Maybe to recover Miss. Rita. More'n likely to see if Wilkes turned up. We've all seen the sighting reports over the years in the newspapers. Booth and Frank and me are Allan J. Pinkerton's most painful failures in his business career and, I suspect, his personal life.

Something had to be done. So, Frank and I did it. We killed them, sunk their bodies in the Rio Grande. Then, we went back to the hotel and built a pretty iron-clad alibi for them being fake detectives who blew town in the middle of the night.

So, Kane. You are right. There is safety in numbers. Not a man here—woman, too, I might add, is one to run from danger. But, we spent some money and some lives to drop out of sight. Frank and I don't want to jeopardize our collective efforts.

Bill and Billy, you with us on this line of thinking?"

Both nodded.

"Miss Rita, I didn't ask you. You are famous as who you really are. Now, whether you want to stay that way is a whole 'nuther question."

"I believe we are a team and should stay together for the mutual good," Rita said.

"Kane, I guess you have a consensus on your plan to stay together until the last one is home."

"Jesse, thanks for telling us about the Pinkertons. You were right not to go into details then or now. You and Frank know how to get the job done better than about anybody. I am surprised there are no replacement Pinks in town looking for the others. Maybe they were here while we were in Mexico. I suspect we will never know. Unless, they bump into us on the trail home, I don't really care," Kane said.

"Let's keep our same cover and the buckboard. You all decide who needs a buckboard and that's who will keep it. No need to try to sell it here. Plus, we can camp some on the way back and bypass towns. I will make sure we have good provisions. Anything personal you need like more tobacco, you better get here in Laredo before we leave tomorrow. Just use paper money or silver and keep your eye-catching gold bags safely stashed away, please," Kane finished.

They broke up and went to smoke or to their rooms. Kane caught Rita for a moment and Booth and the Kid hung closely.

"Miss Rita, have you given any thought on where you would like to be dropped? Maybe a railroad line leading to Denver or wherever your show is going next?"

"Kane, perhaps we might chat briefly in private. There is something I'd like to discuss with you," Rita said.

"Well, since the world has not progressed sufficiently for women to allow us to step into the bar, how about a walk?" Kane suggested.

Once they left her father and Billy wondering and stepped outside, she began.

"I have been doing a lot of thinking. I will always be associated with daddy. While I was proud to carry on the traditions of America's greatest theatrical family, I am tired. Tired of being a target. Tired of being the daughter of the man who killed possibly the greatest president since Washington or Jefferson. Tired of spending three or four days somewhere and moving on. Tired of being cheered for my bosoms instead of my talent. Tired of no place to call home."

She stopped and took a breath. She was verbalizing unresolved thoughts for the first time.

"Daddy is a drifter. He would always be on the move even if he wasn't John Wilkes Booth. Maybe I can give him a home to stop at periodically. Mama is not much different. She will marry someone new, then someone else. She seems to always need a man around to replace the one she really wants." Rita nodded back where they had left her father. She paused for a long moment before continuing.

"I guess you are wondering why I'm telling you all of this, Kane," she said.

"No, not at all. You want me to help you drop off the map. Reinvent yourself with a new identity. Perhaps explore a life with a young man who is already dead," Kane said.

She looked at him and nodded, with more than a bit of surprise on her face.

"I have been watching you. Watching how you interact with your father. With the Kid. Watching how you transitioned from city actress to gunfighter. It was not such a big jump for you. It appears you found the real you, Miss Rita."

"I have not thought about it in those terms, but I believe you are correct. Will you help me disappear and reappear as someone else?"

"Yes. I will. There are some hurdles and lots of questions. Do you wish to start right now?" Kane asked.

"Can we?" she asked. Kane smiled.

"Do you want Rita Wilkes, famous actress to live on? Or, to die? It would be easy have gotten malaria or something in Mexico and it subsequently killed you back in the states," Kane suggested.

"I have a wild idea. It may be stupid."

"Share it and we will discuss it," Kane said.

"There is an actress. She is better than I. She is in a little theater company in Richmond. We are friends and she says every time I see her, 'I wish I had your name and your connections.'"

"Miss Rita, first, may I drop the 'Miss' part?" Kane asked.

"Please do."

"How much or little does she resemble you?"

"She is the same height. Thinner. Her hair is more brown than my black."

"What color are her eyes? They are tough to disguise," Kane asked.

"Her eyes and mine are colored and shaped virtually identically." Rita said.

"You said Richmond. How about accent?"

"Easily handled by a professional actor, Kane. Hair, too. She could have black hair for a while, then 'lighten' it to her natural brown whenever she wishes."

"We could go with the malaria thing to explain loss of weight," Kane suggested.

"Since my incarceration, I have lost weight to the point we are already the same."

"How many people know you both?" Kane asked.

"Nobody I can think of," Rita said.

"If she dyed her hair black, would your former associates from the play at Laredo recognize she is not you?" Kane asked.

"I'm not sure, Kane. I believe so with a bit of coaching, she would."

"How about her family? Parents, siblings, cousins or such?" Kane probed.

"Just an older aunt with age-related memory issues. She could visit her without any explanation about names."

"Where is she?"

"Charlottesville. Maybe fifty, or sixty miles west of Richmond."

Kane chuckled. "I know Charlottesville. I grew up there." He continued his questions.

"Rita, are there any people with whom you have had romantic interludes who would know you?"

"No. I have been on the road too much for that."

"If anybody could keep your secret, it would be your father. How about your mother?" Kane asked.

"I believe she would. I am sure my brother would, too."

Kane thought aloud.

"Looks like we don't have to substitute a dead body for you. One was used for everybody else except Frank James."

"Right."

"Do you think this person would require money to switch identities?" Kane asked.

"No, money might help her get to somewhere else to be me for a play. But, I don't want to switch identities. I want to give her mine."

"Then, Rita, we need to go to Richmond and see her. If she says 'no,' we will have to go to plan 'B'," Kane said.

"What is plan 'B'?" Rita asked.

"You will have to die like Billy, Jesse, your father, and Quantrill did."

"Can you arrange such a death, Kane?"

"Indeed," he said, adding "One last question. Tell me about your relationships and possible plans with Billy. Should he accompany us?"

"Hmm….I wish I knew the answer. We have a connection. Permanent? I don't know and I don't think he does either. It is certainly worth exploring."

"Rita, I like Billy. I believe he's a good young man who had had nothing but mud kicked in his face since birth. He is a killer. Every man in the posse is a killer. But, I don't think Billy takes pleasure in it. I think, from talking with him, he just wants to be left alone on his dirt farm in Texas. He wants to be Bill Roberts, not William Bonney or Antrim, or Billy the Kid. He has not killed even half the men the news rags claim. And, of the ones he did kill, most appeared to need killing. And, he obliged them with a great deal of talent."

"The dirt farm worries me a bit. I am not sure I want to live in squalor," Rita said.

"I would not either. Think, however, about the bag of gold coins Billy now has. You have a pretty good nest egg in the bag I gave you. Together, a new house. A better life. I have not seen Jesse's farm. But, I doubt it is too horrible. Just keep in mind a plantation house will draw unwanted attention. Maybe a town house in a big city is a good place to hide in plain sight. Or, a small farm in Texas or Missouri with comforts built into the house. I would say you and Billy should talk. Tell him what you are going to do. And, tell him you are going to drop out of the public eye and come back to Hico, Texas and give it a try with him if he's agreeable."

"Alright, Kane. I will talk with him tonight. And, I will tell my father the same thing. So, what's first on the agenda?" she asked.

"We head to Dallas from here, where I resign from the Circle. It's a good thing my father has passed. He wanted this to be my lifetime job. He would be crestfallen over my quitting. But, the job caused me to miss the one thing in life I really cared about. And, I am going to give it my very best to rectify it," Kane said.

"I have told you my secret plan. Won't you share yours?" Rita said.

Kane looked at her, his blue eyes penetrating to her very soul.

"I was in love when I was perhaps four years younger than you. It was part of the European training regime my father planned. This part was in Spain, where I was formally tutored in the language and in sword and pistol. He name is Maria Elena. Her family made her marry a viscount. She has a son and daughter. I met the son on this trip. So did you."

"The young lieutenant with your eyes." she burst out.

"The very same. I am going to Spain and try to bring my Maria Elena back here."

"How do you know she will come?" Rita asked.

"In twenty years, she has fulfilled her family's obligation to her husband. She has admirably raised what he thinks are his children. I suspect the daughter really is his, but, I do not know for sure. Maria Elena has professed her love for me monthly for the past twenty years. I believe her. And, I am going to find out."

"What a great story. It would be a play of Shakespearean caliber," Rita said. "Will you let me know how it turns out?" she asked. Kane nodded.

"Why don't we go back to the hotel so you can speak with Booth and Billy?" he suggested.

"You don't like my father very much do you, Kane?" she asked.

"Rita, I try not to judge. Whether I like or dislike Booth is not material to the mission we had. A successful mission, though you escaped on your own."

"With a war party of Apaches chasing me down. I will always consider your mission was both successful and brilliantly executed, Kane." He smiled lightly in acknowledgement, but said nothing.

Rita did not pursue the part about her father with Kane again. Her father has always been her absent hero. Getting to know him in Mexico and on the way back showed a different side. She believed he loved her. She knew now he was a cold man and he hid his feelings and opinions always being the actor. One never knew what she was getting, real or a performance with Booth. She no longer trusted him. If he could not be honest with his own daughter, then with whom? He was surly and moody. Her mother had hinted those characteristics were direct from his father. And, they were not new to Wilkes Booth. He has always been surly and moody.

She had spent her adult life in the theater. She knew how actors were. Often ego-centric and pompous, yes. Moody? Some. Surly? Seldom. They had to play to their audiences, their fans outside the theater and they people who hired them or directed them. There was no room for surliness in her world. She hoped he would visit occasionally. She also hoped he would not stay too long.

Before they got back to the front door of the hotel, Rita asked one more question.

"Kane. You said everyone in the Ghost Posse was a killer. I have seen you perform pretty admirably when the chips are down. But, Kane, are you a killer?"

He paused at the surprise question.

"Yes, Rita. I am a killer. I have killed many times

before this mission. But, I am not a murderer. Let me leave my answer there. It is a topic worth pondering."

"No, Kane. I don't need to ponder it. Your answer was what I already have thought about and arrived at on my own. I appreciate you answering it."

They went into the hotel and Billy was in the lobby. Kid and the actress walked back out the door. She was just as safe walking down the streets of Laredo now as she was moments earlier. Even had she been without the Colt .38-40 which now permanently resided in her purse.

The Ghost Posse left at first light. Rita rode in the buckboard with her father. Billy rode beside. Kane and Quantrill took the lead, with the James brothers riding drag behind the wagon.

It took the procession almost two days to make it to Blevins and drop off Jesse. Frank decided to stay with the group and head on to his home in Oklahoma and Indian Territory.

"It's been good riding with a mission again," Jesse said to the group before he rode into the lane for his farm.

"Billy, why don't you spend the night here and head on to Hico in the morning? I think we are okay here in this part of Texas without an escort, don't you?"

"Well, that would keep Rita from seeing my run-down farm until I can spend some of my new money on sprucing it up before she gets back in a month,"

Billy said giving Rita a big grin and getting similar in return. All dismounted except the two in the buckboard.

"Buck, keep your eyes peeled. Bring Ma for a visit before fall sets in too much."

"I will, little brother," Frank said as two of the most dangerous men alive hugged each other. Jesse shook with his old captain and with Kane.

"Glad we didn't decide to kill each other this time, Jess. We came close when you were a nineteen year old," Quantrill said solemnly.

"Me, too, Bill. It's better watching each other's backs."

Billy shook hands with Kane and silently mouthed "thank you," out of everyone else's sight. Kane knew it was for supporting him with Rita as well as accepting him into this very special group. Jesse gave a short bow to Rita and merely nodded to Booth.

Kane and Jesse walked a few yards away from everyone else.

"Jesse, someone else will be working with you on the Circle business. I am heading directly to Dallas now to resign."

"I'm real sorry to hear such talk, Kane. What are you going to do?" Jesse asked.

"I'm going to Spain and try to correct a mistake I made twenty some years ago."

"You kill somebody over there?"

"No, I left a woman behind. I should have fought for her, but the odds seemed too heavy for my twenty year old brain. But, something happened in Mexico slammed me right in the gut and made me rethink some things."

"Anything to do with that young officer who looked just like you. You were real particular about us trusting him and not killing him. Frank figured it was your son," Jesse said.

"You above all would know you can't fool Frank James, Jesse."

"I'm thinking his ma must be pretty special. You need some help, wire James Courtney, Belkin, Texas. I'm not wanted over there and always wondered what it looked like."

"You are the first person I'd call Jesse. And, the next would be your brother and new young friend. Though, I'm hoping he will be too busy convincing an actress to become a farmer's wife." The two gunfighters clasped hands in a four hand shake and turned away.

Rita put her stuff on Jack Wise's horse and they saddled the buckboard horse for her father to ride the next hundred miles. Billy tied his pony to the buckboard.

He looked at Rita and she gave him a lifetime smile. He gulped, grinned and drove the buckboard to Jesse's farm. Jesse rode beside him.

"God help whatever Spaniards get in Kane's way," Jesse said quietly as he and Billy headed down his lane.

Now, without having to go northwest to Hico, the diminished group headed to Dallas.

After some discussion, both Quantrill and Booth decided to catch trains in Dallas, though in different directions.

Frank James took some of the remaining provisions and rode north. Kane shared his plan as he had with Jesse first. The two parted as good friends.

Booth's parting with his daughter was brief and unemotional. She had expected it would be so. Anything the two needed to say to each other had been said in the buckboard from Mexico to Dallas. And, it was far less than should have been said.

Quantrill shook hands with all and walked to the ticket booth without looking back. He disappeared into rural life and was never identified as the war criminal he really was.

Kane got Rita a room in the hotel where he lived. She was surprised how upscale it was. She had been to San Francisco, Chicago, and New York. This place was easily the equal of any she had stayed in there.

The next day, Kane called a board of directors meeting for the following Friday. The directors were all in Texas, but some as far away as El Paso. They needed the four days travel time.

Kane got to know Rita and watch her mannerisms.

He did not know how to teach actors to act. But, he did know how to prepare someone to go undercover.

She bought travel clothes that were more like a successful farmer's wife might wear and not a famous actress traveling by train to Richmond.

By nine o'clock Friday morning, the trustees had gathered in the board room of the Dallas headquarters. The Knights of the Golden Circle was corporately known as GC Financial.

"Gentlemen, I have called you together to report on the success of our mission. And, at the end, one more piece of business," Kane opened the meeting.

"You will find a complete accounting of expenditures in your folders. We stayed within budget, rewarded the posse members and accomplished our goal. Miss Ogarita Wilkes, nee Booth had escaped from her captor the day before we arrived. We caught up with this brave young woman riding towards us with a war party of hostile Apaches right behind her. She joined us in defeating them in several skirmishes. We encountered both criminal and righteous Rurales and dealt accordingly.

We entered Mexico as a rancher and his men looking to buy a ranch and left the same way. We did not leave any identifiable evidence behind us. Two Pinkertons were present and presented a mission threat. The James boys handled them and they won't be anyone's problem. There again, there will be nothing to tie them to us. All of this is outlined in the mission report before you. For the sake of their future safety, I have redacted the names of the actual posse members from the report. We had one non-Circle knight who you may not be able to figure out from the coding. He was a surprise to me, but totally supported by Jesse James. He proved to be an important asset. His name was Henry McCarty or William Bonney. Take your pick," Kane said.

Kane expected his board to know who Billy was and was not disappointed at the brief questions about him.

"Kane, how was Quantrill? Also, Booth?" his most senior member and chairman, asked.

"Those were the two I worried the most about. Quantrill was quiet and thoughtful. His planning was a boon to us, as was his ability to use dynamite as a weapon." Several eyebrows raised at the statement about dynamite, but Kane kept speaking.

"Booth was an odd duck. He was quiet and un-approachable. Quantrill was beside him during a shoot-out at the ranch were Ogarita was held. He said despite Booth's protestations about only having killed Lincoln, he watched Booth drill the foreman between the eyes at a goodly distance and not blink an eye at it. Quantrill says he believes Booth has killed before Lincoln and after. If you believe it takes a killer to know a killer, I cannot think of a more qualified commenter than Quantrill."

"You mentioned another piece of business before we get down to drinks and lunch."

Kane chuckled and said "I don't remember mentioning drinks and lunch, but they will follow immediately after you announce adjournment, Mr. Chairman.

The other piece of business is I have some personal matters to attend to in Spain. I hope to not be gone more than a month. I am submitting my resignation to the Circle today. It will be effective at a mutually agreed upon time after I return. It is not my intention to leave this organization in the lurch. Perhaps you might look for a replacement while I am gone and I will instruct him in our ways upon returning. I will back away as soon as you are confident he is ready to take the reins."

This delayed the drinks and lunch for another twenty minutes. At the end of discussions, none of which inquired about Kane's business in Spain, they prepared to raise glasses.

"Gentlemen, I know this is a very secret organization. I have an option for you, but only if you would like to exercise it. We spent a lot of money to bring actress Ogarita Wilkes back to Texas. She is downstairs. If you would like her to join us for lunch, I can get her. Of course we cannot talk about any business in front of her, but you may find her a fascinating person. One well worth bringing home," Kane said.

There was a bit of discussion about this departure in protocol, but in the end, curiosity overruled.

Rita both charmed and intrigued the older gentlemen with her stories of being kidnapped, knifing her kidnapper, surviving in the desert and fighting Apaches with her a knife and both her Colt and Winchester. These were stories Texas pioneers could relish and they did.

The chairman stayed on a minute to make interim plans with Kane for the period he was abroad, bid his good wishes to Rita and departed.

"If you don't mind me asking, how did they take your resignation?" Rita asked Kane.

"Shocked, but the group has been around thirty years, so having a new superintendent is not the end of the world. My guess the chairman will install his son-in-law."

"Is he a good man?" Rita asked.

"He is a banker, so he knows the financial end. Could he have led a group into Mexico to rescue a beautiful damsel in distress? Hardly. But, the successor is their problem. I have given seventeen years to this organization. I have saved and invested well. I'm far from rich, but I will be able to live comfortably. Hopefully with my Maria Elena. Time will tell."

"Will you tell me about her?" Rita prompted.

"Well, I have not seen her for twenty years. When I saw her, she was a bit younger than you. Tall, perfectly proportioned. Cold black hair and beautiful blue eyes. Smooth skin. The same light tone as Lt. Miguel Vasquez."

"Kane, what is your given name?" Rita asked as they checked on Hadrian and Billy's pony at the livery stable and told the owner to look after them for perhaps a month.

"Michael," he said.

"As in Miguel?" Rita asked.

"As in Miguel."

"Did he know you are his father?"

"Miguel seemed to get some strong feelings from our interaction. I suspected it immediately, but was not sure until we spoke about where he grew up. He never verbalized his thoughts, but I knew he was wondering."

"Will you ever tell him, Kane?" she asked.

"If his mother does not beat him to it. I mentioned meeting him in a recent letter to Maria Elena. I doubt we will have time to see her response before I board the train for New York, then heading by steamship to Spain."

"But, we will go to Richmond first and see my friend who may become me?"

"That we will. We will spend as much time there as necessary to assure she can pull it off if she is willing," he promised.

"Will you help me perfect my shooting while we

are there?" Rita asked.

"I will. We will purchase a nice leather case for your Winchester and some cartridges and a cleaning kit for it. Also, we'll get a leather belt wide enough to hold your revolver without sagging. Jack Wise might have been skinny, but you still win out in the tiny waist department. We will make sure your gunbelt fits."

"Can we get me one of those stubby little guns like you are wearing under your coat?" she asked.

"Very observant. Yes, we can get a Webley Bulldog for you. The cartridges will not fit any Winchester, but it will work well for a hideaway. I learned to shoot them in London. They are amazingly accurate for such short-barreled revolvers, Rita. And, carry enough punch to do the job at reasonable ranges."

Kane took her to a prominent gun shop in Dallas and they found a Webley. It was nickel plated. The gunsmith promised to have some mother of pearl grips fashioned for it before they left the city for their travels.

The mail would have taken too long for a response from her friend in Richmond, so they chanced her being there when they arrived. Rita had exchanged letters with her a week before the kidnapping and the woman, Sally Hemsworth, was committed to a play in a small theater in town.

Train travel was old hat to both Rita and Kane. They spent the time chatting and reading. The trip was four days, but passed comfortably and in relative luxury.

They arrived in Richmond's Westham Station, west of the city. The train pulled in at ten in the morning. It would be several railroad takeovers and a lot of construction before the new Main Street Station was operable.

Horse-drawn cabs were available and Kane flagged one and told him to go to an address on Grace Street in downtown Richmond. Sally Hemsworth lived in a rooming house there. Rita felt Sally should be there, since her play was presented at night.

They rapped at her door. She was surprised. Kane was pleased. He was very pleased to see how much she favored Rita. Rita said she was a tiny bit older, but Sally did not look it.

"Sally, Mr. Kane and I want to visit with you about a serious opportunity. Is there a quiet place nearby where we can eat lunch?" Rita asked.

"Right down the street there's a tea room in Linden Row. It is said Edgar Allan Poe lived on the land as a boy. Let me get my gloves and purse," she said, staring at Kane.

They walked the block to the tea room and were seated. There was no one else there yet and they were able to talk without being overheard.

"Sally, I doubt the news has made it back East yet, but I was kidnapped in Texas and taken to

Mexico. We had to shoot our way home, literally," she said as Sally listened to a tale her experience could barely fathom.

"Who is 'we?'" Sally asked.

"Mr. Kane and some of his associates came to get me. They had to fight a crooked Rurale patrol, the bad men who kidnapped me, and a large party of hostile Apache Indians. I tried to count the other night. By my best reckoning, perhaps fifty men died in getting me back to the States."

"Fifty. Mr. Kane, did you shoot any of them?" Sally asked.

"A few," he replied.

"Kane is modest. I would say he shot more than his fair share. He is quite the gunman when pushed into a corner."

"Rita, you look beautiful. Yet different. I know you are thinner. Is it because of your captivity?"

"It is. I lived on scraps of bread and water for three weeks. I broke free by stabbing my captor and stole his horse and guns. After a bit of camping, I was being chased by forty Apaches and ran into my saviors who had come for me."

"And, then?"

"Kane and his men killed most of them. We holed up in a village's small church and the rest attacked us. A party of good Rurales came, but most were killed. You should have seen the handsome young lieutenant.

He looked just like Kane, down to the blue eyes."

Kane decided Rita was getting too detailed and interjected himself.

"It was a righteous fight and we prevailed. We were able to get back across the border to Laredo. We later disbanded and Rita wanted to come see you. Something you told her rang a bell and she wants to discuss it with you in more detail, Miss Sally," Kane said, putting things back on track.

"Yes, dear Rita. I cannot imagine what I said would prompt a visit. But, I am surely glad it did." Sally said.

"You have said more than once you wished you were me. You wished you had the connections being a Booth gave."

"I have always thought that, you are beautiful and famous."

"If I am beautiful, what does that make you? We look just alike."

Sally looked at Kane.

"Equally breathtaking. Like twins. Which is why Rita has a proposition for you," he said.

"A proposition? Of what sort?"

"How would you like to become Rita Wilkes. For the rest of your life? Introduce yourself to directors as me. Claim any successes I have had as your own. For an actress who looks like me and has your talent it would be easy."

"Why, dear friend? Half the actresses around would

die to be you."

"Haha. Forget dying. You can *live* to be me. You can *be* me, Sally."

"Why would you give up your career, your fame, the name of America's greatest thespian family?" Sally asked.

"I want to drop out of sight. I am tired of the theater. I had some time to think about my life when I was tied to a bed, then later just locked in, virtually starving. I got tired of a few nights here, a few there. No real home."

"Do you think you were kidnapped because of who you are?" Sally asked.

"Good question, Miss Sally," Kane said. "Allow me to address it." Sally shook her head up and down.

"The man who kidnapped her would not know Rita Wilkes from Lillie Langtry," referring to the newest famous actress to hit the stage.

"He liked what he saw. His interest was carnal, not theatrical." Rita, taking her queue, jumped in.

"I knew what Kane is saying was true from the beginning. The looks, the groping as I was being moved or fed or anything. The lady who fed me left a butter knife with my dishes one day. I took it and she never asked for it back. Once my hands were released after the first few days, I sharpened it and reshaped the blunt point to be able to stab and penetrate.

The man owned a ranch and was a cattle rustler.

He and his men were gone a lot. One day, he came back. He came upstairs for me. He took his clothes off. I could see what he was going to do and led him on. As he sat on the bed, I rammed the knife as deeply into his side as I could. He screamed and ran out to his room. I heard him fall and ran downstairs and to the front door. I was virtually naked. I saw his gun on the table. I took it and stole his horse tied right out front."

"Rita, what did you do then?" Sally asked.

"Why, I rode away. As fast as the rustler's horse could carry me."

"Did the rustlers come after you?"

"No. The cowboys were out working with the foreman. Wise was in his room trying to recover. Then, Kane had followed his clues and his men hit the ranch. Wise came at Kane."

"Mr. Kane, what did you do?" Sally asked.

"I killed him."

"Just like that?"

"Pretty much."

"And," She pressed on, "the rest of his men?"

"They resisted and died."

"Who on earth were your men to be so deadly? And, if I might ask, who are you?"

"My men were a carefully selected posse of gunfighters. Good men in some respects, but all killers. Me? I am nobody. But, a nobody with a vested interest."

"And, Mr. Kane, what is your vested interest?"

"I am a friend of the family. And, Rita's godfather," he lied with a story they developed on the train.

"If you accept, I will be your godfather instead."

"I think I would like that. Quite a bit, as a matter of fact. What will becoming Rita Wilkes involve?" she asked both.

"It will involve days here talking about memories, pet's names, plays she's performed. People she has met. Every detail of the kidnapping. How she survived. The terrible depravity. The malaria which conveniently comes back and keeps her more slender like you. Dying your hair black. Learning her nuances of speech, of which she actually has almost none," Kane said.

"What about her mother?"

"Her mother will be the one person, other than I, who will know. You will not have to worry about her," Kane said.

"And, the Booth family? The uncles and grandmother?"

"The Booth family does not know me. You could pass for me easily. My grandmother is in her eighties and in Boston. The uncles have their own interests. Should you accidentally meet one, they have not seen me since I was five. You look like a Booth. We actually got the good looks from my grandmother. Mary Ann Holmes Booth was quite beautiful. Her husband, from all I can determine was obnoxious,"

Rita said with more emotion than Kane had heard from her previously.

"One last, dear Rita. There are many stories of your father being seen all over. How do I respond to them?" Sally asked. Kane hid a smile. She personalized her question. A sure sign of acceptance of their offer.

"Say if he is alive, he is a piss poor father to have neglected his only daughter for eighteen years," Rita said with vehemence Kane thought was unfeigned.

Sally smiled broadly. She really was quite smart and quite beautiful.

"I hardly ever say things like 'piss poor,' dear friend."

Rita smiled back like a reflection in a mirror.

"Now you do."

"I guess we have a bargain, then and not a piss poor one." Sally Hemsworth said, falling into the exact voice of the young woman sitting across from her.

"There will be a small stipend to help you get started, buy whatever clothes or tickets you need for your new career. I suspect it will take off superbly and you will be making large salaries very quickly."

"May I ask how much the stipend is, dear godfather?"

Kane smiled at her. "Five thousand in gold coins." It was her turn to smile.

"Couldn't I just retire right now?" she asked.

"Of course you could," Rita said.

"But, why not have some fun acting around the world first? Then, if you find someone or just get tired of it all, retire. I would. Or, rather I did." Rita said.

"Godfather, are you taken?" she asked Kane coquettishly.

"Ask me again in another month. I don't quite know right this moment," Kane responded truthfully.

"I have a commitment with the small theater company on Broad Street to finish a run of a burlesque satire. You should make yourself look less like me and come to it tonight. Bring my delicious new godfather, of course."

"How long is your contractual arrangement?" said godfather asked.

"Another week." Kane paused and did some mental arithmetic. He would have time, although barely, to make the departure of the Buenos Ayrean, a steel-hulled steamer to London. His sense of adventure overruled his observation about why he should take a ship made out of a material which could not float under the best of conditions.

"That is pretty tight scheduling for me, but does allow you more time to learn how to be Rita, Sally. If you two work hard at it, I may lessen the risk of missing my boat by leaving a few days before the end of your play," Kane said.

"I've never sailed across the ocean," Sally said. "Are you sure you would not like to have your two goddaughters accompany you?" she said precociously.

"I am sure you could go as twins and be delightful company. But, this trip will be of indeterminate duration and may require a fast exit across Spain to avoid pursuers."

"How exciting." the new Rita said. The former Rita's interest was piqued by the possibility of excitement.

"Perhaps, Kane, we could provide some cover for you on this trip. Sally's idea might be a good one," she said.

"I will consider it. But, for now, the two of you need to work out a brief biography of everything about Rita's life and people she has met and may encounter again. Also personal things, places visited, plays and roles performed. Any interesting details involving them. Then, rehearse, rehearse, rehearse. Just like you are learning the words for Romeo and Juliet or Julius Caesar.

Sally, I promised to hone Rita's shooting skills. Since you will be her and have the skirmishes in Mexico in your made-up history, why don't you join us? I will teach you also. Having a revolver in your bag may not be such a bad thing as you travel around America delighting audiences," Kane said.

"If we could secure a buggy, a friend's family owns acreage out near the James River, 'way west of town. We could take River Road out to it. I've been there many times and can show you." Sally said.

"Let's plan to go there tomorrow. In the meantime, Rita, we need to find a new name for you. Then, we must begin calling Sally "Rita" and you by the new name. And, with no exceptions, even in private. We need to imprint the names upon your brains.

Any name preferences jump out at you?" he asked.

"Let the two of us think about it. Actually, it is a momentous decision. I will keep this name the rest of my life," Rita said.

"Just don't make it too distinctive. Memorable anything is bad when you are trying to drop out of sight. Just seeing either of you is memorable enough, so don't compound it by a name that everyone can remember."

They agreed and he said he needed to go to the main post office and post a letter.

"Perhaps to a beautiful Spanish woman we know?" asked Rita.

"Anything is possible, 'one who needs a new name.' Sally, would you assist Rita with her endeavor?" he requested. "Something like Risa Wilson might be good. Using the same initials are always the easiest to learn and to cover for items with initials embroidered or engraved on them."

"With pleasure, dearest godfather."

Not knowing quite how to respond to her growing intimacies, Kane turned and left. He walked out and left them, hopefully to practice Sally's identity change.

Kane took his leather day book and a fountain pen with him. He sat on a bench in the Capitol grounds and penned a letter to Maria Elena in the formal Spanish they used in their correspondence.

He advised her of his arrival date in London and subsequent one in Sitges. The nearest city was Barcelona. Her husband, the Viscount, had extensive lands in the area. Sitges was also the location of their estate. He told her he was coming to try to rectify his error of leaving alone twenty years ago. Kane was pretty sure his meaning was crystal clear. She should have about a week from when she received the letter to decide what she was going to do.

Give up a wealthy, royal, twenty-year life and a loveless marriage? Or, go to America with her one great love? Kane was stoic. He knew much of his happiness for the rest of his life would depend on her decision. He also knew he would abide by her decision, whichever way it went.

Riding and hunting with a son was something Kane had dreamed of since he first became aware of Miguel's existence. Kane had not thought of a daughter. But, the short time with Rita and Sally showed him why so many fathers doted on daughters.

One of his great doubts now was Maria Elena's daughter. She was the viscount's child. Would she stay? Would she come to America with her mother. More importantly, would Maria Elena leave without her daughter, Gabriela?

He knew from the letters she was devoted to her mother and was, as yet, unwed. Was there a marriage contract? She was old enough. It would be legally binding in Spain. How would an impending marriage affect Maria Elena leaving her daughter?

How would Miguel react? Kane thought well, based on their relationship in Mexico. Did he take Kane's advice and return to Spain? Or, was he still riding with the Rurales?

Maria Elena had gotten married early in her pregnancy with Miguel. She said in a letter the husband thought Miguel was his and had been born a bit prematurely. The baby boy, who looked so much like Kane, also looked like Maria Elena. Viscount Tomás Vasquez had never seen Kane. Her family had hidden as much about his existence and relationship with their daughter as possible. It was the only aspect of their actions which benefited Kane.

Preemptively, Kane had consulted with and retained a powerful and successful annulment attorney. The jurist told Kane it would be an uphill struggle against rich and titled people such as the Vasquez family. He recommended having Maria Elena run off with him, though the viscount could send the sheriff's guards after them with a warrant. Once out of Spain, their woes would not be over. Arriving in the States would lessen their risks. It would take an American lawyer to opine whether taking someone else's wife out of Spain, a crime there, was extraditable in the US.

Kane even inquired about dueling. He quickly found Spain had outlawed dueling almost exactly four hundred years earlier. A quick shoot-out was eliminated. He had a small vial of poison which emulated a heart attack. It was a last resort measure. But, one Kane would not hesitate to employ if backed into a corner.

******

Billy was untutored but highly intelligent. He knew his limits. Home design was high on his list of limits instead of attributes. He found a builder in Hico and had him come to the farm.

The man looked at his house and stable. He immediately determined the house should be converted to a stable and the current stable knocked down.

The replacement house should be on a rise a hundred feet away. It would require a second well. He suggested a new privy down the hill behind it. He recommended a two-bedroom house with a parlor, kitchen with a cooking fireplace and a cupboard. The house would be clapboard with a tin roof. The total cost, with some furniture, would take only about a third of Billy's new nest egg.

"Could you do all this by the end of the month?" he asked.

"Yes, but I'd have to hire more men. It would add a hundred dollars to the figure I just quoted you."

"Consider it done. Five hundred down and rest on completion." They shook, Billy gave him a cash down payment and the man agreed to begin delivering materials the following day.

By the end of a week, Billy had a second well, a new privy and the main house framed up. By the third week, the house was finished and Billy was assisting in the painting of the clapboard. The old house had stalls where there had been rooms and the façade was modified to look more like a stable.

The project was completed as promised and with the agreed upon budget. The man now known as Bill Roberts was pleased and invited his friend Jim Courtney to ride up and see it. He did and brought Mrs. Courtney and a couple of hound dogs. All were duly impressed.

Now, Billy wondered, what would Rita Wilkes think of it?

Having the approval of the man who had become his older brother figure, Billy wrote a letter to Rita at the address she had sent in Richmond. It got to her in time and she told him she was leaving the next day on the train and to meet her at the Waco train depot at a certain time and day. He knew his letter would never reach her in time, so just planned on being there in Waco.

On the appointed day, a handsome young man with a charmingly crooked grin, stood at the train platform. He had on his dark suit and hat, a white shirt and cravat. His boots were shined and he held a bouquet of flowers in his non-gun hand. A short-barreled .45 Colt was hidden in his right waistband. For a man reported to have killed one man for each of his twenty-one years, he was strangely nervous. Actually, he was scared, but would not admit it. He heard the train whistle in the distance and had to run to the privy and urinate for the third time since arriving. Billy the Kid's nerves were shot to hell by a twenty-four year old actress.

He pulled himself together as the train pulled in. Rita swung off and gave a ticket stub to a porter who left to locate her luggage. She approached Billy smiling and gave him a big kiss. Right in front of everybody. It was scandalous. He loved it. She stood hugging him while waiting for her trunk and two bags. He noticed, with approval, she kept her new leather rifle case in her weak hand and had not checked it.

"Did you get your matters settled?" he asked.

She gave him a glowing smile.

"I did. Now, I have a new life. Let's us give it a go and see what happens. I'm game if you are."

"I am game. Wait 'till you see the place. I sure hope you like it. I put a lot into it to make it worthy of you," he said.

"I'm sure it will be fine."

Her luggage arrived and Billy gave the porter a nickel tip after he loaded them into the back of the buggy. Billy helped Rita up into the seat she had occupied with her father in Mexico and Texas. She was much happier sitting next to Billy Roberts, as she knew she had to train herself to call the Kid.

"She leaned over and whispered in his ear. What he heard was not expected.

"You are Billy Roberts now. And, I am Risa Wilkerson. A lookalike friend is going to be Rita Wilkes. Forever, Billy."

"You and Kane have been busy. How is the tall man in black?"

"I don't know. He should be onboard a steamer for London and then for his adventures in Spain. Billy, I so hope he's successful. He's a good man. We all owe him a lot."

"Kin I tell you a secret?" he asked.

"Of course. I expect you to tell me all your secrets."

"He's the only man alive I'd be terrified to draw on. I never saw anybody faster or more accurate."

"Pretty serious words coming from one of the most famous gunfighters anywhere," she said. He was so serious he did not even grin at the compliment.

"I'm just glad he's my friend."

"Me, too, honey," she said. He did smile at those words.

Billy drove slowly, savoring the ride with the beautiful former actress.

When he stopped on his lane at a point with a full view of the newly configured farm, she gasped.

"I never saw it before, but, Billy. This is perfect. I love it," she exclaimed.

"I waited for you to plant the kind of flowers you'd like. The feed store in town has little packets of all kinds of flower seeds. The fella there says he knows which ones grow well in this area."

"You are so thoughtful," she said, meaning every word.

Billy tied the horse at his new hitching rail in front of the house.

He picked her up and carried her over the threshold. The house was large enough, especially with so little furniture.

"I know we will need some stuff. I want to get a wardrobe for you and a dressing table. Maybe some rugs and vases to put all your flowers in. I had the fella who built the place run a pipe in from the new well and you have a pump right in the kitchen. I told him a cooking fireplace, but he said you'd want a kitchen with a wood stove and pump. He said he would move my swing arm from the old fireplace to the new one. I put some pegs over the fireplace for our two rifles. One on top the other," Billy said.

"Just like us," she said with a glint and he turned

red, but burst into a grin so wide it hurt.

She helped him bring her trunk in and then he retrieved the valise.

"When do you want to go furniture shopping?" she asked. "I might wait until the wardrobe is here to unpack a lot of my things."

"I really wanted you to see the place," Billy said. "We can go back in and have lunch and do some shopping today. Maybe they can deliver it tomorrow and you can unpack then," he said. She agreed and after a quick walk around tour, they got back on the buckboard and returned to Hico.

They had lunch at a café and then went to a store which sold furniture and a variety of other things. They chose a wood inlay wardrobe and matching dressing table and chair, some braided rugs and some sundry household goods.

The largest piece, the wardrobe, was neither overly heavy or unwieldy. The store owner helped Billy load it onto the back of the buckboard and tie it down. Billy and Rita, or Risa, as he now called her, loaded the rest. "Tonight," she smiled to herself, "we will sleep in our house almost fully furnished."

They picked up a variety of groceries. One of Risa's worries was her total lack of experience cooking. Her mother had a housekeeper who cooked and cleaned. Risa, as Rita Wilkes, lived on the road and ate at cafés, restaurants and hotels.

She confided her fears to Billy who said he could do basic cowboy dishes.

"They will do for us while we experiment cooking other stuff together," he proposed.

"Sounds like a worthy plan to me, Mr. Roberts," Risa said.

The next day, Risa wrote a final letter to her mother as Rita. She told her about her new name and the new man in her life, one Bill Roberts, a rancher in Texas. She also asked about Mae, the woman who had virtually raised Rita until her teen years. Mae had been housekeeper, shopper, cook and confidant all wrapped in one. She posted it the next day in Hico.

Risa left a lot of things out of her letter. The gunfights and Indian attacks were omitted and any mention of who the posse members were. Especially, her father. Her mother may have spent the years since San Francisco looking for the perfect man to replace John Wilkes Booth, but there was no reason for her to know he was still alive. If he wanted to spend time with her, he had ample means to accomplish his goal. Risa was pretty sure it was not his goal.

She was wise enough to realize sometimes absent lovers were better as dreams than reality. Risa did not really like her parents as people. She was more concerned about Kane, once she reached the conclusion about absent lovers. Kane was the father she would have selected, had the choice been hers. Had there been less age difference, she might have also chosen to rest her head on his shoulder now instead of the sleeping Billy's.

Her mother was an inveterate letter writer and Risa knew she would receive a prompt response in the two weeks it took her letter to reach Connecticut and her mother's return letter to arrive in Hico.

"Hey, what are you thinking about?" Billy asked from what Risa thought was a deep sleep.

"Oh. Did I awaken you?" she asked.

"I felt you thinking. Real hard."

She laughed. Maybe he was the perfect person for her.

"I was thinking about my mother. And, Mae, the woman who really raised me while mother was gadding about as an actress and chasing after the husband of the year."

"Tell me about Mae. She obviously did a good job raising you," Billy prompted.

"Mae. There are so many good things. Where do I start? She is heavy-set. Has the most beautiful smile in the world. When she laughs, you can't help but join in. She is a wonderful woman about fifty now."

"She sounds like a perfect substitute mother. Did anyone ever think she was your real mother?" Billy asked.

Risa smiled. "Not really. Mae has a very dark complexion, even for a Negro."

"Oh. I don't remember slavery and all. Was she ever a slave?"

"No, she was born free, thank God."

"What's she doing now?"

"Billy, I expect she's looking after mom and wherever mom lives. I really do miss her. It was Mae I really visited between plays, not mother," Risa said.

"Did either know you really came home to Mae?" Billy asked.

"Mae knew. I told her. Many times. Mother is so superficial she would never guess. She thinks the world revolves around just her."

"If you don't mind me being real frank, Risa, it sounds like your folks were well suited to each other."

"You are so very right, my dear Billy. They deserved each other. Though, I suspect if they had stayed together this additional eighteen years…." she let her words drop off.

"Then, what?" Billy pressed her.

"One would have killed the other. Or, maybe they'd have killed each other. Neither were suicidal. They each believed themselves too perfect to destroy."

They laid there silently for a while as dawn began to lighten the Texas sky.

"Billy?"

"Hmmm?"

"Tell me about your parents."

"I don't really recollect anything about my pa.

His name was Patrick McCarty. Ma, whose name was Catherine, said he was a good man. We moved from New York City to Kansas when I was a tyke. Pa died and ma and my younger brother Joseph and I moved to Indianapolis. Ma took up with a man named William Antrim. We moved back to Kansas with him, then around New Mexico. He abandoned us in about '74, when ma got the consumption. I stole food for Joseph and me to live. I robbed a Chinese laundry and got caught. I broke out and have been a fugitive ever since."

"What about your brother?" Risa asked.

"Last I heard, he was in Colorado. Like me, he wanders around. I don't think he's ever been in trouble with the law though."

"Tell me about your mother, Billy."

"She did the best she could. Had my real pa lived, I think things would have turned out different for all of us. Ma said he was a hard worker, always had a job and several skills. Said he was good to us and never drank too much. Sure was unlike the Antrim fella she married and who deserted her just before she died. Then, he deserted us. I stayed with him a few days when I was on the lam, but he kicked me out. I stole his guns and have not seen him since. I put some credits on the .45 I took. If I saw him, I'd be tempted to let him taste a bit of its lead."

"I would not want you to do that, Billy. Not to ever

break the law any kind of way again. You have created a perfect life for us here outside of Hico. Why take a chance on losing it?"

"You are right. I wasn't born bad. I had to eat and so did brother Josie. Then, things started rolling down hill and picking up speed like a rockslide. No more. I promise. I have you now. A place in this here world. I am not going to chance ruining it and losing you."

Over the next two weeks, Billy made deals to buy a few heads of cattle. One was a bull so his herd could multiply.

Their plans changed with a letter from Izola Bellows Mills, Risa's mother. She reported she had remarried and lived with her new husband in a hotel in Canterbury, Connecticut. There was no room for Mae, she said, so after many years, she dismissed her. She said Mae worked as a laundress in the hotel, but Izola did not know where she lived.

"I can see why you don't especially care for your mother. What if we went up there and brought Mae back here to live with us? It seems like the right thing to do," Billy suggested.

"That's why I love you, Billy Roberts.," Risa said hugging him.

"We can add a little cottage here for her, once she agrees to come live here," Billy said.

"You just remembered I said she's a great cook," Risa teased.

"Mainly, I remember she's who you came back to see between plays."

Billy arranged for the young girl on the next spread over to feed the horses and mule while they were gone. They left for the northeast the following day.

******

They rode to Dallas and left the buckboard and mule in a livery stable near the train station. Their first tickets took them to Atlanta, the second up to Washington, DC, then New York City.

"I don't remember any of this," Billy said as the city began to speed by after the stop at the newly-opened Union Station.

The trip to Canterbury did not take long after leaving New York. They departed the station carrying their own small valises. The hotel was virtually in sight and an easy walk.

They asked for the rooms of Izola's new husband at the front desk. The haughty clerk told them to sit in the lobby, he would send a note up by bellboy.

Presently, Risa's mother came down the steps and greeted her daughter with a light kiss on each cheek. Rather a light kiss near each cheek. Risa frowned and stepped back.

"Mother, allow me to introduce Mr. William Roberts, rancher from Texas. He and I have been spending a lot of time together."

Izola, who never used the "L" at the beginning of her name, did a small curtsey and presented her hand for Billy to kiss. Billy looked at Risa in a panic and she puckered her lips. Billy laid a big smack of a kiss on the back of the woman's hand, taking her by surprise.

"Why, Mr. Roberts. As Rita's mother, I must ask: have you prospects?"

"Prospect's for what Ma'am?" Billy asked, baffled by this odd woman.

"For life, of course."

"My sixgun has kept me alive so far. I got a farm and a swell girl to live on it. Are those the prospects you mean?"

"Yes, kind of," she mumbled as confused by this brash Westerner as he was by her.

"Mama, Billy has a nice ranch in Texas and money in the bank. He knows how to treat me and to protect me. A couple of things never present in the men chosen in this family."

Risa got a look as if a felony was getting ready to be committed upon her body. Billy saw it and his protective instincts turned on instantly. He flipped his jacket back behind his gun and Risa pressed herself against him, pinning his arm and hiding the Colt.

Izola knew something was going on, but did not know quite what. She changed the subject.

"You must come up and meet Horace. We have

been blissfully wed for almost a month now.

"Does he have any prospects?" Billy asked, receiving a glare from Izola and an elbow in the ribs from Risa.

"He is a successful business man, now retired."

"What did he do, Mama?" Risa asked.

"He, er, was in the gaming business."

"A gambler. I used to play a bit of reno with a friend. But, then he arrested me," Billy blurt out.

"For what?" Izola asked, alarmed.

"I had to shoot a fellow. He ended up dying?" Billy said forthrightly.

"Heavens. You murdered him?"

"No, Ma'am. I just killed him. Murder is a little different under the law. I mean, it's not like I killed the President or somebody." Izola gasped and Risa covered her mouth to hide her mirth over Billy's gaffe.

Without further conversation, Risa slipped behind Billy on the way up the stairs and pinched him on the butt. He managed to stifle his expression and turned to look at her. She pursed her lips again and everything was back to alright in Billy's world.

Izola introduced a gaunt, dour man to them. Risa hoped Horace had a lot of money, because he surely did not seem to have anything else.

The idea about money was soon dispelled as he reached out a bony hand to shake with Billy and Risa saw frayed cuffs on his shirt sleeves.

"Money my sweet butt," she thought. "She waited on the corner for the next bum to come by. Again."

Billy engaged Horace in a conversation about gambling and Horace seemed to perk up. Billy was careful not to mention his favorite gambling partner, Sheriff Garrett. Garrett and the Kid had appeared too many times in New York newspapers to risk it.

"Mama, I have given up acting and, uh, sold the theatrical rights to my name to an actress who looks just like me."

"Was it a wise thing to do?"

"I thought it was, else I wouldn't have done it."

Her mother "Harrumphed", something she did often and well.

"My name is Risa Wilkerson. It's close enough to Rita Wilkes to be comfortable. It's how you should always address me now. Billy and I are happy. If we tie the knot and it becomes Risa Roberts, I will let you know."

"Well. You cannot live in sin."

"You mean marrying three men without divorcing any of them is not sinful? Mama, you should look in the mirror before saying such things to me."

Receiving no response, Risa ploughed on.

"Where might I find Mae? Is she working here today?" Risa asked.

"I expect she is. Not having her has put an awful lot of strain on me, what with keeping this place straight, keeping Horace properly groomed like a gentleman and all."

Risa looked at the dust on the furniture and at Horace's prodigious Adam's apple bobbing up and down his yellowed celluloid collar.

"Yes, I imagine it pushes you to the extremes of your energy." Mae would be dismayed seeing this dump.

"Well, it's been nice," Risa lied. "Here is a note with my new name and my address. My identity switch has a lot to do with security. The man you sent to rescue me, thought it prudent. Thanks for contacting the panic folks, by the way. It was literally a lifesaver."

"I have, of course, always been there for you," her mother stated, actually believing herself.

"C'mon, Billy. We need to get going. People to see and things to do."

Risa walked over to Billy and took his arm in mid-conversation. She nodded at her step-father *du jour* and pushed Billy towards the door.

"Bye." Risa called over her shoulder as she and the Kid headed for the stairs.

They checked every floor and found Mae sweeping on the third floor. Diligent and face down.

"Mama Mae." Risa called. The room virtually lit up as the woman looked up and gave a radiant smile. It was followed as quickly by tears of joy as she dropped the broom and ran to the little girl she raised from birth.

They embraced and both cried. After a while, Billy cleared his throat loudly and got their attention.

"Miss Mae, I'm Billy Roberts. It's nice to meet ya."

"Honey, is this fine looking young man yours?" Mae asked.

Risa glowed and said, "He sure is."

Billy found himself in a bear hug.

"Mae, how are you? We've just left Mama and it looks like she has hooked another dead fish."

"Honey, I knew it the second I looked at the loser. I don't know what's in your mother's mind. And, letting me go after looking after her and her children for a total of thirty years."

"Miss Mae. Risa and I have a deal to offer you," Billy said.

"Now, if you are going to be her man, you need to learn her name right."

"Mae, I have ceased to be Rita Wilkes. I am now Risa Wilkerson. So, Billy has it right," Risa said.

"Mae, Risa and I want you to come to Texas with us. I will have a cottage built on the ranch near our house. It will be yours for the rest of your life."

"Mr. Billy, I won't have a job. How can I pay rent?"

"I'm just plain Billy. And, family doesn't pay rent. You have been more of a mother to my Risa than the woman we just saw. All she seems to care about is herself. When you spotted my girl, I saw pure love.

You are her family and now you're mine, too."

"Lemme think about it. Okay, I just did. I will come."

"When do you get off here? And, how much notice do you have to give the hotel?" Risa asked.

"I get off at five. They can fire me without any notice, so I figure I can fire them without any too."

Billy wanted them to all go to dinner together an hour later. He was unaware of the White Only signs in restaurants, even in the north.

"That's the stupidest thing I ever heard," he said indignantly. They settled on a so-called Colored restaurant. The Kid had never had soul food, but became an aficionado.

"Can you teach Risa how to cook this?" he asked Mae.

"You bet," Risa answered first. "She taught me damn near everything else I know."

"But, young lady, I didn't teach you how to cuss, so you better unlearn those words."

A day later they were doing the reciprocal of their trip up to Connecticut. Several days later, the buckboard turned into the Robert's ranch. Mae stayed in the guest room until her cottage was finished. Billy never ate better, with both women cooking, or felt more love. But, he still practiced with his four and three quarter inch barrel Colt every day. He might farm like a Billy Roberts, but he drew and shot like a Billy the Kid.

******

Rita Booth, nee Sally Hemsworth, began writing to Kane immediately. Her first letters referred to him as "dearest godfather," and graduated to "darling godfather."

He received the first three in New York, having missed his departure by several hours. He took rooms at the Fifth Avenue Hotel to kill two weeks until his ship returned and he could use his fare.

Kane thought about defraying the living expenses for two weeks by tearing up his steamship fare and buying fare on a different ship. He decided to stick with his original and enjoy a play or two and unwind after the excitement in Mexico and Texas.

He wrote the two Rita's and told them of his plight. The original Rita told him her new name was Risa Wilkerson and she could be reached as such care of the Roberts Ranch, Hico, Texas. Kane smiled at the address. He hoped the two had a long, happy life together.

The next letters would have been of concern to one embarking on a trip to regain his lost love. Except, the Sally version of Rita was a wonderful letter writer. She was bright and an outrageous flirt. Kane had noticed that from the very first moment.

By the end of the second week, his name had become "Darling Michael." He wondered how in hell she learned his first name. Then, he remembered.

She had asked for a carte de visite. He said he did not have one of the original large photo format, but gave her one with his name, business address and a small photo.

She immediately kissed it and tucked it in her décolleté. Her friend rolled her eyes at her fellow actress and the blushing gunfighter.

The new Rita presented him with one of her own, except hers had the accent on the photo and the written information took second place. In response, he kissed her carte de visite and tucked it in his shirt under the knot of his tie.

The actress formerly known as Rita Wilkes broke out in uncontrolled laughter and was soon joined by her friend, who pulled the three together for a combined hug.

As Kane packed to move out of the hotel and on-board his ship, he tucked her card in his vest pocket, across his chest from his gold watch.

He rang for a bellman. They left room 462 and headed for the lobby. A hansom cab was flagged and Kane gave the driver the pier number at the port. Within an hour, he was checking into his stateroom. The long delayed endeavor had begun.

CHAPTER 11

MARIA ELENA
1883

The Atlantic, England,
Spain and the US

Kane had wondered how he would feel sailing on a steel hull ship instead of a wooden one. He found from onboard he could not tell the difference. His stateroom was comfortable and he had the requisite formal wear for dinners. He knew the food was going to be world class and planned to walk around the decks daily, regardless of weather.

Within a day or two at sea, he regretted not bringing the Rita's. Billy could have waited a month or two longer. Their wittiness would have added to this or any trip.

Then, he admitted it to himself. He had been devoid of the company of a beautiful woman for twenty years. And, he missed it. He had cut a swath through

Europe as a twenty year old. Until he met Maria Elena. Then, it had come to a screeching halt.

No other woman existed on his green earth but her. Yet, now he wondered. Would the chemistry be there? The feelings? It has been two decades. Lots of water had flowed over the proverbial dam.

By the third day, he sent a cable to Richmond.

"Regret not bringing darling goddaughters. Would have added mightily to voyage. More soon via SS Buenos Ayrean."

Rita in Richmond received the cable the following day with glee. She picked up on the adjective immediately. She did not want the tall man in black to be unhappy. But, she wanted him to return alone. She could make him happier than anyone. She knew it.

Kane had walked ten revolutions around the outer deck walkways. The days were gray and windy, with a cool mist blowing. The smell was of saltwater. They were mid-Atlantic now.

He returned to his stateroom and stripped off the heavy oiled wool sweater and lighter wool trousers. Kane laid across the bed for an hour. He arose and put on a supplied robe and walked down the interior corridor to the men's shower. He cleaned up and shaved. He wondered if he should go back to wearing a mustache, then decided against it.

Returning to his room, he donned a tuxedo and starched shirt. Once dressed, he clipped the inside the waist holster with the Webley on and pulled his coat on. He re-draped the coat over the small revolver and walked to the main dining room. He sat at table 14. Kane selected the seafood entre, but with the inappropriate red wine. He did not like white wine. To hell with somebody else's ideas about what went with what.

The food was good, the conversation rather boring. He deflected lots of questions about where he was from and what he did. Finally, disgusted, he smiled and admitted being from Charlottesville, Virginia and was an undertaker. The occupation caused additional chat to be directed at either the banker and his wife or the department store owner from upstate New York.

With a pleasant look on his face, Kane completely tuned out the rest of the conversation and enjoyed his sea bass *en Papillote* with an uncouth but delicious cabernet.

He walked down dinner and sat in a deck chair and smoked a Cuban cigar. Life was not bad. Not bad at all.

He had a cable envelope under his door. It was from Maria Elena.

Translated to English, it said: "Dear Miguel. I look forward to seeing you. Send a location to meet a bit away from Barcelona. I will go ahead and tell you now. I cannot return with you. The laws and customs here are too archaic. I plan to ask him for a divorce without mentioning you, my lover of two decades. It is easier on his massive sense of *machismo*.

I look forward to our few hours together. Perhaps I will be surprised at his answer and they will be years, not hours. Love, Maria Elena."

The words could not have been more disheartening for Kane. Maria Elena had spoken about her husband frankly for years. He was a stubborn, pompous ass, his minor nobility gone to his head.

Viscount Vasquez would no more grant his beautiful wife a divorce than he would give up his several mistresses or his thousands of acres on the Besos River plains.

"River of kisses." Kane balled his fist. "I'll give him a kiss. With this on his bulbous nose. He will have to breathe out of his damn ear."

He walked the decks more and did exercises in his room to work off anger. His lunches were large so he could skip the formal dinners.

The ship landed in London in the morning and he took a boat to Paris. There, he took a train to Barcelona. He took a hired buggy to the village of Sitges, a beachfront town twenty-two miles from the city. He knew the Vasquez estate was about five miles away. Coming to Sitges would be simple for a horsewoman like Maria Elena.

The room was very simple. A table with a pitcher and bowl a three-candle appliance on the wall near the door, a chair, wardrobe, and a bed.

The view of the Mediterranean out the window was, however, superb. Kane opened the window and the curtains and let the warm ocean breeze in.

He wrote and posted a brief note with his location. She knew his handwriting sufficiently well it was no need to sign it.

She would receive the note the next day.

He laid across the bed and read a cable from Rita. It came just before the ship sighted the English coast. By its length, he feared it cost her a week's salary from her play. But, then, he had given her five thousand dollars in gold coins.

She said she, in her new persona, had accepted a month run of a play off-Broadway in New York. So, alone or with Maria Elena, she would be there when he got back. She hoped he or they would come to see the great Rita Wilkes perform. Kane could tell she was not as flirty as in each previous communications. He reckoned what she thought she knew about the Maria Elena coming to America with him was dampening her enthusiasm.

"Well, my lovely actress. What I do know about Maria Elena coming to America is dampening my enthusiasm also," he mumbled aloud in his room.

He walked down to the beach in his shirt and trousers. Leaving his shoes, he started away from the center of the village and began a slow trot in the sand.

He had not run for a while and it felt good. He must have gone a mile before he turned back and returned at the same pace.

Kane determined to do this daily or even twice daily while in Sitges. He had run in formation during his military school training in Europe, especially here in Spain.

The running and the fresh Mediterranean air encouraged thought. He tried to make it productive thought.

Should I stay with the Circle? The chairman has probably already chosen his son-in-law to replace me. Besides, I have had enough of being a financial administrator and running a secret order. I will sign whatever non-disclosure agreement necessary and pack my desk. Other than a gold fountain pen and a Webley Bulldog in a hidden drawer, and some framed diplomas and certificates from around the world, the packing will be quick.

What will I do? Depends on Maria Elena, but I pretty much know the answer about her. I have the land outside of Charlottesville papa left me a couple years ago. Jefferson designed a wing of the house. It is not gargantuan, but has four bedrooms and appropriate outbuildings. It's brick and the couple of yankee cannon ball holes have been repaired. A manager is farming it and it turns a net profit, even just after the end of Reconstruction in Virginia. I have lived in Texas and saved my good salary and invested it. I could live comfortably just on it. Travel? Maybe. My friend JA left the

McLaughlin farm in Caroline County, Virginia and went to Hawaii. He's still there living among native girls on the beach and eating pineapples.

My biggest problem is what fun to have and with whom to share it.

So, Michael Kane. Kick yourself in the ass and quit worrying. Things will work out well. They generally do.

******

Former Lieutenant of Rurales Miguel Vasquez never got along with his father. At least the man he had known to be his father until a bit over a month ago.

Then, Michael Kane, the man in black, showed up. It is said we do not recognize as much as others when someone looks just like us. But, Miguel did. He felt like he was looking into a mirror. Kane was several inches taller, but given a few more years and they would be eye-to-eye. Perhaps it was the eyes which were the real giveaway.

His mother, a pure Castilian, had blue eyes also. It was probably why her husband had not questioned a blue-eyed little son. Perhaps he should have.

There was an almost instant energy between him and Kane. Kane was his father. He had taken Kane's advice and left the ill-run Rurales. They would excel years later. A Russian colonel would take over the Rurales and change them.

Miguel had come home to consult with and protect, his mother.

And, to speak with her as never before. Kane as much as told him she had answers. "Show her the Colt. The initials." He would, perhaps today if his father was away. The elder Vasquez being away was a pretty sound probability. Between his investments and his mistresses, he was always away. He was a very active man for his early sixties.

He did not hesitate leaving his beautiful forty year-old wife to run a large estate and look after Miguel's wild sister. The sister was more the father than the mother.

She was slender, not stocky like the father. Gabriela had his curly hair and dark eyes. Miguel always looked after her. She required a lot of looking after. She was beautiful and provocative. Miguel had beaten more than one teen aged boy who had responded to his sister's entreaties. He was always surprised she did not become pregnant. After a while, he began to wonder if she could not. It was not for lack of trying.

Despite the stern brotherly admonitions, they were close and loved each other dearly. He would never desert her. Miguel felt badly about his six months in Mexico. It benefited the career he planned. His father seemed to go on forever with no indication of turning the running of the lands over to his son and rightful heir under Spanish law.

Miguel had the man who picked him up at the train station drop him at one of their remote stables. They were spread out enough to require stables and *vaqueros*, or cowboys, near herds and not just by the main *hacienda*. He wanted to ride in on his favorite horse. It was an Andalusian mare so dark gray it appeared black. Kane's black, Hadrian, reminded him of Azteca in muscularity. Azteca was a smaller female, though probably with every bit as much heart.

He saddled Azteca. She was a little fat. The men had not exercised her enough. He would make sure she got plenty over the next few weeks. He was not sure exactly what he was going to do once the visit part was over. He might go to Madrid or Barcelona and sell his police service. He knew he would get nothing but scoffing from his father. "It's not what a titled man should do." The Rurales were associated with the Mexican army, so they passed muster. Serving in the military was good experience for being a titled Spaniard. If he only knew the lack of caliber of the men Miguel led and their uniforms and poor armaments, Vasquez would not boast about his officer son.

Miguel transferred his clothes and gear to saddlebags and saddled up. He rode the four miles to the main house quickly, Azteca virtually dancing with happiness over having him aboard and being able to trot and even a brief gallop.

As he slid off the horse and tied her to one of the

single posts out front, his mother came out and ran to his arms.

"I recognize Azteca's gait anywhere." she said as she hugged him.

"It is so good to see you, my son. You are taller and even more handsome."

"And, you are far too young and beautiful to be an officer's mother." he said.

"Come in and get something cool to drink. Your sister is gone off somewhere, your father is also. It's just me and the staff."

"That is perfect. Let's get our drinks, mother and find a place to chat. I want to share some experiences and show you something I believe will interest you. All without being overheard," Miguel said. His mother looked at him, trying to fathom what they were going to talk about. She knew he had met someone who struck him deeply. She thought she knew who it was. If so, fate was intervening.

Maria Elena issued orders and they adjourned to a terrace with an umbrellaed table.

They sat and exchanged time-filling pleasantries until a maid brought out a pitcher of lemonade and some glasses. Once she had left, Miquel spoke.

"Mother, I would like to show you a gift. It is a revolver a tall man in black gave me. He saved my life several times. It was like having a guardian angel." She nodded and he withdrew the Colt and unloaded all five rounds.

He handed it to her butt-first. She immediately saw MK engraved on the bottom of the butt. Her eyes dilated and a tear ran down one.

"His name was Michael," Miguel said.

"Kane," his mother answered.

"Yes. Mother, we looked like twins except he is at least twenty years older."

"I suspect my son, you know why God put him there to save you?" she asked.

"Because he is not only a guardian angel, he is also my father." He replied. It was a statement, not a question.

"Yes. You, I and no one else on this earth knows he is your father."

"You are wrong mother," he said, causing her to look up with alarm.

"He knows. He knew instantly."

"Miguel, it is said the very luckiest of people have one great love in their lives. Michael Kane was mine. Perhaps is mine. Please tell me everything you can about him."

"He led a rescue mission of the most deadly group of men I ever saw. Warriors all.

I rode up on them with a patrol of my riff-raff troops. I began to question the leader, who was Kane. He just goes by his last name. He speaks as perfect Spanish as you or I. When I asked how they were going to pay for something, he said gold. Apparently, my stupid men decided to go criminal and one lifted his rifle at me and told me to raise my hands.

I was watching Kane, who may have been six meters away. I heard the Rurale behind me begin to cock the hammer of his rifle.

Kane drew and fired so fast I could not see his hand. The man was dead on his horse. Kane's other men drew and killed almost the whole patrol, before he called for them to cease fire. Mother, it was unbelievable." Miguel said.

"And, Miguel, you said he stepped in another time?"

"Yes, mother. Apache Indians, fierce fighters, were attacking a village Kane was defending.

One shot me in the shoulder. I fell off my horse. One of Kane's men fired and killed my aggressor. As I was laying there, another Apache jumped off his pony and approached me with his knife.

Kane met him and left his gun in its holster. He drew a large American knife called a Bowie knife. He and the Apache circled, virtually around me. The Apache made his move and Kane stood his ground. Then, he made a fencing move with the big knife. It was a move I and I suspect he, learned at *Academia General Militar*. His lunge was so deadly, no parry was required. The man died where he stood. Kane knew and did not even bother to check him. Mother, he is the deadliest man I ever saw. He then ripped the bandana off his throat, folded it into a pad and pressed it against my shoulder wound. He told me, in perfect Castilian, to hold the pad against my shoulder because he still had work to do. When his work—killing—was over, he picked me up like a little child and carried me into the church for aid."

"Oh, my dear Miguel, he told me so many times in letters how much he wanted to hold you, to teach you, to know you. He never married. He never had other children. Imagine the feeling he must have had when he first saw you."

"I was busy being officious at the time, regrettably."

"You said 'rescue mission'. Will you elaborate?" she asked.

"A famous and beautiful actress was kidnapped by an American cattle thief who had a ranch in Mexico. I have since found she was the daughter of John Wilkes Booth, the man who assassinated President Abraham Lincoln. They rode in and saved her. She ended up stabbing her kidnapper and shooting Apaches with them. She is quite a lady."

"So, a hero's mission."

"Yes, surely a hero's mission."

"You said she stabbed her kidnapper. Good for her."

"Aha. But she only wounded him long enough to get away. Later, I heard he aimed a shotgun at Kane. It was Kane who killed him."

"Was Michael wounded in all of these battles?" she

asked.

"Yes, once. In the last Apache attack, he was hit in the head and knocked unconscious. Before several Indians could reach him, the girl and a young gunman intercepted them. The girl—the actress—ended up killing all three. The last one was with a knife."

"We ladies love our daggers," his mother said, shocking him.

"So, Mother. What happens now?"

"Kane is coming here. Anytime. He may be nearby now. I can almost feel his presence. He wants me to leave with him. You know Spanish laws about women. About divorces. Your father has thought you are his son for the last twenty years. Our marriage has been loveless. The only good thing to come out of it is your half-sister. Can you imagine her if Kane was her father, too?" Miguel nodded, sadly.

"Something of relief to me has come out of this," he said.

His mother looked up with interest.

"I do not feel half as bad now about always hating my father. He is a pig and is not my father."

"Do not speak so loudly or so quickly. There are two good reasons to call him your father. One is the title you will inherit. The other is this rancho. It is worth millions of *pesetas*. He will not live forever. He is in his sixties and eats, drinks and whores to extremes." Miguel was surprised to hear this from his mother's lips, but knew it was true.

"If I were to leave and he learned a description of Michael, for whom I named you, he would go crazy. He would kill me and probably try to kill you. At the least he would disown you. Being rich is better than being poor."

"But, you said you were going to ask him for a divorce."

"I know I said it, Miguel. But, our talk has made me think more clearly. It would be foolish and cause a blow-up which would rip this family open. Only your sister, Gabriela, might be unscathed. And, there is no guarantee of her getting off either. Vasquez is crazy when he is mad. He beat me regularly when you were little. Finally, I told him if he ever did it again, I would wait until he is asleep and slice his manhood off. He believed me."

"Were you kidding him?" Miguel asked.

"I was in dead earnest, Miguel." She reached under her full skirt and withdrew a small dagger. She stabbed it into the wooden table top and left it vibrating as he looked at it. Finally, he spoke as he removed the dagger and proffered it hilt first to his mother.

"We ladies love their daggers," he quoted. His mother smiled and said nothing.

"I doubt when you turn him down, Kane will stay in the area long," Miguel spoke, thinking aloud.

"Yes, I fear you are right."

"Does he know you will turn him down?" he asked.

"Yes, he knows I will not leave with him. I told him I would ask for a divorce, but he is a smart and lettered man. He knows Vasquez would never grant it. He knows, too, it is almost five hundred kilometers to a direct route to London to get back to America with me or without me. That is a long way with the whole Spanish army and police chasing you."

"Once he visits, would you tell him I would like to spend a bit more time with him and get to know him?"

"Why not see him first? I would rather you know a whole father than a broken-hearted one."

"Do you know where he will stay?"

"Not for sure. But, I would say Sitges is a strong probability," she offered.

"Do you mind if I ride over there today?"

"No, I would like for you to find him and get to know him. More importantly, you should make plans to visit him in America. Let him show you the American part of your heritage. From everything he has told me, I believe you would find it fascinating," Maria Elena told her son.

"And, tell him I will be free to visit him on the trail southwest of Sitges tomorrow at noon," she added. Miguel acknowledged.

"May I take my leave before my so-called father gets home?" She nodded and he stood, gave a crisp bow, and left.

*****

There were not many small hotels in Sitges. Miquel located the correct one very quickly. He went upstairs to the room, one of six.

Miguel tapped on the door. He waited to hear the four clicks of a colt cocking, but did not. Had his father become careless?

"Enter," came the deep resonant voice. He recognized it immediately.

Miguel pushed the door open.

Kane was sitting in a chair. He had a pleasant look on his face.

"I've been waiting for you, Miguel," he said.

"I thought perhaps so, father. May I call you 'father?'" he asked.

"I would like nothing better, son. Nothing at all. I am afraid there is not much seating. Please sit on the bed."

Miguel noticed the bed was made up with military attention. He sat down, not knowing where to start.

"Mother said to tell you she could meet you on the trail southwest of here tomorrow at noon," seemed a good option, so he went with it.

"Thank you. I fear the news will not be good."

"Her life is complicated by a pig of a husband and a wild daughter who drives us both crazy trying to keep her out of trouble. She also runs the estate in father's frequent absence."

"So I have gathered from the letters we have exchanged over the years," Kane agreed.

"Have you written often?"

"I believe the count is up to two hundred fifty two," Kane replied.

"So, roughly monthly. I am amazed my pseudo father has not intercepted one."

"I am, also, Miguel. I gather the two of you are not close?" Kane asked.

"We have never been close. I knew you were my father from the moment you killed the peasant Rurale who was going to kill me. But, even as a small boy, I hated the man who was supposed to be my father. How, I asked myself, could my elegant and learned mother marry such an uncouth pig?"

"It all goes back to Spain's predilection for arranged marriages and *machismo*. And, the latter is the worst. There are arranged marriages everywhere in the world. The mania over male supremacy seems worst in Spanish countries. At least in my travels it has," Kane said.

"Father, Mother says I should visit you in America and learn about your part of my heritage. May I do that?"

"Of course. I do not have a thousand hectare estate to leave you, but I have a beautiful one. Your late grandfather inherited it from his father and grandfather, and so on back to the 1700's," Kane said.

"It is over the border in Texas?"

"No, it is in the area of Virginia where the rolling hills turn into blue mountains," Kane said.

"Why don't you live there?"

"I will soon. My job, predetermined by my father, kept me in Dallas. I like Texas. It was also a place less affected by our war between the northern and southern states of about twenty plus years ago." Miguel was interested in war, having graduated from Spain's military academy. He decided, however, to not press the line of conversation and learn more about his father.

"What is it you do, sir?"

"I run a financial institution called GC Financial and various other names. Our mission has changed over the years. Now, much of it is charitable work. I resigned to come here, convinced I could bring your mother back to America and be happy for the next thirty or forty years. I see now, it probably will not happen."

"You seem to be very deadly with a revolver or knife. Where did you learn?"

"The revolver from my father and some of the best instructors in England and Spain. The knife from fencing classes at your very own alma mater. Hand-to-hand combat in France and Germany."

"Even wounded, I recognized your classic lunge from my own training. The Apache never had a chance."

"I saw from your eyes you did. And, it was another clue adding to your immediate suspicions about my real identity," Kane said.

"What should I do, father?" Miguel asked.

"My answer pains me, son. You should stay here and learn everything possible about running the estate. My economics training was in London. I highly recommend you consider a few economics, finance and business courses there. Your mother's husband will not live his lifestyle forever. You will want to be prepared to be the next viscount. And, to do it well, unlike him. I detest titles and royalty to my very fiber. They are why America separated from England a hundred years ago. But, your legacy here is large. If you are able to dispose of it at a good price and bring your mother and sister and all of us live together, wonderful. I just do not see it happening."

"Sadly, nor do I," Miguel lamented.

"I dreamed of teaching my little boy to shoot and fish and ride. You surely can shoot and ride, the fishing I don't know about."

"I can fish, too, Father."

"Good, I only wish I had taught you."

"Me, too. Luckily hired help and academy instructors did. Vasquez only gave me a prominent name. But, one he has added no luster to over the years."

"I have known some people who rose above their birthright and became highly respected in their chosen endeavors," Kane said, thinking of Billy the Kid.

"Father, I have an odd question," Miguel began. Kane's expression told him to proceed.

"When I tapped on the door, I expected to hear four clicks as you cocked the Colt identical to the one you gave me."

"A Webley is self-cocking," Kane said, brushing away the Stetson covering one on the floor beside his chair. It was in easy and fast reach of his hand. He picked it up and unloaded the .455 cartridges before handing it to Miguel.

"It is ugly, but feels just right in my hand," Miguel said.

"And, therein lies its beauty. It is also highly accurate. Especially for a small, short-barreled revolver."

"I should buy one of those," Miguel said.

"Get two, you may want to give one to a son one day," Kane said smiling as he noticed his Colt under Miguel's covering jacket.

"I need to get back to the estate. Can we meet again before you leave for America. There are so many questions, I have not begun to think of them all yet."

"I have at least as many unplanned, Miguel. I hope we can meet. Either way, take my card and contact me soon. Letters and a visit. A long visit, son. Please," Kane said.

Two men who looked so much alike stood and embraced. For the first time in twenty years, Kane had a tear in his eye. The other time had been very nearby when he bade goodbye to Maria Elena.

Miguel Kane walked out of the door. He did not look back. His father stood watching, imbued with great pride and, greater regret.

******

The real Rita Wilke's mail was now forwarded to Richmond. Where the new Rita would get it. She received an offer to play a role in A Midsummer Night's Dream off Broadway in New York. The new Rita absolutely could not turn it down. It also put her in the city when Kane returned with or without the Spanish woman. Rita's intuition told her it would be without.

She packed, took some cash and placed the corpus of her gold from Kane in the State Planter's Bank of Commerce and Trusts.

Rita boarded a train and headed north.

She reported to her theater, bag in hand. The director and the theater own both welcomed her warmly. She was told a room awaited her in a nearby hotel and a meal arrangement was included. Her stipend for the first month run was easily four times the small theater's in Richmond. She asked for and received a list of the full cast.

One person seemed familiar. Once she had

checked in to her hotel to begin studying the script, she pulled out the list of players with whom her real predecessor had worked.

She found the woman, who had a mid-level role. The woman's part was Hermia, one who would be in different scenes, at least as Rita remembered the play. She was to play Titania, queen of the faeries. Rita smiled at the filmy costume in which Michael would first see her act. She was set for the costume fittings two days hence.

Rita went to the restaurant in the hotel and ordered a light dinner and returned to her room to begin memorizing the play.

This was her first break into big time. Broadway. Or, almost Broadway. A month run with possibility of extension. And, she had a featured role. Thank you, original Rita and, than you darling Michael. She finished moving in, placing her English revolver from Michael in a drawer between folded blouses.

Rita turned up the gas lights to their brightest, put on a dressing gown and settled on the sofa in her room with the script. She began reading with relish.

The next several days were a blur. The costume fittings were simple with her trim frame. Titania's gown was deliciously filmy and sexy. She was quite sure Michael would love it. It would be far enough from the audience they could not see how illegal it would be close up.

She was on her way to make the person she was pretending to be more famous than ever. And, to somehow win the heart of the tall man in black. Rita had every confidence she would pull of both objectives with ease.

******

The next day, Kane put on country riding tweeds instead of his usual trail black. He shaved more carefully than usual and brushed his dark hair well before donning a tweed cap in lieu of his Stetson. He slipped the Webley into its waistband holster and the Colt into his right saddlebag. Checking his watch, he saw the time was eleven forty-five. He retrieved the black horse from the livery and rode southwest out of town at a walk, scanning all around.

He saw a beautiful white horse in the distance. He could tell the rider was his Maria Elena and his heart beat picked up.

He lightly tapped spur less heals into his horse's sides and picked up to a canter.

As he approached, Maria Elena waved and she saw a flash of white when he smiled.

He rode up to her and scanned the area for observers. There were none. He had expected Miguel to ride security for his mother. If he was out there, he was good. Damn good.

"Darling Maria Elena," he spoke softly, his voice deep but full of emotion.

"My Michael. It has been too long." Her voice had not changed a whit over the decades. Still sweet and musical.

"Where can we go and sit?" he asked. She turned her horse towards a nearby hill with trees atop.

"Come."

He rode beside her, questioning his emotions. Had they lessened because he now knew he had lost her?

"I met with our handsome son again yesterday. You have done a wonderful job turning him into a man. I salute you and only wish I could have helped."

"You and I both know it would have been guaranteed defeat for two twenty-year old's to go up against the Vasquez family. We would not have had a chance of winning.

We had to play the hands, we were dealt. But, we did not give up. We stayed in touch. You learned how he was in every step of his growth. And, out of nowhere, you appeared and saved his live. Not once, but twice. Is there not a hint of a miracle in your appearance and your skill?" she asked.

"As you know by now, there is no chance of us finding happiness together in this life. But, take solace. You will have a life with your wonderful son. He adores you. He *is* you. I saw it from the first. The way he walked. How he framed his sentences.

The set in his eyes. It gave me such happiness in an unhappy life. And, it will give you happiness now all your years. I know it will.

There is no need for you to meet my daughter. She is so much her father it would sadden you. She is wild and takes all Miguel and I can do to hold her back. Her father is useless with her as in most things. I just pray daily his horse with throw him and step on his head."

"Maria Elena, I can do something about him. I can kill him and escape. As always, I have worked out an overland escape plan—albeit for us. It would be to ride fast for three hundred miles of mostly open country to Santander, then a ship to Plymouth. A totally different way than I came here."

"No, Michael. I want you to remain safe and not a fugitive. We both owe it to Miguel, who needs time with you in America." She took a small Swiss watch from a jacket pocket.

"I must ride back soon. We must say goodbye again. This time, Michael, is the last time. Vasquez is getting paranoid. I fear for our letters. I fear your son will kill him.

Kiss me goodbye. Again. And, we will part. We will keep in touch now on through our wonderful son. I have burned twenty years of love letters. You should too. We know what we have felt and what each says. They are too risky, especially for me."

She leaned over and kissed him sweetly. But, not

passionately. There was love, but no heat. He returned the kiss and squeezed her hand.

"You are free, Michael. You are rich and handsome. Find some young beauty who will worship you. Marry her. Give Miguel brothers and sisters he can help you raise. Let me fade away in your heart and your mind. One great love. Always there. Never uppermost. Let me just be a permanent sweet memory." She said this with perfectly dry eyes. It was clear to Kane she had rehearsed her lines many times over. Her words were not delivered with love. Just sad resignation. This was not the way it was supposed to be.

"Your words about us, Maria Elena. I cannot fault them. Fate has put us in this untenable strait. Let our love reside in our son, not each other. You know I love you. I know you love me. That is more than most people ever have. It will simply have to be enough for us."

He stood and helped her up from the hill where they were sitting and talking. Kane move her horse to the downhill side so she could more easily mount.

She leaned down and kissed him one last time and rode off. Her canter became a gallop. A great Spanish horsewoman on a beautiful Andalusian. Poetry in motion. He watched as she disappeared from view. Dry eyed. Sad. But, strangely relieved. He could not fathom why and decided to put figuring it out until later or, never.

Kane mounted and rode back to his hotel in Sitges. His work was done here. He would see his son again. He was sure of it. He would leave tomorrow and return to America. And, to what? To a new life he had not yet defined.

******

Maria Elena arrived back at the estate well after her husband. She heard him raging. Drunk again. He was calling for her. She went up the stairs to their bedroom.

He had a letter in his hand. It was one she had just received from Michael and had not burned yet.

Viscount Vasquez was screaming and blowing saliva from his mouth as he yelled.

"You are deceitful. A whore. The wife of a viscount and you act like this."

"You should talk, pig. You have at least three slut mistresses I know about. You have had them and little bastards with them for years. How dare you call me names over a friend I have not seen in twenty years."

He strode over to her, though unsteadily due to his state of inebriation. He swung a strong backhand blow. His hand caught Maria Elena across the jaw and knocked her over on the bed. He staggered over and grabbed the front of her white blouse with both hands and lifted her to her feet.

The viscount moved his hands from the front of her blouse to either side of her throat and began to squeeze with all his strength.

"The bastard is going to kill me and get by with it in court," she thought as she began to lose consciousness.

With one last effort, she drew the dagger from her leg holster and followed up on the threat she had made to him.

She rammed it into his groin with one last burst of superhuman strength and twisted down. She did not hear his scream as she fell dead on the bedroom floor.

The viscount was in excruciating pain. He could feel blood rushing down both pant legs. He knew he had been castrated by the sharp dagger still stuck in the front of his *pantalones*. He staggered away, strangely sobered by the pain. The dagger moved in him with each step.

He knew he needed medical help. There was no way he could ride a horse this way. He screamed for a buggy and leaned against the wall, dizzy, while a horse was harnessed.

The viscount collapsed into the buggy and slapped the reins against the horse's back. The horse took off and Vasquez steered the buggy towards town and a doctor.

Miguel was riding along the road from town and saw the buggy coming. His father did not seem to see him as he drove the buggy by at speed.

Miguel could see blood all over the front of his trousers. His mother. The threat.

He spurred his horse and galloped to the house, jumped off and ran in.

The senior house maid stopped him at the base of the stair.

"You do not want to go up there, sir. It is your mother. She has been murdered by your father."

He brushed past her and bounded up the stairs. His beautiful mother lay on the floor. He could see the bruises on her neck. It was obvious she had been strangled to death. There was also sign of a blow against her right cheek. She had also been struck.

Blood was smeared on the floor. The viscount's wound. He looked for her dagger and did not see it.

"Do not touch anything. There is nothing you can do to help her now. Did you hear them fighting?"

The woman nodded.

"Your father was yelling. I could not understand what he was saying. I could hear him hit her. Then, it got more quiet until he screamed. It was ungodly."

As he ushered her outside the door, Miguel spotted a letter on the floor. He turned and picked it up. Miguel pushed it out of sight in his jacket pocket unobserved.

"Not as ungodly as I will make him scream," Miguel thought to himself as he ran out the front door and mounted his horse. He galloped into town and dismounted at the *Guardia Civil* station.

He burst in the front door. The sergeant recognized him as the viscount's son and a reserve officer of the Spanish army,

"Sir." he said as he popped to attention.

"Come with me to the doctor's. My father has murdered the Viscondesa. You must arrest him now."

"Honorable senor Vasquez, I cannot arrest a viscount. A magistrate would be required."

"Then, come with me to the house and interview the staff. View my mother's body, her marks and the crime scene. Write it up for the magistrate or whoever. I want my father arrested for murder."

The sergeant, still not convinced he was doing the right thing, left with Miguel. When they arrived, Miguel walked him through the notes necessary to provide evidence in a murder case. The man left for his office and to have a telegram sent to Barcelona to request assistance.

Miguel mounted Azteca and rode for Sitges again. This time to see his real father.

Kane was packing as Miguel knocked. He knew something was terribly wrong when his son came in, embraced him and began sobbing.

"Son. What is it? Your mother?" Kane asked.

"Yes. The bastard murdered her."

"Talk to me, Miguel. We need to make a plan."

"I had the worthless Guardia sergeant make a crime

scene writeup. I led him through it. The viscount hit her in the face, then strangled her to death. This letter was on the floor."

Kane looked at the bloodstained letter. It was from him.

He walked over to the gas lamp and burned the letter.

"Miguel, how did the blood get on the letter?" he asked.

"She stabbed him in the groin."

"Where is her knife?"

"It was a dagger. She wore it all the time. It must still be sticking in him. I searched and it was not in the room where he killed her or on the hall, steps or outside while he waited for the buggy to be harnessed," Miguel said.

"The current system here in Spain means he will have a trial, be charged and excused. He is a viscount. A powerful one. He will be free. So, I have to act. You cannot.

You absolutely have to act the role of a grieving son and the future viscount. Deny anything bad about your mother. But, support your father. Trust me to exact justice. Trust me, son.

Now, go home and console your sister. Is she there?"

"God knows where she is. But, she does always come back. I will be there for her. She might be too much like her father, but it's her mother she adores. And, me, I believe."

Kane held his son at arms-length, hands on shoulders.

"Go. Be there for her. I have to stay behind scenes and plan. Please keep me apprised of everything judicial, alright?" Miguel nodded and started for the door.

"Remember, son. If you are the next viscount, you can travel wherever you wish. You and your sister can come to America and stay as long as you want. Don't do anything irrational. Play your role. Grieve. Let me exact vengeance. I am good at it."

"Yes, father. I will. I promise." He left. Kane heard him ride away and sat in the room's only chair, face in his hands, thinking. Planning.

*****

The planning sped up. That night, Miguel was in the restaurant downstairs in Kane's hotel waiting for him.

"What's the status of things?" Kane immediately asked his son.

"The undertaker is preparing Mother for a fast burial. My sister, Gabriela, is a wreck. She really loved Mother. And, though she is like him in some ways, is not particularly enamored of her father. She thinks he is loud, abusive and a lout. Now, she also thinks he is a murderer who should hang by his neck until dead."

"I like her more every moment," Kane commented.

"I fear the government will do nothing. He will come up with some story, self-defense or something and get off without even a slap on the hand," Miguel said.

"Perhaps if you and I took the train to Madrid tomorrow. You could try to get an appointment with a member of the General Council of the Judiciary. Plead your case of long term abuse of mother and you. Extreme drunkenness unbecoming a viscount. Mother lived in fear of her life at all times. Mother was an absolute saint. You know what to say."

"I will do it. Will you ride up with me?"

"I will. There are a couple matters I need to address. I may come back earlier, so just hop a train when you get through. We can meet here for dinner. If Gabriela wants to come, that is okay. Only downside is suspicions being aroused when she sees us together."

"I thought about that. Perhaps we should wait until the viscount is done one way or the other, and I will tell her the whole story. But, not before. She is smart, but not the most stable and trustworthy sister in Spain."

"I leave it to your discretion, son," Kane said.

They met at the depot in Barcelona in the morning and took the Madrid line.

The honorable lieutenant Miguel Vasquez charmed his way into a chief judge's chambers and pled the case against his beloved father. He told the judge the father was a danger to his sister and was on a path of self-destruction. His neglect of the Vasquez lands would cause economic hardship locally and loss of many jobs if left as it was.

"Young man, do you want to be named the viscount?" the judge asked.

"Not particularly, your honor. I want to be a soldier. To serve Spain. But, I have a duty to protect my family. If it is giving up my dream to become a soldier and becoming a rancher instead, I will. My father was a good man. Now, he has gone bad. His murder of my sister's and my mother is an unforgivable act for which he should be held accountable. No matter how much it personally grieves me to say it," Miguel said.

"You wouldn't be here in Madrid before me if you thought justice would be done in the Barcelona court, would you?" the judge asked.

"No, sir. I would not. I think my father will claim self-defense, invent something about my mother—who was a saint—and get off with perhaps a slap on his hand. Then, I will be back here petitioning you again because he killed my sister. He must be stopped by the law."

"Would you like to see him hanged?"

"No, sir. I love my father, despite the monster he has become. He needs to be incarcerated to protect society and himself. It would be my fond hope one day, he could walk out and meet me at the gate and we could go home together," Miguel continued his planned series of lies.

"I have seen this thing in the news. Here is what I will do. I will prepare a warrant for murder and have him arrested and tried. Will you accept whatever a fair trial decides his fate to be?"

"I will sir, if he gets a fair trial in an area where he has so many friends in high places."

"Young man, do you question the Spanish court system?" Miguel realized he had gone too far and backed off.

"Of course not, your honor. Whatever the court decides, I will support."

"Consider it done. A warrant will be sworn today and sent to Barcelona for service. A trial will be held and justice will be served, as always is the case."

"Of course it will. And cows will jump over the moon," Miguel thought as he thanked the jurist and took his leave.

******

Kane had been equally busy and equally disingenuous. He went to Spain's finest gun shop. He had discovered it when living in Madrid years before. Kane was pretty sure nobody there would recognize him as a German hunter.

"*Sprichst du Deutsch?*" he asked, inquiring if the clerk spoke German. The man shook his head negatively and Kane broke into his best idea of what German accented Spanish might sound like.

"I am going stag hunting. It is in the mountains. I need a rifle with very flat trajectory and the ability to drop a stag at four hundred meters."

"We have Remington rolling block target rifles in a number of larger calibers. There is also one Ballard in .44-75. It is a very long range cartridge and has flatter trajectory than, say, the .45-70 US Army cartridge. The particular rifle also has Vernier sights, which are very adjustable for distance, wind and any other conditions."

"May I see it?" Kane asked, knowing what it was and it was perfect for what he had in mind.

He hefted the over ten pound rifle and peered through the sights.

"*Ja das ist gut.*" he exclaimed in German before translating to "Yes, that is good." in Spanish.

"How much?" The man told him and he advised he would take it with a box of twenty cartridges.

Kane figured he needed about three shots to set the sights for angle and distance and one for the job, leaving sixteen rounds for fun.

With his new single shot long range rifle wrapped in waxed paper, he walked to the train station and bought a return ticket to Barcelona. Miguel was not on the train.

"Just as well," Kane thought. It would be better to not include the boy on anything he might have to lie about under oath later. Kane had a distrust of Spanish courts. And, any other courts anywhere.

Arriving at Barcelona, he retrieved his horse and rode back to Sitges in time for dinner.

Miguel awaited him in the restaurant.

"How was your day?" he asked the young lieutenant.

"Mixed. I pled my case to a high judge. He issued a warrant for Vasquez for murder. So, he will be at trial. I am convinced he will be let go under the "good old boy *machismo* rules.""

"I suspect you are right. But, at least he will be tried. I take it the trial will be in Barcelona?"

"Yes, at the national court house there," Miguel responded.

"What is on your schedule tomorrow?" Kane asked.

"I am not sure. I guess I need to address things Vasquez did not do and Mother can no longer do relative to running a thousand hectare ranch."

"You need to. It is not your only legacy, but it is a valuable one. Just a hint about the other: do you know who Thomas Jefferson was?" Kane asked.

"One of the early Presidents of the United States and architect of the Declaration of Independence."

"Exactly. And, an architect of more. He also designed a wing of a home in our family for years. It will be yours one day." Miguel perked up upon hearing about the home.

"How many hectares go with it?" he asked.

"We go by acres. A hectare is about two and a half acres. So, it has around two hundred hectares."

"How can you ranch on so little?" Miguel asked.

"It is not a ranch. Crops are grown there and it is perfect for thoroughbred horses. The land is rolling hills to mountains. It is so beautiful it will take your breath away."

"I would like to see it."

"I trust you will see and own it one day."

"You have a plan don't you, father?"

"Not quite. But, I'm working on one. We each have a plan. To remind you, you are the grieving son. Grieving for your mother and because your father went so crazy. You want to be supportive of him to keep your titles and legacy. What you do with them is your call. Keep them and live here with your sister until she marries, sell it and move to America with me. Travel the world. Your choice. But, make sure you get it to finance whatever you decide to do. Your mother would want you to have it. And, remember, whatever happens at the trial, be Vasquez' son."

"There is a hint in there. Why don't you trust me?" Miguel asked.

"There is a hint and I do trust you. I also know better than to tell you something you might be forced to testify about later. Something which could make you an accessory. What I don't tell you is not lack of trust. Rather, it's caring for your welfare. You have to trust me on this." Kane said. "I have lived in a dark world for a long time. A world I don't want you to live in."

"Shouldn't it be my choice, Father?"

"Yes, you are right. It should be your choice. But, not on this. This is stuff which can make or ruin your life. I take chances for a living. Let me teach you how before you jump in with both feet."

"I think what you are saying is fair enough. I will comply."

They spoke quietly, ate and Miguel departed. Kane went back to his room and contemplated.

He had a small bottle of poison brought to Spain for such as contingency. The problem is how to deliver it.

The viscount had been moved to Barcelona to a hospital. The local physician's surgery was not equipped to perform the partial reattachment of the part Maria Elena's razor sharp dagger had almost severed. And, then, there was the large blood loss.

Kane lamented the bastard had not died on his own. Now, he would need help.

Kane hated to imperil the rest of his life for such a worthless human. However, he owed it to Maria Elena. One final act of love. And, to his son.

Kane was the protector. He was the fixer. And, he

would serve in his dual roles here. If it was the last thing he ever did.

The next morning, Kane went back to Barcelona. He went to the hospital on a pretense of nausea and was given some powders to take. The patients were on an upper floor and it was busy. There was no way he could find Vasquez and give him the poison.

While he was at the hospital, Guardia showed up. Kane moved into place and listened as they presented themselves officiously at the front desk.

"We are here to deliver papers to your patient, the *Vizconde* Diego Vasquez," the senior of the four proclaimed.

"He is in a great deal of pain after his surgery. You must wait while his doctor is summoned," the receptionist said in his equally officious voice.

Perhaps five minutes later, a man in a white coat appeared.

"I am *Vizconde* Vasquez's physician. Please tell me what is going on here. My patient is a very important man and is very ill."

"That may be. But, we have a murder warrant to serve and we will serve it now. If you stand in the way, you will be arrested for subverting justice. Do you understand?"

"Come with me," the doctor snapped and began to walk down a corridor.

As all eyes were on the excitement at the reception

desk, Kane picked up one of the vases of flowers decorating the lobby.

He followed the physician and the Guardia as they proceeded to Vasquez' room. Kane contemplated killing all of them and making his escape, but decided the risks were too high.

A man with a large belly pushing up the sheets as he snored was in the next room. Kane went in and silently placed the vase beside him and stood listening.

He heard the policemen deliver the warrant and the guttural yelling as Vasquez protested and threatened their badges, careers and everything else he could summon in his rage.

"What an ass." Kane thought.

The policemen left, but the doctor stayed to calm Vasquez with a sedative. The hall was too busy for Kane to hang around and deliver the poison. He would have to use the Ballard.

Assassination in mind, Kane walked the several blocks to the courthouse. There were several courtrooms. All were on the second floor. He took a tour of the building and noted where defendants sat.

Conveniently they sat across from a front-facing window in each courtroom.

Now, he had to select a sniper's nest level with or above the windows to allow a shot, regardless of which courtroom was used for Vasquez's trial.

He left the tour and went outside, mentally marking the three windows in his mind.

Kane stood and stretched and appeared to be thinking about where to tour next as a tourist.

In reality, he was scanning across the street. There was a building related to the court. Perhaps a clerk's office, he thought. The windows lined up perfectly.

He walked in and asked "Is this where one files trusts?"

The man to whom he addressed the question quickly answered.

"No. This office handles criminal filings. The one for civil matters is behind the courthouse. Go across to the courthouse and circle behind it. The building looks much like this one."

"Thank you," Kane answered in Castilian sounding like a native. "I am an architect by trade. These are such efficiently and elegantly designed buildings. Are the top floors offices? Are they luxurious?" he asked.

"The floor above is a waiting area for attorneys. The courthouse has become so busy it can no longer accommodate them as they await trials. The top floor is merely file storage."

"I see. I am sure one day attorneys will also fill it. They are insidious creatures. Then, you will have to walk down the street to get your files," Kane said flippantly.

"You are so right. I fear the day is almost upon us."

"Thank you for your help. I am Francisco de la

Cruz by the way. I live here, down in the old part, Sarrià-Sant Gervasi," Kane said, using an area where he used to have a friend.

"Ah, it is nice there. You must do well as an architect."

"Not so well as you think. It is my wife who has the money. My soon to be former wife. That is why I am creating the trust I mentioned. To protect what little I have."

"Good luck, my friend. Women can be a painful necessity."

"Ah, but I love them anyway," Kane said, smiling at the man before he walked out the door.

Clearly the design of the courthouse and the clerk's building had coincided. The third floor windows were symmetrical and placed in line with, but a floor above where the defendants sat during trial.

Kane walked across from the door of the clerk's building to the door of the courthouse and memorized the distance. Then, he walked down the sidewalk fifty feet and looked at an imaginary line from the third floor windows of the clerk's building to the court-rooms across. He burned the degrees of the angle into his mind, smiled slightly and walked off looking for a tapas bar for a snack before returning to Sitges.

He met Miguel for dinner and reported the warrant service at the hospital to his son.

"You should obtain a defense attorney. Contact

your Vasquez's attorney and see if he can handle criminal trials or recommend someone. Then, stay in touch with whoever you retain. He will be the best source of information as the probability of a conviction or of the judge finding him innocent for some trumped up reason. He will also keep you apprised of the timing. The latter will be crucial for me to know.

With my dark hair, I can grow a beard quickly and will. It will help blur my appearance in people's memories," Kane said.

Within the next several days, Miguel retained a criminal attorney. The attorney visited Vasquez in the hospital and then checked the court's docket.

He immediately petitioned for and got a postponement.

The trial had been put on the docket far faster than normal because of the title of the defendant. The clerk had assumed, probably correctly, he would be quickly exonerated and the dead wife blamed.

The trial was set for two weeks hence, by which time the ill-tempered viscount and his sore groin should be ready. The *abrogado defensor*, or defense attorney, hired at the suggestion of the family lawyer was confident in a quick acquittal.

Miguel told Kane how painful it was to hear the attorney build a case against his innocent mother. Kane sympathized but urged him to hold the course. Justice, he told his son repeatedly, would be served.

During the weeks before the trial, Kane grew a beard, carefully sculpting below his cheeks and chin and shaving his neck. With his daily runs on the beach tanning his complexion, he looked every bit the Spaniard. On an almost daily trip to Barcelona, he picked up a long black coat and a throw pillow. He also purchased round glasses with dark lens to protect against the sun.

Several times, he put the disassembled Ballard rifle in a bag and rode miles down the beach to a hill he had found. He took three fresh melons in his saddle-bag. He placed them several feet apart just where the incoming tide stopped. In twenty minutes, the area would be inundated.

Once at the hill, he walked off the distance from the three melons to the hill. He made sure it was the same as the distance between the clerks building front door and the front door of the courthouse.

He then eyeballed the hill and climbed up the height of the third floor storage room windows in the clerk's building and the windows in the courtroom. The angle was perfect for the shot.

He as on the side of the hill. From his perspective, he could tell nobody was in the area.

Cross-legged, he reassembled the Ballard. He loaded a long cartridge in and closed the breech. Cocking the hammer of the single-shot, he took a breath and let it out as he held the gun aimed.

Kane fired and the melon on the right disappeared in a haze of fruit bits. Then, the second and the third. From the measured distance, the sights were set perfectly. The hundred yards was virtually point blank for the .44-75 Ballard caliber. Kane reassembled the rifle and put it in the bag. He sat for a while, watching to insure nobody was present, climbed down and left.

*****

The trial began and its ultimate result was apparent from the beginning. Miguel played his part well and his father bought it lock, stock and barrel. As did all observers. He was the grieving son, but one loyal to his father and loyal to the notion, men were generally right and woman seldom were. In reality, he found the concept repugnant.

At the end of the second day, he met with Kane and told him a verdict was expected when the trial commenced the following day.

Kane told his son he would see him in America and to continue to play the part of the devoted son, no matter what happened. Miguel knew what would happen, just not when or how. He knew Kane would not leave Spain with Vasquez still alive.

They parted with an embrace and a hand shake. No more words were needed.

Kane moved out of his hotel with the story he was

"leaving Sitges for Madrid, then on to Germany." In reality, Kane had just left an alibi and moved to a modest hotel in Barcelona. His plan was to ride and camp between Barcelona and Bilbao. He would buy a horse and leave it at the port at Bilbao before boarding a ship to Portsmouth, England.

Kane did not know whether the Guardia would telegraph to all points and detain people trying to leave Spain. It was a risk he had to take.

The trial was a popular one and, as Kane hoped, left the clerk's building empty as the staff and attorneys all clustered in the courtroom watching the trial. For a titled man to be charged with murder was big news, no matter how foregone the verdict was.

On the day of the verdict, Kane's face was covered by a new black beard. He donned his black outfit and packed as many of his clothes as he could take on the horse he had bought the day before. He left it tied several blocks away from the courthouse.

Kane put on the long black coat with his Ballard hung upside down on his back. With his height, the rifle was hidden. He put the dark glasses on. His identity was virtually hidden. He walked around to the rear door of the clerk's office. It was locked. He took out a small pen knife and picked the lock. He entered quietly and made sure nobody was there. He went to the second floor and found it empty. The file room on the third floor was empty also. He watched the three windows. People were scurrying around behind only one. The trial had to be there, as it was yesterday.

From his darkened room, Kane began to see people filing into the court. He saw Miguel go in. Presently, Miguel stood at the window across the street and one floor below. Miguel stretched his arms and left the window. The empty defendant's chair was in plain sight across the room.

Kane put the throw pillow on a table he pulled over six feet away from the window. He did not want his Ballard rifle barrel sticking out the window. The rifle must be completely inside. He must shoot from the shadows. Anyone looking up at the window after the shot could not see anything.

He went to a window facing the back of the building. He unlocked it and tested it. The window was not tight. It slid up and down smoothly. Kane tied two riatas together with a bowline and wrapped the standing end of the rope to the leg of a table holding files which weighed a great deal more than Kane. He tied a loop he could slip his foot into and coiled the rest. Kane left the coil by the closed window.

He looked back out of the front window. People were milling around in the courtroom. It has not been called to order. Then, he saw Vasquez being brought in. He was limping from his wound, but seemed confident. "We will see," Kane thought.

People stopped moving around and Vasquez sat.

The judge must have walked in and called the court to order.

He could see Vasquez leaning a bit forward, looking nervous.

Kane knew his window of opportunity was brief before all hell broke out in the courtroom.

Kane sat at the table and put the rifle to his shoulder. The throw pillow was his rest. The Ballard was loaded.

He pulled the hammer back. It clicked into the cocked position. He pressed the set trigger. The second trigger required only a touch of several ounces to fire.

Something happened and Vasquez stood. Kane could see him mouth "yes."

At that moment, Kane pressed the set trigger and felt the Ballard buck against his shoulder. As planned, the lead slug went though his Adam's apple and he died standing at his chair.

Kane did not wait to see anything further. He slung the Ballard upside down over his shoulder and put the long coat, dark glasses and long black coat on. Grabbing the riata, he tossed it out the window after stepping into the loop with one foot. He let himself down a few feet at a time, repelling down the side of the building.

On the ground, Kane jerked the rope still in the building and coiled it as he walked away from the scene at a normal pace.

He could hear noise from across the street and knew he must vacate this part of Barcelona before police combed it for an assassin.

Kane walked down the street, a tall bearded man in a long coat and slouch hat. Two blocks down, he shed the coat behind a bush and slid the rifle into a scabbard on his horse. He mounted and began his almost four hundred seventy kilometer trip to the docks at Bilbao.

By night, he still did not see pursuers. He wondered how Miguel was. He knew his son would see the poetic justice in a throat shot. The throat is where Vasquez killed his mother. The forty-four caliber bullet would have severed the spinal cord immediately and left Vasquez a dead man standing.

"Sleep in peace, my Maria Elena," Kane said aloud as he rode. He sobbed for a few miles then stopped. He never cried over her again. His duty was done, she was dead and so was her killer. He had a son to mentor and maybe a daughter. All he had to do now is board the steamer at Bilbao without being arrested and sail to Portsmouth England from there on to New York. He had a play to see. One William Shakespeare wrote two hundred eighty three years ago.

CHAPTER 12

HOME IS THE KILLER, HOME TO THE KILL
1883

England, New York
and Virginia

Kane rode hard and camped light en route to Bilbao. He saw mounted men in uniform once, but had no idea if they were seeking him.

In what he thought had to be the most remote part of his ride, he climbed a hill on foot and buried the Ballard and its cartridges under a pile of rocks. It was a good gun and he hated to give it up. But, it and the bullet it fired were distinctive to the murder of a Spanish man of title. So, it had to go, the empty brass he had fired still in the chamber.

At a small town outside Bilbao, he bought a valise for his clothes and put his horse in a livery. He told the livery man if he was not back in two days, the horse was his.

He hired a buggy driver to take him to the port. Kane dismounted the buggy several blocks before the port and watched it for a while. There were a couple of Guardia around, but Kane thought this was normal.

An hour before departure, Kane walked up the gangplank and introduced himself as Frank Antrim and handed the purser a ticket. He was shown a small room for the short cruise and put his valise in it. He then waited down the deck from his room and surveilled it. He did not return to the room until he had walked the entire boat and made sure there were no uniformed Guardia aboard. Plain clothes ones would be more difficult to spot, but Kane knew how to spot the law and was confident.

He went to the dining room, still dressed in more informal tweeds and ate a small meal. He drank a lot of water after the ride and returned to his room and slept most of the way to Portsmouth.

From Portsmouth, he went to Liverpool.

Kane replenished his formal clothes and bought a decent suitcase. A day later, he boarded a New York bound ship as Samuel Hemsworth.

His first thing once settled in his room was to write a cable to Rita Wilkes, c/o Harkness Hotel, Room 202, New York City. Before requisite stops, it said: En route NYC. Alone. Love you. Look in audience in week or so. Michael.

Kane walked it up to the communications room

and left it to be sent once they were sufficiently off-shore to be in proximity to the undersea cables. He thought about a turn around the decks, but decided he had enough stress and exercise over the last week. He picked up a Cuban cigar and sat on a deck chair in the strong wind. He watched the gray ocean slip by under the wooden hull of the steamer. He wondered how things were in Spain. Was his son a viscount yet? Was it automatic? How did the daughter, Gabriela, take her father's death? Not having ready answers, he fell asleep. When he woke up some time later, he found a steward or someone had put a blanket over his lap. He pulled it up higher and went back to sleep. The movement of the ship through the waves and the wind were just perfectly conducive for sleeping.

******

Miguel was named viscount immediately. It passed down by heritage and took no royal action. He engaged his sister in the management of the estate and various family enterprises. He wished he had some instruction from his mother on how she so effortlessly ran it. Or, so it seemed to him. Gabriela had been devastated with her mother's murder and turned against her father for the act. She was suspicious of his assassination. And, assassination is exactly what it was, she knew.

Since Miguel had adequately played the part of the dutiful, though sad son, and was sitting there when his father took a round in the throat, no suspicions were cast on him.

Nobody saw the assassin. The judiciary and Guardia suspected it was either a hit put out by a business associate Vasquez had treated unethically, or by a cuckolded husband. It was widely known he had sufficient number of both to form a waiting line.

Without any evidence beyond the accuracy and professionalism of the shooter, there was effectively no case. A "wait and see if something turns up attitude" prevailed on the shooting. Since everyone liked the son, the powers in Spain considered the whole thing to be an improvement.

Once Gabriela began to deal with her mother's death, she matured beyond her late teen years. She had taken over the house and adjacent stables and supervised the staffs for both. She oversaw maintenance and shopping and non-business budgeting. She had done these things automatically, even before her father's death.

The siblings became closer. Finally, Miguel had an inevitable talk with he had put off. It had been a fast several days since the shot rang out by the courthouse in Barcelona.

Miguel was unsure of her reaction to him only being a half-brother. If she wanted to press the matter in court, she could end up with his title.

Her becoming the viscondesa did not worry him at all. Her ability to take over the full management did. Thinking the land might be sold sooner than later, he had their mother buried in the churchyard of a large Catholic church in Barcelona. The funeral had been small and private. Titled families did not air their dirty laundry in public.

He had his father buried in a newly-created cemetery at the home. Miguel did not give a damn who owned the abusive murderer's rotting remains in the future.

They were sitting at the large dinner table after it had been cleared.

"I need to tell you something. Something you can, if you choose to use to your own gain and hurt me. I have always been truthful with you and loved you throughout your escapades. I always will. No matter what. Please listen and don't make up your mind about anything. Ask me whatever you want. I will answer it if I can."

"Sounds very serious, Miguel. Should I be worried?"

"No, I don't think so. Here goes. When mother was about your age, she had a lover her family would not approve. He was neither Spanish nor Catholic. He did not have a title, though his family was affluent and prominent. They wanted her to marry someone titled and had worked out the marriage with your father."

"My father? Why not our father?"

"Because he was not my father. Unknown even to her, she was pregnant when she married Vasquez. Because I look like her, he never questioned it. The fact I never got along with him did not bother him either. Because he did not care."

"You said 'not a Spaniard,' what was he?"

"An American. When I was a Rurale officer several months ago, I came upon a group of Americans in Mexico. I questioned them. The spokesman struck me so deeply. He was me in twenty years. It was amazing. When my untrained ruffian troops heard the Americans had gold, they wanted it. They knew I would not condone thievery and turned on me first. As one was ready to shoot me in the back, I saw the man who looked like me draw from horseback and shoot him in the head, killing him. It was amazing. As was the way his men opened up on the Rurales. Except for me. He saved my life. Later, I led a better group of men into an Apache Indian attack on a village. The man was defending the village. I was shot and fell off my horse. One of his men killed my shooter. As an Apache approached me with his knife, the man like me engaged him with a large knife called a Bowie knife. I saw him make a move I learned at Spain's military academy. He had gone there, too. He saved my life a second time.

I truly believe God put him there like a guardian

angel for me. We became close. It was clear who he was to me, but he never said.

Before he parted, he gave me one of his beautiful matched Colt revolvers. It has his initials on the bottom of the grip." Miguel handed her the revolver to examine after unloading it.

"MK," she read aloud, absorbing what she had just heard.

"You did not tell me you had been wounded in combat. Have you healed? Recovered?" He nodded.

"Gabriela, he told me to leave Mexico and go home to Mother. He said she needed me. And, to tell him about her and show her this gun.

I did a few weeks ago. She told me the story. He is my father. So, now you know the truth, you can contest my title in court and become La Visondesa of all of this," he spread his arms around each point of the compass denoting their lands.

"I would never do such a thing to you. You will always be my brother. We had the same mother. She was the one we both loved."

"I did not think you would, but it is your birthright. I would be a gentleman, hug you and ride away without contest if you chose to claim all of this, Gabriela."

"Forget the birthright. You earned it by all you tolerated from my father. The man you thought until recently was your father.

Tell me about your father. What is he like?"

"He looks like me. Exactly, but twenty years from now. He is about forty. He and mother were twenty years old. Vasquez was already forty something when he married mother. Kane is very tall. I may catch him, but he is several inches above me now. He has blue eyes and dark hair. He was trained in England, Germany and Spain in the martial arts and business. He runs a large financial organization in Texas," Miguel said.

"So, he is not a cowboy?" Gabriela asked.

"Not by occupation, but he could be. He looks the part."

"Miguel, did he kill Father?" There it was. The inevitable question. Miguel strained his mind to give a truthful answer.

"It would seem impossible. Someone would have seen him. For him to show up within days of Mother being murdered would seem geographically impossible. For a distinctive looking American to do it and get away…I just don't know how he could have. Besides, he saw me the day before and left for America. He was gone when it happened."

"Would he have the talent to do it? You said he was fast with a gun."

"I saw him shoot that revolver in front of you. That is a lot different from being a sniper who can surgically kill someone from hundreds of meters away."

"Did he perhaps learn in the army?" she asked.

"Good question, Gabriela. Except he was not in the army. Ever."

"Did Father kill Mother because of him?"

"They had one of their violent arguments we knew so well, Gabriela. There is no evidence regarding Kane was mentioned. Mother had kept him a secret for twenty years. And, she had not seen him for twenty years. The facts, the clues, are not there," he spoke painful truth, but mis-directed his sister by how he structured his words. It was true there was no evidence. They destroyed it. Kane had not seen Maria Elena for twenty years. But, he had seen her just before Vasquez choked her to death.

"So, who killed Father?"

"The judiciary and the Guardia have virtually given up on the case due to lack of any solid evidence. They told me it was a professional assassination. Their best guess, knowing his reputation, was he was killed by a jilted husband or wronged business competitor. And, whoever it was paid a professional from out of town to do it. The fact it was done just after he killed our beautiful, sweet mother may just be a coincidence.

Personally, Gabriela, I would like to shake the hand of the man who made such a shot and removed a horrible creature from the earth. I will always remember how he beat Mother and me."

"And, you, Miguel, kept him away from me, though it cost you dearly in beatings."

"It was a brother's responsibility to a sister he loves."

Finally, after her coolness in listening and questioning, she broke down crying.

Miguel hugged his little sister as he had since she cried as a baby. He had always protected her and always would as long as she let him.

He did not know if she would change her mind after reflection and claim the birthright rightfully hers. He did not care. He was thinking more each day about going to America and at least exploring his true birthright.

Miguel's preference would be to sell the holdings and take Gabriela with him. To meet Kane. And, to see the world beyond Spain.

******

Kane was on the third day of his Atlantic voyage to New York. He was not a fan of cities. He considered them dirty, loud and having too many people. But, the ship was destined for there. And, Rita Wilkes was there, in name only. The woman was intriguing. He was not sure how long she would keep the name and the career it all but guaranteed.

He did not want to lead her on. He was very interested. Almost guiltily, he was smitten from the first moment he met her at the door. He believed it was true for Sally also. He could not even remember if he and Maria Elena had shared such a feeling when they met.

Sally Hemsworth was beautiful and fun. He wished she was not only a slight bit older than her namesake. He was forty and though such age gaps in marriage were common, he would have liked her to be within ten years of him.

Kane was rightfully saddened by Maria Elena's sudden death. He knew now them being together was a reality only in his mind. Certainly not in Maria Elena's. He was glad he saw her. He was glad he spent more time with Miguel. He was glad he avenged her and got away.

Though if he had been backed into a corner, he would have swallowed the white powder in the small bottle in his vest pocket. He was not a good candidate for a Spanish noose. Prison would not have been even a consideration for what he did to a member of Spanish nobility.

Kane finished his fifth round on the deck and plopped into a deck chair. The ship was rolling. As autumn approached, the Atlantic seemed angry.

He did not mind the action of the sea. He found it soothing. He liked the gray, blustery days far better than the bright sunny ones.

They were good thinking days. The cool mist made breathing more pleasurable. It even made the wonderful Cuban cigars he found tastier, though lighting them required more patience with a wooden Lucifer.

The barefoot runs on the beach at Sitges had increased his vigor and endurance. He thought he might keep them up. However he drew the line at running barefoot in the snow. Indians did it, he knew and were notoriously healthy. There was a lot to be learned from them, he thought.

He arose and put on his formal wear for dinner. Though at the captain's table tonight in his meal rotation, he ate lightly. A shrimp cocktail, a green salad and some red wine.

Kane was feeling better every day. And, looking forward to watching the full A Midsummer Night's Dream before walking to the stage and laying roses on its edge for Titania, Queen of the Faeries.

He was unsure of what he would do. Probably wait in New York until the play obligation had run its course. Assuming, of course, his intention was agreed upon. Then, ask her where she wanted to go. Rita may already have signed a continuation agreement for the play or agreed to another. She might love the new fame he knew she would garner.

What he really hoped was she had her fling at Broadway and was ready to leave with him and the life of a Virginia estate wife. Or, Texas. Or, wherever she wished.

He admitted to himself again he missed the green

hills and blue mountains of Western Virginia. His land had been central until half the state seceded. Now, a new state line was a bit over a hundred miles from his land, depending on whether you go over a mountain or two or around them.

Kane liked the raw excitement and danger of the West. Virginia and the Eastern US in general were too tame. But, depending on Rita's wishes, he had options. A whole world of options.

******

The ship landed in New York City on a Saturday morning. Kane took a hansom to a hotel and managed to get a room, though well before normal check-in. He took a walk through Central Park while the hotel freshened his wrinkled formal wear for tonight.

He circled around to Broadway and had lunch. By the end of lunch, the ticket office was open and he secured a front row seat for A Midsummer Night's Dream, just off Broadway. A flower vendor had a stand near the theater. Kane learned he was open in the evening for sale of flowers to theater patrons to give to favorite actors and actresses.

Kane ordered two dozen of his freshest, best roses and had them held in his name. Returning to the hotel, he wrote out the text of a wire to the chairman of the Circle advising him he was in town. He also inquired about his black horse, Hadrian. The chairman was looking after the big horse at his ranch during Kane's absence. He wrote a letter to Miguel, wishing him well and giving nothing away which could be used against either by authorities.

A final letter was to Billy Roberts. Kane told him he had returned alone. He said Maria Elena was dead. Kane ended by saying he had to return briefly to Dallas to finish up some business and hoped to visit and might bring Risa a surprise friend on the visit.

Kane walked the letters down to the front desk to post and walked outside and around the block. He was still full of nervous energy and walked it down by briskly circling the block five times. He ate a light and early dinner in the hotel's dining room and adjourned to his room.

An hour before the play, he called for a hansom cab. He climbed in and rode to the theater.

Kane dismounted the cab, his height and mien, now without the disguise beard, drew attention as he walked into the lobby and presented his ticket. He was seated and waited eagerly to see Rita perform. The play was one of his favorites of the Bard's and he enjoyed the often unsubtle humor.

The play began and he impatiently awaited the conversations between the non-fantastical players to finish. Then, the lights dimmed and steam provided a foggy setting for the woods. A beautiful Titania appeared and began speaking. Though heavily made up for the stage, Sally Hemsworth portraying Rita Wilkes, portraying Titania was perfect.

If ever there was a faerie queen, it was she.

By the end of the play, Kane wondered if he could ever lure such a talent away from the stage.

As the players came out to take their bows, he approached the edge of the stage and set the two dozen roses on it. She looked down, looking for him as she had done for several nights and saw him.

Even her talent could not have expressed sheer joy as was in her face as their eyes met. She mouthed a kiss, seen by any close enough and curtsied. He was back in his seat on the front by their second curtain call. And, third.

As people began to stand and rustle about, a theater employee motioned for Kane to follow him. The man led him to Rita's dressing room, small but unshared. Kane knew unshared was the sign of a star.

The man tapped on the door.

"Miss Wilkes, your visitor is here," and left.

The door opened and Rita appeared and dragged him in. Into her arms. She kissed him as he had never been kissed. Minutes went by without speech.

"Darling Michael. Have you come to rescue me and take me away from all this?"

He knew her words were sincere and not theatrical.

"I have. If you will come with me."

"I have been waiting to hear those words since meeting you on my doorstep in Richmond." she whispered.

"It will take me ten minutes to wash off theatrical makeup. I am famished. Can we eat something?"

"Yes. How about Delmonico's for a steak?"

"Do they have whole steers?" she smiled.

"For my Titania, they have everything."

She used face cream to remove the heavy make-up and removed faux flowers from her hair and brushed it. Rita stood and smiled at him and slipped the gown off her shoulders. She had nothing beneath it. He returned her smile and took her into his arms once again.

"I suspect I should wear something to the steakhouse, shouldn't I?" she said in a few minutes.

"We could forget the steakhouse," Kane suggested.

"Only if you wish to hear my stomach growling like a bear all night."

"The night is yours to choose. The rest of your life, also."

She kissed him and dressed in conservative city evening wear.

They went outside and he hailed a hansom.

"Delmonico's, please," and they were off.

Halfway through her steak, she became serious.

"Michael, what happened to Maria Elena?"

"Her husband, the viscount, got mad and strangled her to death," he said.

"Over the two of you?" she asked.

"Probably, though when we met earlier in the day for the first time in twenty years, we mainly spoke about our son."

"The young Rurale officer?"

"Yes. She told me she would not return with me, but wished our son to visit and establish a father and son relationship."

"Darling, were you heartbroken?" she asked fearfully.

"Strangely, not at all. I guess a twenty year relationship needs to be nourished by something other than letters. Seeing each other, hearing each other. Presence. Ours was long devoid of those things. I was greatly saddened by her murder. But, only a bit more than I would have been at the murder of any friend. Am I so cold to feel in such a manner?"

"No, Michael. You are passionate and far from cold, unless, as the real Rita told me, you are on a mission. Then, she said you are focused," she said.

"May I ask you one more question about Spain?" He nodded.

"What happened to the husband? The viscount?"

"Justice was done. He died."

"He was arrested, tried and hung?"

"He was arrested, tried in a mock court and shot in the courtroom."

"The son?"

"No, the son was there in the courtroom. The bullet was fired from a distance, through the window and into his throat. The very part of the body upon which he murdered Maria Elena."

"Did you…" he held a finger to her lips.

"Justice was done. Just as would be if anyone ever harmed a hair on your beautiful head. Let the details be a mystery."

"I will. Have you thought of me?"

"Constantly since the doorstep in Richmond."

"Yet, you went to Spain."

"I needed closure. I got it. Now, I look forward to spending as much of our lives together as you will permit."

"Is that a proposal?" she asked with apprehension.

"If you want it to be, yes. I don't have a ring, but there is a place here called Tiffany's. I believe they could alleviate the ring problem."

Her eyes widened.

"Yes, I believe they could. Perhaps we could go there. Are they still open?" she asked, knowing the answer.

"What are you doing around ten in the morning?" he asked.

"I hope finishing breakfast in bed with you," came the reply.

"We have a date then. Tiffany's tomorrow morning. After a very long breakfast."

Rita beamed at him.

"Rita, you are a clear hit in this play. Do you want to pursue acting? Or, be the beautiful country wife at a Revolutionary War era estate?"

"The latter please. I always wanted to star on Broadway. I came within a block of it. Good enough for me. Tell me about the estate."

"My family home since the 1700's. Damaged a bit, but restored after the recent war. Rolling hills. Very green. A great place to ride and fish and entertain," he listed.

"Tell me it is brick with white columns."

"It is brick with white columns. A wing was designed by Thomas Jefferson."

"After a life so filled with adventure, what will you do, Michael?"

"Enjoy keeping my wife the most satisfied woman alive."

"Umm…. Satisfied in every respect?"

"Especially 'every' respect," he smiled.

"Yes. I could quickly learn how to live as a country lady. When do we leave?"

"As soon as you can sever ties here, I need to settle job matters in Dallas and figure how I am going to move Hadrian from there to Virginia."

"Hadrian?" she asked.

"My black stallion. The chairman of the board of my organization is keeping him on his ranch for me. I left him there when we departed on the rescue mission."

"Rita told me the group you put together was probably the most dangerous men alive, but would not share a single name."

"She was right. Uttering a name could get one or all of them killed in short order. I will not tell you either, unless we outlive all of them. The youngest is your age. Twenty-four like the other Rita."

She reddened.

"Did I tell you I was twenty-four?" she asked.

"No, I just reckoned you and she were the same age."

"I am older. By six years."

"You are thirty? That is wonderful. I was feeling a little guilty over cradle robbing. I am relieved."

"How old are you? Forty?" she asked. "That's what Rita told me."

"Yes, at least for several more months."

"My contract ran out last night. The play will continue for another several weeks. The will have to use my understudy. It seems so fast. With the week voyages over and back and your time in Spain and wherever else you were, you have been gone a bit over a month," Rita said.

"It was a fast six weeks. I am glad to be home."

"But New York is not home," she said.

"Wherever you are is home, darling. Maybe when we get away from where you have to portray your actress self, I can begin to call you Sally again. I like the name. It fits you better." She smiled assent.

They finished dinner and chatted over red wine. This time it was appropriate to the dinner. Before or after. The doorman flagged a hansom for them.

It was a long night at his hotel. They did not sleep much at all. But, a good night. A very good night.

The next day she advised both the theater owner and the director of her intent not to stay with the play. The emotional director became highly agitated and began to berate her.

Kane reached over and took the knot of his tie in one big hand and lifted him off his chair.

"You continue like this and I will throw your skinny ass out of that second story window. Unless you land on your head, you will probably survive, but it will hurt a lot. Do you understand me? Or would you like to continue to flap your wings like a baby bird and I will give you the opportunity to see if you can fly?"

Some people never learn. The man, screeching, began to curse. Kane, still holding him by the neck, slapped him almost unconscious with one open-handed blow.

He turned to the owner.

"Call the police if you like. But, know this. I will own this theater after the court battles are over. And, I will own both of you. And, you will not like it." He had used he ploy successfully after the robbery attempts in the hotel in Laredo and liked how well it worked there. It worked equally well here.

The man nodded and told the awakening director if he did not shut up, he would never work in New York again. Kane set him back down, none too gently.

They left and walked down the street, Rita's arm in his.

"We need to go straight back to the hotel. I found that very exciting in a surprising way.

"Does that mean I have to beat up someone before bed every night?" Kane asked.

"Well, no. But I always wanted a husband who did not have to wait for bedtime to show his love for me," Rita said softly.

"Thank you God for blessing me," Kane thought to himself.

"I know what you were just thinking," she said.

"Oh, you do?"

"I thank Him, too."

They walked on, one woman smiling and one man amazed. Nobody had ever been able to read his thoughts so readily before.

They stopped at Tiffany's and she chose a ring. He chose a similar one with a much bigger diamond. She liked his choice better. She tried it on and kept it on.

"No need to wrap it," she told the clerk.

"Does this mean I have to get on one knee right here?" Kane asked.

"Of course it does. Do you think I am going to take

this ring off and take a chance of you changing your mind? Oh, no."

They were engaged minutes later. In response to Rita's question to the Tiffany clerk about whether this had ever happened in Tiffany's before, he responded "every day."

They had the hansom wait while Rita quickly packed her clothes and personal items to move to Kane's hotel until they departed New York.

"Do you still have that English thing I got you. You know, the one like the other Rita's?" Kane asked as they settled in the hansom. It was none of the driver's business about it being a Webley revolver.

"It's right here," Rita said, patting her purse. He smiled.

"Michael, when we go to Dallas, will we be close enough to stop by Hico and see Rita, or rather, Risa?"

"Of course. We will only be about a hundred miles away. My only request is accept the name her new husband, or whatever their relationship is, gives you and don't try to guess his identity. A slip could cost them their lives, dearest."

"You have brought me into an exciting, mysterious world, Michael. But, I love it."

They moved her into his room very easily and very temporarily. The sooner Kane could put the noise and crowds of New York behind them the better.

They left on the train for Dallas the next day and

arrived several days later. Their next rooms felt a bit more like home.

The chairman, a former senior Southern officer named Shelby, was in the office he maintained for periodic visits next to Kane's. Kane found his own office occupied, as he expected, by Shelby's son.

The son would be a good administrator. He was a bank president. What he was not, however, was a field operative. But, times and the mission of the Circle were changing. He would be fine. Kane knew him and greeted both men warmly.

"I just dropped in to see how things are going. Rita is out in a carriage waiting. I need to pick up a couple personal items from the office."

"Bring Miss Rita up to say hello," the Chairman Shelby insisted. Kane knew this would be a good test.

"Excellent. She knows this is an investment trust and that's all anyone but we know. I'll get her and we can collect a few items from my wall and desk."

He went down to the small carriage he had rented for them.

"You are invited up to say hello to Chairman Shelby and his son, who is replacing me. Rita met the chairman briefly at a lunch after your safe return. Don't speak with him about the organization. Answer any questions about Booth as you wish."

"Rita actually told me a lot about how disappointed she was spending time with her father. She was eternally grateful he joined the hunt to rescue her, however. Is the son aware he is alive?"

"A great question the answer of which I do not know. Let me set the stage for your possible answers with a question to Shelby about what Joe Junior has been read into if I can do it smoothly. If not, we will just play everything by ear."

They went into the building and up to the suite of GC Financials' offices.

"General, you remember lunch with Miss Rita Wilkes. And, Rita, this is the Joe Shelby, who is my successor. Both are friends," Kane said.

"Miss Rita, I am so happy to see you again," the senior Shelby said as he kissed her hand. The junior gave a short bow and smiled

"And, I you. Should I call you Chairman as before, or General?" she asked taking a calculated risk.

"Those were trying times during which to get to know one another. You were starved from captivity, browned from the sun, and I was told blooded from saving Kane's life by shooting and knifing Apache warriors in a skirmish. Now, things are more relaxed. Call me Joe."

Confident his fiancé could hold her own with the two star struck men, whose official domiciles were in Mississippi, Kane walked into his office. He removed his diploma from London and certificates from the Spanish Military Academy and others in France and

Germany. He placed them on a reception desk, currently unoccupied.

"Kane, Rita just showed me her ring. Congratulations are in order. And, lunch with champagne for sure. Do you have time?" his former boss asked.

"For you, General, of course. Name the place. We can walk if close or meet there. Rita and I have a two-place buggy tied out front."

"Walk? Cavalry generals don't walk to the privy, son. But, the hotel within an easy walk does, I am told, offer good labels of champagne."

They had a convivial lunch keynoted by many questions about Rita's play in New York.

At one point, the general mentioned he had testified on Frank James's behalf in the first part of the year and claimed his testimony got the outlaw exonerated. Rita would have merely thought the fact interesting. That is, until she saw the look of warning Kane gave his former boss. The subject changed immediately and she took note.

She had never had champagne before and was beginning to reflect its affects. Kane looked at his watch and told the men they had an immediate appointment. They left before she fell out of character.

He helped her into the buggy, smiling at how happy she was, no matter why.

They went back to Kane's room and packed his diplomas away. He also put Rita to bed, where she slept soundly until he woke her to get ready to go to the train station.

An hour later, dressed in black and his Colt in a briefcase, they boarded a train which stopped in Waco. There, Kane rented another buggy and took the beautiful actress and her headache to the Roberts ranch near Hico per directions on a letter.

They arrived the same time as a messenger from town did. The messenger carried a telegram.

Billy, rushing through introductions, immediately took Kane aside and handed him the telegram.

"Need help now. Stop. Come Blevins. Stop. Your friend. End."

"Kane, that ain't like Jesse. Something big happened. We need to go right now."

"I agree, Billy. Let's leave the girls to talk. Can Risa put together some trail meals for our saddlebags?" Billy nodded.

"She and Mae, who you haven't met, can cook up a storm. I have a good horse and saddle for you to use. And, a rifle, too. You got that fast Colt?"

"I do, my friend. Let's get ready to ride."

They went back to the women. Mae had joined them. After brief introductions, Billy told the women what they needed for the trail and went to the stable to prepare the two horses for travel.

"Ladies, Billy just got a scary telegram from one of your rescuers. He is the coldest operator I ever knew.

For him to send that kind of telegram means something horrible has happened. He said he needs help right now. I'm glad we arrived when we did. He's my friend as well as Billy's. We have to ride immediately and may be gone several days.

We have a seventy mile ride, according to Billy," Kane explained as he strapped on two big Colts, hidden in his briefcase. Rita's eyes got big when she saw him in his full man in black outfit with twin revolvers in shiny black holsters.

Billy rode up on Reno and had a strong looking dun in tow. Risa and Mae put food in their saddlebags. Billy already had rifles, blankets and canteens on the horses.

He jumped off and hugged his two and Kane hugged and kissed Rita. They remounted and took off at a gallop, never looking back.

"Michael didn't look back," Rita lamented.

"They never do, honey. It's the way of Western men. It doesn't mean he doesn't love you. It means he is now in stay-alive mission mode. That's what you want him in," Risa said.

"Michael said I cannot ask you any questions about Billy. A slip could get you killed. He must be somebody really important to be so young."

"He may look twelve, but he's my age. And, yes, he is somebody really important. There are several territories and a state or two which would hang him if they caught him. He's a good man and we cannot let the fact he's alive be known. He was part of the Ghost Posse which came to save me," Risa said.

"Why Ghost Posse?" her longtime friend asked.

"Some, like Billy, are supposedly dead. That's all I can say and don't let on I even told you so much. Those men risked their lives for me. I owe them all a debt I can never repay, except with silence"

"Michael Kane is a man of many secrets, himself" Rita said.

"I gather. Whatever happened with the woman he went to Spain for? You wrote me about it."

"She's dead. Her husband strangled her."

"I guess he got hung."

"Wrong. Assassinated through the courtroom window the moment he was declared innocent."

"Kane?" Risa asked.

"He won't say."

"What about the young Spanish lieutenant who looked so much like Kane?"

"He was all Michael and Maria Elena talked about during their brief meeting. Him, and her refusing to return here with him. The lieutenant who looks like him is his son."

"I knew it. Was it pure coincidence they met in Mexico and Kane saved him twice?" Risa asked.

"Apparently. Certainly good fortune for both."

"Did the son kill Maria Elena's husband? And did

he know the man was not his father?"

"No and yes. He was in the courtroom. The shot came from many yards away through a second floor window of the courtroom. It took a real expert."

Risa got a knowing look on her face. Her friend recognized it immediately. So did Mae, who was sitting silently part of the conversation.

"How did Mr. Kane get back here?" Mae asked.

"Mae, I honestly don't know. The man is like a wraith."

"More like an angel, is what I'd say," Mae added.

"You know, you're right. He's certainly my angel. I never loved anybody so much."

"Heck, you loved him at the doorstep when you first met him," Risa added. "And, you are sure he is not rebounding?"

"I'm sure. Their only actual meeting in twenty years was about the son. No romance. The spark was gone. Apparently, it had been gone for a long time. He was saddened and angered by her murder by a regularly abusive husband."

"Without speaking any names, do you know who they are riding so fast to help?" Rita asked.

"Yes. He was a member of the Ghost Posse. I don't know who he was before," Risa said.

Rita held back her question about Frank James. She would let Michael Kane decide what she knew or did not know rather than putting more stress on her friend.

"Mae, how did you end up here?" Rita asked, changing to a safer subject.

"This angel I helped raise came and saved me and brought me home with her and Billy," Mae said.

"Saved you? How, Mae?"

"I worked for her mama most of my life. Then, she married another no-account gambler and let me go. Rita, I mean Risa, heard about it and they came up to Connecticut and saved me. I have never been so happy as I am now with my girl and her new fella."

'I am glad for you. I have known Risa for years. She has always been my best friend, though we have seldom lived in the same state."

"Yes, Miz Lizola does not let any grass grow under her feet for sure," Mae said.

******

The two riders got to the Courtney ranch just before six hours had passed. They found Jesse packing saddlebags. He had already cleaned his Colt and Winchester.

"Jesse. What happened?" Billy jumped off Reno and clasped his friend. "And, look at the gunsel I brought you." pointing to Kane.

Jesse patted the young man on the shoulder and turned to Kane.

"I screwed up, Kane. Big time. Somehow some

fellas followed me from a major cache of Circle funds. They waylaid the old robber himself and knocked me in the head on the way back. They got forty thousand in gold. Money the new fella, Shelby, sent me a coded message to withdraw and hold for a messenger from him.

I was just at the cache for a minute. This was a real small part and not far in. I'm hoping they saw it was a lot and figgered it was all I had. But, we have to check for sure, then get on their trail."

"Jesse how long ago did this happen?" Kane asked.

"This morning. It was ten of them. They were toughs. Looked like they knew the ropes."

"How far away is the cache?"

"It's about five miles, Kane," Jesse James responded.

"Let's go there first. When we get close, you point where it is and the three of us will come in from different directions to make sure we don't ride into a trap. They may have doubled back to check for more treasure."

Jesse nodded and they all mounted up and Jesse's wife, Mary Ellen, ran out and kissed him goodbye.

The rode off and split near the cache. Jesse rode straight in like he usually did, Billy circled right and Kane circled left. All had their Winchesters out and ready.

Jesse signaled all was okay and rode in to inspect the cache. The other two faced outwards and watched for approaching riders. After a minute or two, Jesse rode back out by a quarter mile and signaled the other two. They rode to meet him.

"There are no tracks near the cache except for mine. They did not go back. I have no reason to think they know where it actually is. Men, we have to kill all ten of them. Otherwise, they will be back to the area scouting around. We can't chance it. They gotta die."

"Billy, this is all real secret stuff. I ask you to promise not to share anything about caches or treasures to anybody. Rita included. You were the only person not clued in about this secret organization and its emergency funds stashed away around the country. Jesse trusted you. So, I trusted you. I still do, but I want you to promise anyway. Afterwards, we won't bring up promises ever again," Kane said.

"I promise, Kane. I'd do anything to help Jesse and never anything to hurt him. You, too. First, because I like you and second because you scare the living hell out of me."

Kane grinned. "I do strike people as scary. But, you should know by now I'm as innocent as a little hound dog puppy."

Jesse James broke out laughing at Kane's protestation of his innocence.

"Let's backtrack to the place you got jumped Jesse and look for their tracks. They have a five or six hour head start and plenty of light before they need to stop," Kane said.

They rode back almost a mile and Jesse stopped. The men could see a profusion of horse tracks and Billy spotted a little blood on the ground where his friend had laid after being cracked over the head with a rifle butt.

"It's a wonder they didn't kill you, Jesse," Billy said.

"Yep. And, they are going to wonder why too. It will be their last thought," the former outlaw replied.

Kane led the way as they began trailing the robbers across country. This was a good omen. Tracking on busy roads was virtually impossible. But, it looked like these ten were going to stay away from the roads. Were they possibly wanted for something else?

At one Y in the trails, they stopped, probably to decide which branch to take.

Kane held the other two back and dismounted. He carefully studied the horse shoes. There was nothing distinctive on any, unfortunately. But, he did verify ten mounts like Jesse had guessed.

Kane blew the air out of his nose, held his head up and drew in fresh air. He followed his nose, walking away from the profusion of tracks. He found where one of the men had defecated. He poked it with a branch. It had hardened and he reckoned it was hours old.

"Jesse you are right. There are ten. Nobody but one who had to relieve himself dismounted here. If they ate, it was chewing jerky along the way. What could you tell about their horses? Trail gear?"

"Yes, Kane. They had saddlebags and rifle scabbards. A couple had dusters hung over their saddles. I figure they were passing through, not locals. While the trails through here aren't bad, it would have been easier to stay on the road. They are avoiding notice."

"Jesse, though they don't have cattle with them, has there been any rustling you know about in this area recently? They might have dropped off a herd and be riding back to steal another," Billy asked.

"Don't know of any, but that don't mean it's not so. You could be right, Billy. I think I was a fool of opportunity for them."

Kane pushed on and they followed. They trailed the robbers until dark.

Darkness was usually the enemy of a tracker. A tracker could slow down and either miss the trail if they turned off, or ride right into their camp and get cut down.

Or, with luck and moonlight, the tracker could track slowly and maybe make up for some lost time. Like five or six hours' worth. Having a strong moon in their favor, they chose to ride on into the night.

Kane tracked until one in the morning. He reckoned they had made up five hours in the dark. Not six only because they had to go slowly and search for tracks in the moonlight.

"We better call it quits for the night before we

ride up on their camp and scare hell out of all of us," Kane said.

"I don't smell smoke, so they are either ahead too far to smell it, or right here with a cold camp," Jesse said.

"I agree. But, if you can live without coffee, we have some fine food packed here. Mae does something she calls soul food. It's the best stuff I ever ate." Billy said.

"You mean Rita Wilkes did not cook up all the food they loaded in the saddlebags?" Jesse asked, suspecting the answer before asking.

"Ha. Risa is learning, but she's right at the lesson for boiling water."

"Wait a minute. You keep calling her 'Risa,' what's up here?"

Billy looked at Kane who nodded.

"Well, Rita Wilkes fell in love with a handsome young cowboy. She was tired of living all over the place, so she picked a friend who looked like her to become her and make the kind of money her name enabled. Mr. Kane here supervised the whole shooting match. Rita Wilkes became Risa Wilkerson. Her lookalike actress friend became Rita Wilkes. But, she fell in love with the man in black over here and I have no damn idea how this story is going to end."

"And, the new Rita—my Rita—was her friend Sally Hemsworth," Kane said.

"I can't stay away from y'all for a month without getting a year behind," Jesse exclaimed. "So Rita is Risa and Sally is Rita?" Billy nodded.

"And, where did Mae come from?" Jesse asked while all were unsaddling.

"She worked for Lizola, who goes by Izola because she thinks the first is ugly and is too dumb to know the second is just as ugly," Billy said.

"Okay, I am in for the whole hand," Jesse said. "Who is Lizola?"

"Booth's wife and Rita's ma."

"How do you keep all this straight?"

"Just smart, I reckon," Billy replied.

Turning to a less complex conversation, Jesse said "Kane, I notice you have two matching Colts again. I thought you gave your left one to the Rurale officer who looked like you."

"I did. He's my son. I missed it, so I got a duplicate recently in New York when I picked up Rita. Really Sally, actually."

Jesse shook his head. So much for less confusion.

Makeshift blanket and saddle bedrolls laid out, the men dug into the food. It was friend chicken and cornbread. They had to wash it down with water, but Billy's new well was pure and the water really good. They alternated watches and started off in the dawn.

At eight o'clock in the morning, Kane raised his hand. All stopped.

He whispered "I heard something up ahead.

They dismounted and moved forward on foot,

rifles in hand.

Their ten fugitives were right in front of them in a clearing. Apparently not aware of anyone following them, they slept in. Now, they were making coffee. It smelled like the nectar of gods to their three pursuers.

"The three of us can shoot faster with our six-guns. He slipped a cartridge in the chamber kept empty for safety in both. Jesse and Billy followed his example.

"Let's walk in slow and quiet about twenty feet apart. Make it as hard as possible for them to hit us," Kane whispered.

They moved as silently as possible. Twenty feet from the camp, they stopped and set their rifles on the ground by their strong or primary gun hands.

"Hello the camp. My name is Kane. You have some gold belonging to us."

"And, I am Jesse James."

"And, I am Henry McCarty. But, folks call me Billy the Kid."

The ten men getting ready for the day froze.

They heard the names. They knew two. The two looked like newspaper pictures of who they claimed to be. They had no idea who the man in black was.

But, collectively they decided it would be stupid for ten men to surrender to three men who did not even have their guns out.

So, they compounded stupidity and all drew.

Their three adversaries drew two guns each. Kane's

right gun went off. Then his left simultaneous with Jesse and Billy's righthand guns. The two outlaws would never again have to wonder if Kane was faster. Then, they were all shooting so fast, no one cared. The men in camp were falling, usually before they could shoot. Several fired wildly and died to accurately placed shots from the three.

In less than twelve seconds, ten men were down and the three across from them were standing. One on the ground moved and Jesse shot him left handed. All three holstered empty revolvers and picked up their rifles and levered the actions. But, readying the rifles was unnecessary.

The greatest gunfight in history was over. One which made the Earps shootout near the OK Corral pale by comparison. But, this one would never be famous. Maybe Frank James, the two Rita's, and maybe Miguel Kane would hear a bit. Probably not. It was Circle business transacted by three of the deadliest men who ever lived—Men who secretly retrieved the Circle's gold and went home to live quietly to very old ages.

Men who lived the legend never told. The legend of the Ghost Posse.

NOTE FROM THE AUTHOR

My great grandmother, Alma Maury McLaughlin Joyner, lived until I was about twelve years old. She lived on the McLaughlin farm in Caroline County, Virginia. She grew up during Reconstruction. McLaughlin's Pneuman's End Creek Farm grew tobacco and sweet potatoes. No hoop skirts and mint juleps there; the first floor was dirt.

I asked her every question a little boy could think of about growing up during that troubled time. She answered plainly and without agenda. One of her favorite stories was about walking next door (a mile through copperhead snake filled woods) to the Garrett farm and sitting on the porch with old Mrs. Garrett. The older lady would tell her about the night the Yankees came and burned down her tobacco barn and killed Mr. Booth. Her biggest problem with the event was losing a season full of curing tobacco, a barn and the army never repaid them.

Given such a childhood, I studied Booth and came to believe some of the stories about him. Was he the man who committed suicide in Enid, Oklahoma in 1903? He apparently had a wife, though she had a penchant for not really divorcing her several husbands before marrying another. His daughter, Ogarita Booth Henderson, was an actress. She and her brother both closely favored the handsome, but troubled assassin.

Similarly, was James Courtney, who died in Blevins, Texas in 1943, really Jesse James? A lot of modern forensic evidence seems to support it.

Brother Frank, by the way, never was convicted of any of his crimes, between friendly juries and statutes of limitations. He spent much of his later years as a shoe salesman.

Sheriff Pat Garrett and Billy the Kid were best buddies, known as Big Reno and Little Reno because of their favorite game of chance and their widely different heights.

I was always suspicious of Pat killing Billy. They had been too close.

Was Brushy Bill Roberts, who died in Hico, Texas in 1950, really Billy? Again, there is some University of Texas computer forensics evidence supporting it. As of this writing, neither Billy's alleged grave nor Brushy Bill's has been allowed to be exhumed for DNA proof.

One of the most hated Confederate raiders was William Quantrill. Even Jesse and Frank James broke off from him because of his scorched earth policies. Did he escape from a federal hospital wearing his visiting wife's dress? Was his wife the sister of the James's friend Cole Younger? A lot of these folks appear to have lots of things tying them together. Confederate general Joe Shelby's testimony helped get Frank James acquitted.

Then, there was a secret order called the Knights of the Golden Circle. Originally, they were expansionists from both sides of the Mason-Dixon Line. Did they really escape with the Confederacy's gold just before Richmond fell in 1865?

So, given all these possibilities, what is a fiction writer to do? I guess make up a story on the presumption they were true. But, even if they are true, this is purely a work of fiction. If the presumptions are false? It is still fiction.

I hope you have as much fun reading it as I did writing it— GWT.

A LOOK AT: ARIZONA GUNMAN

A WESTERN STORY OF GOOD OVER EVIL, LAW OVER CRIMINALITY.

County Sheriff James Duncan is fast and honoable. An Arizona lawman who rides rough country, often going up against dangerous men and gangs alone. Dealing with bank robbers, kidnappers and rustlers with his fast gun. Much of his tracking ability comes from his Scottish father, who served as an Indian scout. Valuable experience as a Rough Rider with Teddy Roosevelt, then as an Arizona Ranger.

Outlaws and corrupt government tend to stand in Duncan's way, but he manages to overcome all obstacles with integrity and really fast guns.

AVAILABLE NOW

ABOUT THE AUTHOR

G. Wayne Tilman is a full-time author. He retired from the Federal Bureau of Investigation several years ago. Prior to the FBI, he was a Marine, bank security director, deputy sheriff, investigator, and security contractor.

He holds baccalaureate and master's degrees from the University of Richmond and has been an adjunct faculty member there, as well as the University of Phoenix, St. Petersburg College and Florida Metropolitan University.

Some of his law enforcement subject matter expertise includes threat assessment, continuity of operations, security and executive protection, counter intelligence, international terrorism, and small arms. He has been an instructor in those subjects in a number of training academies, conferences and seminars. Mr. Tilman holds the internationally-recognized Certified Protection Professional board certification, generally accepted as the highest in the security profession.

He also earned a US Coast Guard 50 Ton Inspected Vessel Master Captain's license.

G. Wayne Tilman's primary interests are family and writing. His avocations are bushcraft (survival/primitive camping), hiking, boating, kayaking, shooting sports, and travel.

He wrote his first novel over thirty years ago and has now written thirteen novels. Genres include espionage thrillers, mysteries, and Westerns.

G. Wayne Tilman's impetus to write in those genres comes from both personal experience and heritage.

A direct ancestor was a sheriff in Virginia Colony in 1680. Another ancestor was the lawman who brought in outlaw Bill Doolin singlehandedly and helped to decimate the infamous Doolin-Dalton outlaw gang, sometimes known as the Oklahombres. Bill Doolin was the Desperado of song fame. Closer to home, his mother was a counterintelligence agent for what is now the Defense Intelligence Agency or DIA.